THE UNITED FEDE:

GRUB WARS

BOOK 2

THE PRICE OF HONOR

Colonel Jonathan P. Brazee
USMC (Ret)

Semper Fi Press

A Semper Fi Press Book

Copyright © 2017 Jonathan Brazee

ISBN-10: 1-945743-18-2
ISBN-13: 978-1-945743-18-4 (Semper Fi Press)

Printed in the United States of America

Acknowledgements:
I want to thank all those who took the time to offer advice as I wrote this book. A special thanks goes to beta readers James Caplan and Kelly Roche for their valuable input.

Cover art by Matthew Cowdery
Graphics by Steven Novak

Dedicated to

Private First Class Brian Abrams, USMC
10-31-1969 to 6-2-1989

RIP, Devil Dog

KRAKOW

Chapter 1
Hondo

"We know they're out there," Sergeant Hondo McKeever passed over the squad net. "It's just a matter of time, so be ready for it."

Eight of Hondo's twelve Marines, along with Doc Torrington, his corpsman, had never seen combat before, had never seen Klethos in the field, and he could almost feel their nervousness. The blinding snow didn't help things. Each PICS had more than enough sensors to pierce the blizzard, but even the best composite image failed to create the same comfort level as actual eyes on target.

Hondo had his squad positioned on both sides of a small gulch where a stream had worn through the rolling hills before funneling out into the vast, windswept plains. It provided the only cover for several klicks to reach the higher ground occupied by his Marines, so it was a logical avenue of approach . . . too logical, probably, meaning it might be avoided. Still, it offered the squad its best shot within its AOR.

A stronger gust of wind hit him, making his PICS compensate with its gyros to keep him motionless, something he didn't think he'd ever experience before. With the wind and minus 40-degree temperatures, a Marine not protected by a PICS wouldn't last long. He subconsciously checked his readouts yet again. Hondo had molted twice during battles with the Grubs, which might be a record for someone who survived the experience. It was too damned cold for him to want to make it three times.

A flicker on his display caught his attention. He increased the gain on the temperature gradient scan, trying to capture whatever was out there. The flicker could have been nothing, caused by a tiny fluctuation in his PICS electronics. It could have been a reading from one of the small mice that roamed in tunnels under the snow. But Hondo's instincts screamed enemy.

"Gradient array," he ordered, then watched his display as his Marines went to their assigned bands, each PICS taking a narrow frequency as their sensors tried to pierce through the storm.

"I've got something, Sergeant, at fifty-three thousand," Private First Class Uriah Joseph passed, his voice filled with excitement.

"Second Team, blanket the fifty-thousands," Hondo ordered, then switched to 52,000-55,000 himself.

Immediately, that flicker he'd seen before turned into eight ghost images, moving quickly up the right side of the ravine. If they kept up the pace, they'd reach the squad's position in about five minutes.

"Here they come. Remember, this is nothing. We've all done this before, so keep your heads in the game."

The problem was that most of his Marines hadn't done this before, not against an actual opponent. Half of his squad had been civilians eight months ago, called up in the wartime draft. This was the first time in over three hundred years that the Corps was not 100% voluntary. Officially, the Marine Corps had not lowered its standards, but Hondo wasn't sure that all of his Marines would have made it through boot camp before the surge.

"Wolf, watch Pickerul," he passed on the P2P.

PFC Tammy Pickerul was one of the weaker members of the squad, and her pulse was racing. Hondo didn't need the Marine to panic and expose them all to the advancing enemy.

"Roger that. She'll be fine," Corporal Curtis "Wolf" Johnson, the First Team leader, replied.

I hope so.

Hondo switched his scanners back on the squad for a moment. There was barely a reading that there were 13 Marines and a Navy corpsman waiting in the snow. Hopefully, no one else would know they were there, either.

He switched back. The "ghosts" were becoming more pronounced. There were eight of them, which was expected, moving quickly and using the weather as cover. Three hundred meters away, they were within range of the Marine weapons, but Hondo held off. He could employ his weapons systems without visuals, but he wasn't sure how the blizzard would affect the light M99 hypervelocity darts or the M48's target acquisition lenses. He wanted them in his kill zone so they'd have no chance to escape his ambush.

Keep coming, he tried to will them along.

He'd been concerned that with so much frontage, they'd pick another route to the high ground. But here they were, heading right into his trap.

"Steady," he passed over the net as the opposing forces reached 200 meters.

This was in-your-face range on the modern battlefield. Hondo still held off, however. With the elements affecting them in ways he just couldn't calculate, he wanted to leave nothing to chance. He'd risk the Marines being spotted first.

The decision was taken out of his hands. On his display, he could see that the opposition force had broken into a run, charging the right leg of the ambush.

"Open fire!" Hondo passed as he fired his M90, letting the scope AI target the still-unseen ghosts.

All around him, Marines fired with hypervelocity darts, 30mm rockets, and 40mm grenades. Two Marines' avatars grayed out, KIA, but five of the ambushees fell to the withering fusillade.

We're going to do it, he exulted as he targeted the left-most surviving Klethos.

He poured over a hundred darts into her, trying to overwhelm her defenses, his inner warrior singing a battle cry. He knew he should hold back and direct his fire teams, but at this point, the team leaders should know what to do, and Hondo couldn't restrain himself. He wanted to tally a kill.

His incoming alarm shocked him out of his battle lust. He was being targeted. He superman-jumped to the right, landing in a deep pile of snow, and spun around. Four ghosts registered right behind him. Hondo switched to his grenade, but before he could fire, his display whited out, and all his weapons went offline.

"Shit!" he screamed into his dead mic.

A moment later, the display ghost coalesced into an actual Klethos warrior as she ran past him, intent on hunting more Marines.

Where the hell did they come from? Hondo wondered. *They had three quads? Klethos don't do that.*

But they did. And they'd used two quads to spring the expected ambush, somehow sneaking in the third to ambush the ambushers.

Hondo was KIA, out of it, but he could watch what was going on as both Marines and Klethos fell. As the squad leader, this was on him, and to be caught like that wasn't going to stand him well. He'd fallen victim to over-confidence. He'd assumed that the Klethos would act in one way and ignored other possibilities.

Within moments, two of his three team leaders were KIA as well. It was up to Wolf, Doc, and two Marines to take out the remaining two Klethos. Watching on his display, Hondo could see that the corporal was letting his Marines get maneuvered to the restricted ground higher up in the gully, and he let out a scream of frustration at not being able to send out a warning.

"All hands, all hands, return to your camps immediately," came over his comms. "This means humans and Klethos. I repeat, all hands, human and Klethos, cease training and return to your camps immediately."

Hondo's PICS came to life, restoring all functions. He didn't know what was going on, but orders were orders.

"First Squad, the exercise is over. Form up on me."

On his display, he could see the two remaining Klethos continue their attack. he switched to the range freq, then keyed in the Klethos leader.

"This is Sergeant McKeever. Did you get the orders to stop the exercise and get back to camp?"

"Affirmative. I am retrieving our warriors," she responded.

Which was sometimes easier said than done. It could be difficult to regain control over a Klethos warrior in full battle fury. During exercises like this, the Klethos were not allowed to take their swords or pikes into the fight, and their rifles were simply turned off when the AIs determined they'd been killed. They might still be in warrior-mode, but there wasn't much they could do to a Marine in a PICS.

"Nice job, by the way. I never expected that you had three quads with you," he passed to the Klethos squad leader.

"We're learning to be more devious," she said with what Hondo could swear was a smug tone.

Hell, I guess that's good news, he had to admit, even if he was pissed to have suffered the brunt of it.

Hondo didn't know who would have won in the end, but he'd have bet on Wolf and the rest. But who "won" an exercise was not the issue; as the squad leader, he should have been better prepared for a flanking force. It was a lesson learned, but an embarrassing one.

"Sergeant McKeever, return at Run Alpha," Lieutenant Singh passed to him.

"Roger that."

"Run Alpha" was the nickname for the fastest speed given the terrain, and in this case, the weather. Whatever was up, the command wanted everyone back ASAP. Hondo looked up to the sky, half-expecting to see the light spheres of descending Grubs. He'd been on Purgamentium when the Grubs had attacked, and he'd been lucky to survive. With fewer than 150 Marines on the planet, he doubted they'd be able to survive a Grub landing.

"Let's move it," he ordered as the last of his squad reached them.

In a loose column of twos, he led the squad back. He couldn't see much, not even the ground in front of him, so he had to rely on the PICS' ability to remain upright no matter the footing.

"What's up?" Sergeant Cara Riordan, the Second Squad leader, asked him over the P2P.

"Don't know. How far are you out?"

"Forty-two klicks, and it's snowing like a son of a bitch here."

"We're in whiteout here, too. We're sixteen klicks, though, so I'll beat you back. I'll let you know what I find out."

"We didn't even see our Klucks. How about you?"

"We'd just engaged when we got the recall. I think we would've won," he said.

Well, technically, we might have won. I don't have to tell her about getting caught with my pants down.

"Good on you," she replied.

"They're learning, though," he added, feeling a little guilty. "Gave us a good fight."

"As big and tough as they are, they're still not Marines. Well, we've got a long ways, so I'll see you in the rear with the gear."

"Roger that. See you."

Forty-two klicks weren't particularly far. A Marine in a PICS could make that in less than an hour in good conditions. With the blizzard, however, Hondo thought it might take Second Squad almost two to get back. He and First Squad would be back long before that.

He'd just settled into Run Alpha when Lieutenant Singh opened up the P2P and said, "I'm switching over to live-arms, Sergeant. I'm leaving the hot switch on, too, but giving you control."

Hondo nearly stumbled in surprise, his gyros whining to keep him upright and moving. During training, the PICS were in training mode, with energy beams barely registering at 1% output and slug-throwers simulated. Switching over to "live-arms" meant that the lieutenant was powering up the energy weapons and releasing the magazines for rounds. In three minutes, the PICS would be fully combat-capable, only needing Hondo to release each PICS' AI to go hot.

"What's going on, Lieutenant?" he asked, trying to see through the blizzard to spot descending Grubs.

His display lit up with each of his three team leaders trying to connect via P2P, wondering why their PICS' weapons systems were powering up. Hondo ignored them for the moment.

"We've got a problem back here," the lieutenant said. "Pick up the speed. I need you here ASAP."

What kind of "problem?" You're not telling me shit.

There had to be a reason the lieutenant was being tight-lipped; Hondo just couldn't imagine why.

"Roger that. I'm going to go Risk Five."

"Go to twenty," the lieutenant ordered.

Twenty? This is serious.

Run Alpha had a ten percent safety cushion. At a Risk 20, there was a realistic chance that he could lose a PICS by pushing the terrain and weather.

"Roger, that, sir. We're on our way."

He gave the order to the AI, and he could feel a tiny surge as each step he made covered slightly more ground.

"First Squad, listen up. As you can see, we're going live. I've still got the hot switch, but we need to be ready for something back at camp. Before you ask, I don't know what's happening, only that we'll be the first ones there, so be ready for anything.

"I've also gone to Risk Twenty on Run Alpha. Let's all make it back without a breakdown, so, no chatter. Unless you've got a problem powering up, I don't want to hear from you. Concentrate on your movement."

The AIs were handling the mechanics of the run back, but Marines weren't simply passengers. They, not the AIs, fought the PICS. If staying alert could otherwise keep a PICS moving, then he wanted their full concentration on the run.

That means you, too, he had to remind himself as his mind raced with possibilities.

He reached the higher ground, and each stride lengthened. He was running at close to 40 KPH, which was pushing it given the conditions, but his PICS seemed to handle it OK. Halfway back to camp, the blinding conditions improved as the blizzard faded, and he could actually see the ground in front of him. He was tempted to goose up the risk limit, but he was already pushing it, and with only another six or seven clicks, saving a minute didn't seem worth the risk.

Ten minutes later, the camp's expedition shelters loomed out of the waning snow.

"I'm at the front of the gym," the lieutenant passed to him. "Come in strong and meet me there. Do not go weapons hot, though. I want your impact, but no accidents."

It'd be nice if you told me what's going on.

"Roger that. We'll be there in two minutes."

Hondo switched to the squad net and passed, "I'm not sure what the situation is, but the lieutenant wants us to make an impact. Form on me, squad wedge. First Team, right, Second, middle, and Third, left. Do it now."

Within moments, the Marines had shifted to the wedge. Hondo started to move out, leading the squad between the expeditionary shelters towards the big Class D shelter, a large expanse that housed supplies, the armory, and the PICS shack. The Marines had put together some field-expedient weights that were kept in the corner, and it also had the largest protected open space in the camp, big enough for a b-ball or rocket game. That was why they simply called it the "gym."

As they came around the corner, Hondo could see the lieutenant and the staff sergeant, dressed in cold-weather gear, and two Marines in PICS. Facing them, ten meters away, were 15 soldiers, all bundled up in heavy cold-weather gear as well. Behind the visitors, a Malakh personnel carrier sat, its GET-70 gun almost, but not quite, pointing at the lieutenant. Hondo could feel the tension in the air.

"Is someone else coming here for training?" Wolf asked, as Hondo led them well around the other soldiers to fall in beside the lieutenant and staff sergeant.

"Not that I know of," Hondo answered. "Can you tell who they are?"

"Not with all the cold-weather gear covering their uniforms. But those are GE-55's," he said.

"Which a quarter of all armies use, like the Malakh," Hondo said before it dawned on him. "Shit, they're Brotherhood."

"We're not in—" Wolf responded, before the lieutenant cut him off over his personal amplifier.

"I trust training was good, Sergeant McKeever?"

Hondo knew that whatever was going on had nothing to do with their training. The Marines had been very careful not to get within ten klicks of the border.

Krakow was a split world. The larger, less-populated continent was in the Federation, while the smaller continent was an independent protectorate of the Brotherhood. The battalion was officially on the planet for cold-weather training, but it was an open secret that they were there as a reminder to the Brotherhood and the rest of the cowards that there was a war out there, one that threatened all of mankind. They might be refusing to fight, but the Grubs wouldn't make that distinction when, not if, they made it to human space.

"Yes, sir, it was fine," he answered, not quite knowing what his platoon commander wanted.

"As I said, Lieutenant Singh, we don't care about your so-called training. It's the Klethos. With them here with you, they are in violation of UAM 12.06.14. So, let's stop this charade."

"I'm not going to give you who is and who isn't with us here, as I'm sure you know. What I do know is that you are in violation of Berkshire territory, Major."

"And as I said, let's stop this charade. Under the planetary charter, either government is free to inspect the other's territory when there is a Class A or B violation. This is a B."

"What's going on, Staff Sergeant?" Hondo asked on the P2P while the two leaders were going back and forth.

"Power play by the Brotherhood shitheads. They're hitting all the platoons up and down the training area. The battalion CO's on the hook for orders, so right now, we're just trying to keep things calm. So, look like you're about to kick their asses, but don't get aggressive."

"Listen up. Those are Brotherhood host, and they're making a political play with us and the Klucks," Hondo passed on the squad net to his Marines. "They're doing this up and down the training area, and the battalion CO's waiting for orders. Staff Sergeant Callen wants us to stand behind him and the lieutenant looking fierce, but don't do anything else."

"What if they fire first, Sergeant?" PFC Joseph asked.

"If they do, we protect the lieutenant."

"We're not hot," Joseph said.

"You're powered up. If it comes to that, you'll be hot, weapons free."

"That's what I'm talking about," the young Marine said.

"Can it, Joseph," Corporal Takimora, his team leader, cut in. "You heard the sergeant. We don't start anything."

Joseph started to respond, and Hondo killed his mic. This wasn't the time for arguments.

"Let's do it," he passed, before cutting Joseph's mic back on.

The private first class took the hint and shut up as the Marines took their positions backing the platoon commander. Lieutenant Singh was spouting some sort of BS, which Hondo knew was simply to stall until they had confirmed orders.

"Shit, that's Conroy," Corporal Johnson said.

Hondo pulled up the readouts on the two PICS Marines who were already standing by the lieutenant. One was Corporal Julli-Patterson, one of the company clerks. The other PICS didn't have a Marine listed on his readout. Hondo turned to see who it was, and the baby-face of Gilead Conroy was clearly visible through his visor.

Gilead was a civilian armorer, not a Marine. He seemed competent enough at his job, but without a shred of doubt, he was not qualified, nor cleared, to be in a PICS in what could be a confrontation. Lieutenant Singh had to think this was an extraordinary situation to have approved that.

That realization hit Hondo hard. This was something bigger than he'd assumed. There'd been posturing even before the Brotherhood pulled out of the UAM task force, and it had gotten worse, but it had not devolved into a hot conflict . . . yet. He turned his attention to the Brotherhood major.

"I'm willing to stand here all day, if it is necessary," the Brotherhood officer said.

"And I repeat, sir, that this is in violation of Federation integrity. You are on Federation soil," the lieutenant answered.

"And as I will repeat, we are here as provided by UAM 12.06.14, which give us the authority to be here."

"The best I can tell, even if that is pertinent here, that only allows you to ascertain if there are Klethos on this world. I'm sure you have us on orbital surveillance to be able to determine that."

"With this weather?" the major said, spreading his arms as if to encompass the area. "You give us credit for more capabilities than we actually possess."

"Bullshit," Wolf passed through the P2P.

"Steady," Hondo told him.

It was bullshit, though. Brotherhood surveillance was probably the best in human space. A little snow couldn't defeat it. The lieutenant wasn't admitting that there were Klethos on the planet, but the Brotherhood would know for certain that they were there. Heck, that was one of the reasons the battalion was training along the border, to remind them of the threat and what was being done to combat it.

None of the host on the ground looked to have much that could threaten a Marine in a PICS. That didn't mean they didn't have anything—the Malakh was more than powerful enough to take on PICS Marines. Hondo pulled up the threat brief, noting the vehicle's weaknesses. There weren't many. While not the equal of a Marine Aardwolf, nor a Brotherhood Magen, for that matter, it still packed a powerful punch. Its armor was impressive, as well. Facing the Marines, its more vulnerable rear was protected.

Hondo pushed the threat brief to the rest of the squad. If anything did go down, they needed to be ready.

The major was talking again, pushing the UAM rule, when Hondo's proximity warning lit his display.

There's no way Cara made it this quickly, he told himself as he queried the approaching force.

Only it wasn't Second Squad making it back to camp. To his surprise, it was the 12 Klethos, closing in fast.

The Klethos weren't billeted in their small camp. They had their own area 50 klicks away, but they were heading toward the Marines.

"Lieutenant, we've got the Klethos arriving in camp," he passed to the lieutenant, knowing his commander's PA wouldn't have the same range as his own PICS' array.

The lieutenant stopped mid-sentence and almost turned to face him before gathering himself.

"What the hell are you talking about, McKeever?"

"They're here. Or almost. Five minutes, tops."

"Son of a bitch. I told them to go back to their camp. What the hell are they doing back here?"

The original plan was that after the engagement, all hands would return together to the Marine camp for the debrief, but the lieutenant had specifically told them to go back to their camp. Hondo told his AI to run the recording, and sure enough, the platoon commander had said, "I repeat, all hands, human and Klethos, cease training and return to your camps immediately."

"I think they misunderstood, sir," Hondo passed.

"No shit, Sergeant."

"It was the original plan, sir," Staff Sergeant Callen said. "You know how the Klucks are. I bet they're just going with that."

"And now we're screwed."

"Is there something wrong, Lieutenant?" the Brotherhood major called out. "You were saying?"

"I was saying that I think it's time for you to leave, sir. You've duly made your point. Those much higher on the ladder will take over. We're just the tools to get the conversation going."

The major gave the lieutenant a piercing stare while Hondo willed him to take his host and leave. For a moment, he thought the major would do that, but suddenly, he spun around and looked at the Malakh.

That's it. The Malakh picked up the Klucks, too.

The major turned back, a broad smile visible under his goggles.

"No, I think we're going to stay, Lieutenant."

"McKeever, send someone to stop the Klethos. I don't want them in this camp," Lieutenant Singh passed on the P2P.

"Roger that," he replied, then passed, "Wolf, go stop the Klucks. Tell them to go back to their own camp."

The corporal stepped back, then broke into a run, heading for the Klethos.

"Is your Marine going somewhere. Lieutenant?" the major asked, satisfaction dripping from his voice.

"I thought you said to cut the charade, sir."

"So I did, so I did."

"What now, sir?" Hondo asked on the platoon command net.

"We see if Corporal Johnson can stop the Klethos. I've just given them the same command, but they're not responding."

Hondo had both respect and disdain for their allies. On the one hand, they were fantastic warriors, never expressing fear, and tough as nails. Without being in a PICS, no Marine could stand up to one and win. On the other hand, their tactics were rudimentary at best, and they had a habit of shirking from technology. Credits to doughnuts, they'd turned off their communicators.

There was a subtle shift in the 30 host who faced them. They were now half-oriented to the approach the Klethos would take if they entered the camp.

"Weapons hot, Sergeant McKeever," the lieutenant passed on the P2P.

There was the slightest surge as his magazines locked into the feed slots. Around him, he could sense more than see his Marines as their focus intensified.

"Lance Corporal Haus, watch Pickerul," he told the senior Marine in First Fire Team now that Wolf was gone.

Pickerul's pulse was racing. For a brief moment, Hondo considered taking her cold, but if it did come down to a fight, he couldn't leave a Marine unprotected.

The Malakh's five-kilojoule GET-70 powered up and swung to cover the Marines. The armored vehicle had picked up the PICS going hot. Things were escalating, and Hondo felt as if they were losing control of the situation.

"Easy, Marines," the lieutenant passed.

All pretense gone, neither he nor the major were speaking to each other. This was about the Klethos, as it had been from the beginning. They were all waiting to see that would happen.

And that didn't make sense to him. If they really wanted to "arrest" the Klethos, not that Hondo thought they had the authority, why send only 30 host to face 15 PICS Marines, 16 if they counted Gilead? Sure, they had the Malakh, and it could cause damage, but there were too many

PICS for it to succeed. They had to be assuming that the Marines wouldn't risk an incident.

Bad assumption, he told himself.

But they could be right. As far as he knew, the battalion CO hadn't received any orders as how to proceed. The Federation leadership might decide that the sacrifice of a couple of hundred Klethos was a price they were willing to pay. They could negotiate their return later when things cooled down.

Hondo was watching the progress of the Klethos. They stopped when Wolf reached them, and he let out a sigh of relief.

Too soon.

A minute later, Johnson started back along with a single Klethos.

"What are you doing?" he asked the corporal.

"The leader wants to see the lieutenant. I can't stop her."

"Get her to turn on her damn comms!" Hondo said. "The lieutenant'll tell her."

"She won't do it. She says she has to see him face-to-face."

"Sir—" Hondo started, when the lieutenant stopped him.

"I see it. Tell Corporal Johnson to get that Kluck to turn on her comms."

"I did, sir, but she won't do it. She wants to see you."

The Klethos could be stubborn—no, not *could* be stubborn, *were* stubborn. If the Klethos squad leader decided that she had to come in, she was going to come in or die trying.

There was a pause, then the lieutenant got on the hook with the team leader, linking in Hondo. "Corporal Johnson, go back to the other Klethos. No matter what, they are not to approach the camp."

"What about the leader?" Staff Sergeant Gary Callen, the platoon sergeant, asked, also listening in.

"Not much we can do about her now, so the key is to keep the rest out of the way."

"Nothing from battalion?"

"Nothing new. Just keep the situation from escalating."

Everyone, Marine and host alike, settled into silence as they watched the Klethos' avatar approach their position. Hondo peered into the still-falling snow to spot her.

Which isn't my job, he reminded himself.

"First Squad, focus on the Brotherhood host, not the Kluck," he passed. "All Mod Threes, your only target is the Malakh if things go to shit. Hopefully, they won't, but we need to be prepared. If something goes down, Corporal Ling, take your team and get in back of the Malakh. The rest of us, keep the host ground-pounders occupied.

"Doc, you and Gilead get the lieutenant and the staff sergeant out of danger if rounds start flying," he passed, keying the civilian into the circuit.

"That's not going to happen," Staff Sergeant Callen passed.

Hondo rolled his eyes. He should have figured the platoon sergeant was monitoring the squad net. He wasn't surprised that Callen wouldn't leave—the man was a certified hard-ass—but neither he nor the lieutenant were in PICS, and they'd be cut down in a second by the Malakh.

"Ignore that, Doc. Just get them out of here," he passed on the private P2P.

Hondo tried to think of anything else he could do in preparation. Without an operations order, this was all on the fly. If it came to a fight, he'd have to rely on the training to get them through it.

"Here she comes," Corporal Ling passed.

Loping along on her ostrich-like legs, the Klethos warrior emerged from the snow, an apparition from instinctual nightmares. She never even glanced at the assembled host as she ran up to the lieutenant.

"Why did you stop us?" she asked the lieutenant, barely audible.

Hondo turned up his gain to hear.

"We have a situation here, and I want you to go back to your squad."

"We have the debrief of our engagement to attend."

"Later," the lieutenant said, his voice calm as if reasoning with a child. "We will do that later."

"That is not the schedule," she insisted. "We are here now."

Oh, come on. Can't you see that now is not the time to be hidebound?

"Lieutenant Singh, unless I am somehow mistaken, I believe that is a Klethos soldier standing there," the Brotherhood major said, sarcasm heavy in his tone. "As you are in violation of UAM 12.06, subparagraph 14 gives me the authority to take the spawn into custody. If you'll step aside?"

Four host took a few paces forward, ready to approach the Klethos.

"No, I will not step aside. I do not recognize that 12.06 applies here, and until our own SJA weighs in with the contrary, I will not allow you to take any action here on Federation soil."

The lieutenant turned back to the Klethos and said, "If you will return to your squad, we will debrief later."

"It's not going anywhere," the major said.

The Klethos slowly turned around, for the first time looking at the Brotherhood host. She seemed to contemplate them for a moment, then with a human-like shrug of all four of her shoulders, seemed to dismiss them.

"We will return for the debrief," she said, and without another word, started to run off.

"Stop!" the major shouted, and the four host who'd stepped forward moved to intercept the Klethos.

"Sergeant McKeever—" the lieutenant started to yell, when a shot rang out.

An instant later, the camp was filled with fire.

"Ling, go!" Hondo shouted as he fired his M90, sending hundreds of hypervelocity darts into the host, who had almost to a man taken the Klethos under fire.

The Brotherhood personal armor was good, impervious to the standard-issue M99, but the PICS' M90 packed more of a punch, and several of them fell.

With a blast of ionized air, the Malakh opened up. Hondo didn't have time to see if anyone was hit as he charged forward to protect the Klethos. She staggered under the onslaught of fire, but with a tremendous leap, she was in among the host, kicking and swinging with what looked to be a small knife.

Under normal combat conditions, the Klethos would be able to suppress human weapons, and armed with both her own rifles and sword, she'd be almost invincible. This was a training scenario, however, and she'd been stripped of her capabilities so as to minimize the potential for accidents.

Still, she managed to drop three of them with the small knife she wielded. All of the host seemed to be focused on bringing her down, which was a fatal mistake. Ling's Third Team was trying to flank the Malakh, but that left two teams to rake the host with darts, grenades, and shoulder rockets. At least a dozen were down before the Klethos finally fell.

With her KIA, Hondo paused to find out the lieutenant's orders, but to his shock, he and the platoon sergeant were down, killed by the Malakh's first shot. The personnel carrier fired again, taking out Doc and Julli-Patterson.

Hondo was now the senior Marine. He stood back a second to get a grasp of the situation. Corporal Ling and his team were racing around to the right. Haus was down, his avatar greyed out. That left him with eight Marines, including himself—nine, if he counted Gilead—to face about 15 host and the Malakh and keep them occupied while Ling got into position.

He fired his shoulder rockets at the Malakh, knowing they probably wouldn't penetrate the frontal armor, but hoping it would catch the crew's attention.

"Push forward, First and Second," he ordered. "Get in the mix with them."

On foot or not, the host soldiers had weapons that could take down a PICS, but none were as effective as the Malakh's big GET-70. If the Marines were intermixed with the host, the Malakh crew couldn't fire at them without killing their own side.

Something hit him in the left arm, and lights flashed on his display. The arm, and the attached M90, was out of commission. He didn't pause but continued into the host. He didn't need the M90 at this range; his right fist was more than enough against ground troops. He swung at one soldier, who ducked to the ground under the swing. Hondo tried to step on him, but the man managed to roll out of the way.

He might not have his M90, but his shoulder rockets were still functional. He initiated the magazine switch-out as he spun around, making sure no one was on him.

A surprised host soldier jumped back, a limpet in his hand. A limpet was used for breaching bunkers and buildings, and it would have done a number on him if the soldier had managed to place it on his PICS. As the man backpedaled, Hondo took a PICS-sized stride forward and swung his right arm, his gauntlet almost knocking the man's head off his shoulder.

His display lit up with yet another energy blast, surprising him. He pulled up the trace, and he realized his mistake. By intermixing with the host, that left the Malakh only one target: Corporal Ling's team. Lance Corporal Weinstein, with the Weapons Pack 3's Chimera, was down hard.

That left him two WP 3's. Both had fired at the Malakh, but the close-in defenses and active armor had defeated the missiles. Lance Corporal Acevedo had tried a pop-up, coming down on top of the vehicle, but the missile had been shot down. They had to get a side aspect for a mobility kill or a rear aspect to destroy it.

For half a second, Hondo considered taking a limpet from one of the dead host—one of them probably had enough punch to burst through the side armor. He discarded that idea as it would require one of the Marines to molt.

He did have a bullfrog, the heavy-duty incendiary device that was designed to destroy an abandoned PICS or other equipment. He pulled it out of his thigh slot, and with a careful toss, threw it on top of the Malakh. It bounced once, then slid down the sloped sides, falling to the ground before erupting into a blinding hot ball of fire.

Another blast of energy lit up his display, this time knocking Private Jorgenson out of commission. She was alive, but she was out of the fight. With only three host still on their feet, the Marines had lost their cover, and the Malakh had fired into them.

"Second, on me!" he passed. "Keep seven meters off."

According to his readout, the Malakh had four close-in anti-personnel pods on each corner of the tank, set to activate when someone broke the seven-meter zone.

"Antman, hold fire until you get around to the back," he told Lance Corporal Acevedo. "And I'm serious about the seven meters.

"Davis, cover us," he ordered the last WP 3 Marine.

Davis had three more Chimeras. He fired the first. At this close range, it only took a second to reach the Malakh, but Hondo could see the close-in defenses rise like a cloud of gnats, detonating the missile short. Hot plasma continued its trajectory and splashed the vehicle in a shower of sparks, but didn't penetrate.

A split second later, someone's M146 shoulder rocket hit the same spot and made it through to the tank itself. It detonated with a blinding flash, and his face shield display compensated, revealing a gouge in the armor, right where one of the four CIAP pods was located. Hondo painted the spot on the AI, then ordered everyone else to concentrate their fire there.

Without any host left standing, the Malakh let loose a stream of 12.4 rounds from the supplementary turret, but those didn't have the punch to take out a PICS. The big GET-70m, though, started to swing towards Hondo. He wasn't sure if that was simply bad luck or if the carrier's battle AI had figured out he was in command from the comms web. He supermanned a jump forward, trying to keep ahead of the tracking gun as it closed in on him.

He forced down the rising panic, knowing that if the crew was tracking him, then that left Antman free to get a kill shot.

But it wasn't Antman who closed in. Rushing through the gap Hondo had left, PFC Pickerul, of all Marines, rushed forward to the Malakh, angling right for the gouge on the front right corner. Hondo's heart caught in this throat, as he expected the CIAP pod to let loose and cut her down, but it never engaged. With her own superman, she jumped up onto the vehicle, scrambling to stay on her feet on the slanted surface.

Immediately, the GET-70 tube reversed direction off of Hondo, and the Malakh surged forward, only to stop with a jolt. Pickerul was knocked to her hands and knees, the PICS' servos struggling to keep her in a vertical aspect.

"Cease fire!" Hondo screamed out over the net to protect her from friendly fire.

The Malakh jerked forward again, knocking Pickerul toward the turret as the GET-70 closed in on her. More to keep herself on top of the vehicle than anything else, she reached up with her left gauntlet and clamped her arm over the barrel. As it kept traversing, the barrel pulled her along, actually assisting her with regaining her feet.

The Malakh's gunner fired, and Hondo held his breath. An unprotected Marine would be killed by the power surging down the focusing tube, but Pickerul's avatar remained a stead bright blue. She wasn't hurt.

With one arm clamped around the tube, she fumbled in her thigh slot and pulled out her own bullfrog.

"Get some, Tammy," he muttered to himself, as she activated it with one arm and slid it under the tube, right at the base of the turret.

She started to bail when the Malakh jerked hard to the right, making her almost lose her balance again—and more importantly, knocked the bullfrog from the one flat spot, making it roll off the sloped top and onto the snowy ground, where it detonated like a tiny star.

Shit, shit, shit!

PICS Marines only carried a single bullfrog, and hers was gone.

"Pick!" Wolf shouted over his externals as he came running up to join the fight. "Take mine!"

"The CIAP!" Hondo warned him, but the corporal stopped ten meters short, and with a soft underhanded toss, flipped his bullfrog up just as the Malakh spun hard to the left like a bull trying to throw its rider.

Pickerul stretched out, tipped the bullfrog spinning back into the air, and somehow managed to snag it as it came back down. The Malakh bolted into reverse and spun around with Pickerul simply hanging on. When it lurched forward, Pickerul reached under the tube to the base of the turret again, this time jamming the bullfrog forward as hard as she could. She waited a moment, and when the fuze lit off, she supermanned yet one more time to jump off the tank as the bullfrog detonated. Sparks followed her, arching up in the air to shower the snow around the Malakh with an eerily beautiful display.

The top hatch flung open, and bodies began to pile out.

"Hold your fire," Hondo passed, as three hosts tumbled off the Malakh and into the snow, hands raised as soon as they got to their feet.

"Corporal Takimora, secure them," he ordered his Second Team leader.

"Pick, that was freaking awesome," Antman passed over the squad net.

"Cut the chatter," Hondo passed.

It *was* freaking awesome, but Hondo had to get a grasp of the situation. In a little less than two minutes, 30 Brotherhood host had been wiped out. If mankind's two major powers hadn't been at war, Hondo might have driven them to it.

This is serious shit, Hondo. What the hell have you done?

First things first, though. Whatever the consequences, he had to secure the scene.

"Ling, secure the Brotherhood grunts. If any are still alive, get them into the gym. Davis, check Jorgenson and the others. I've got to report this."

He took a deep breath, but his P2P crackled on before he could contact battalion himself, and the battalion operations officer said, "Good job, Sergeant. Secure the area and wait for someone to reach you."

He should have known that battalion would have known what was happening—they just hadn't wanted to get in his way during the fight.

"I've got dead, wounded, and prisoners, sir. I need transport."

"Can't do it now, Sergeant. Fighting has broken out all over the training area. Keep the dead out in the snow, bring the wounded inside, then just wait. Three, out."

With that, the operations officer cut the connection.

All over the training area? What the hell is going on?

He had his orders, though, and it looked like they were on their own for now. He looked over the battlefield. The lieutenant, platoon sergeant, and Haus were KIA, probably beyond resurrection. Doc, Weinstein, and Julli-Patterson were KIA, too, but they had a chance of being zombied, at least. The Klethos squad leader was dead. They had three prisoners, and 30 host, including a major, were dead, even if most might be zombied and resurrected.

Hondo had no idea as to the consequences of what had just occurred, but it couldn't be good. With a war against the Grubs taking up most of the Federation and its allies' resources, he wondered if they had a new enemy: a human one. He hoped not, but that was something to be hashed out far above his pay grade.

EARTH

Chapter 2
Skylar

"The Minister wants you at the conference, ma'am," Jack said, sticking his head in the door.

"You knew he would," Keyshon told Skylar Ybarra, Assistant Vice-Minister for Alien Affairs.

"Yeah, I thought he might, but this isn't an alien thing. This is human against human," she said.

"Twenty-four Klethos were killed, and the Liaison Quad is asking for answers," Keyshon reminded her.

She leaned back in her chair and closed her eyes for a moment. The confrontation on Krakow had taken everyone by surprise. From what she'd been able to glean over the last hour, the intent of the UAM forces had been to goad the Brotherhood, but not to the point of a shooting war. Reports were still coming in, but no fewer than seven fights had erupted from the 15 confrontations. Forty-two Federation Marines had been killed, as had one-hundred-and-twenty-four Brotherhood host.

And the twenty-four Klethos her chief-of-staff had just mentioned.

Some, if not many, of the dead would be resurrected, but no matter how it was spun, this was the single largest loss of life in a conflict between the Federation and Brotherhood since . . . well, since forever.

Skylar was still numb. She'd been reviewing one of her committees' reports on the most likely Dictymorph expansion route into human space when word of the fighting on Krakow reached her. She couldn't think of worse development, save a Dictymorph landing on Earth itself. Humanity needed to band together to face the threat, not fight among itself.

"Ma'am, you really need to go," Keyshon gently reminded her.

She opened her eyes and brought her chair upright. He was right, as he usually was. Sky was quite young for her position, and she'd made a few enemies among the more established bureaucrats. She might be an expert in Klethos psychology and knew as much as anyone about the Dictymorphs, but she was a neophyte as to the inner workings of the Federation ministries. Keyshon, on the other hand, had been with the Second Ministry for over 60 years, working his way up from the very bottom. If he resented being under a woman a third his age, he never let on, and he'd been invaluable to Sky as she established herself.

"OK, I'm ready. I'd like you with me, though," she told him.

He nodded, then told Sierra, "Let them know we're on the way."

Sky stood up, straightened her oh-so-conservative suit, and followed Keyshon out of the office where an anxious-looking proctor waited by the entrance. As soon as she saw Sky, the woman opened the door, one arm back as if she wanted to push her through.

The three walked down the hall, the proctor subtly speeding her pace as if she wanted to sweep up Sky in her draft. Sky knew she had time, but the Proctor Service was not known for their flexibility, and this one would want her charge in her seat with time to spare.

The Second Ministry's headquarters was in Pittsburgh, far away from the hustle and bustle of DC or Brussels, and Sky was glad of that. The minister himself had taken a stratojet to Brussels to back up the chairman, but the rest of the ministry was gathering in the conference room. Sky nodded to Dr. Tolker, her closest ally in the ministry, then took her seat at the table. Her proctor hooked up the earbud, checked the connection, and then with what Sky thought was a sigh of relief, left the room, her job done.

The UAM's grand hall was visible in the projection over the conference table. It was three-quarters full, with the main meeting to commence in another twenty minutes.

"Glad to see you made it," the minister said through her earbud.

The minister had taken a special interest in Sky, another thing that distanced her from her colleagues. He'd been the one who'd elevated Sky from a lowly FS-13 scientist to the ministry's rep to the first task force against the Dictymorphs. That task force had ended in the disaster of the attack on Purgamentium, but somehow, Sky hadn't been stained with the fallout, and in fact, had been elevated to her present position.

"Yes, sir. Not much choice with the PS's escorting us."

"Is Keyshon with you?"

"Yes, sir."

There was a short pause, then the minister said, "You need to fly off on your own, Skylar. You don't need him."

Sky blushed, then quickly looked around to see if anyone noticed. She knew she was using Keyshon as a crutch, but she hadn't thought anyone else realized it.

"I just thought—" she started before he cut her off.

"You just thought you needed him there with you. Look, if I'd wanted him, I'd have given him your job. He's a good man, a good assistant, but I chose you. Next time, I expect to see you and only you, understand?"

"Yes, sir, I understand."

She looked up at the projection. Except for the Brotherhood section and those of their allies, the hall was filling up, and she had to query her AI to find the minister. It zeroed in on the man, and he was looking right at the universal pick up. As soon as it locked in on him, he gave the slightest nod, then turned to the woman on his right.

The minister was right. He'd put her in the position, and it was about time she took charge and said screw the rest if they had a problem with it. She was about to tell her chief-of-staff that he could leave, but since he was there already . . .

Next time, I'll fly solo, she promised herself.

She studied her PA for the next five minutes, scanning for updates. Nothing new of any import was streaming in.

"The Klethos quad's arrived," Keyshon whispered into her ear.

Sky didn't have to search the hall to spot them. Four Klethos, wearing the minimal harnesses that for them was full regalia, strode into the hall, then leaned up against the oversized backrests that had been installed for them in the observer section. She switched to her PA and zoomed in on them. When agitated, a Klethos' neck fringe tended to straighten, reaching full peacock display when entering battle musth. These were seasoned diplomats, however, and their fringes were down and flat against their backs.

"Make sure you get our own recording of them," she told Keyshon. "I'm going to want our K-team to analyze their reaction to whatever goes down today."

"Yes, ma'am," he said. "I'm on it."

Sky went back to her PA, messaging Dr. Harry al Upton, her K-team leader, to focus on the quad.

Which he's undoubtedly already doing, she had to admit to herself.

Captain Throckmorton, her Navy liaison, had been gently advising her to keep from micromanaging her team, but because she didn't feel comfortable as a leader, she had a habit of trying to do too much herself.

"Here they come," someone said.

Sky looked up, and with almost military precision, the Brotherhood contingent marched in together, led by the ambassador. He continued to the front row, his people breaking off to fill their section. He ignored the chairman and the president of Greater France, a huge breach of protocol. The murmurs from the gathered worthies was evidence that his slight was noted.

The ambassador started towards the secretary general, then halted for a moment, his head cocked in the manner of someone listening to a call.

"Looks like First Bro's handling the strings," Yelcy Smith said.

Not that Sky had expected anything different. The first brother might not have made the trip to Earth, but he and his conclave would be directing every word the ambassador made.

After a slight nod, the ambassador turned back and sat in his designated seat, his eyes impassive as he stared somewhere over the secretary-general's head.

At exactly 1300 GMT, the secretary-general stood and made her way to the main podium. She paused for a moment, leaned forward, and dramatically swept her gaze from one side of the hall to the other.

"As per the request of the ambassador of the Alliance of Free State, I hereby call this extra plenary meeting of the general assembly to order." She paused again, her famous dark brown eyes boring into the assembly. "We are here after a series of unfortunate events, events that could—"

"Madame Secretary," the Dentonian ambassador stood and shouted out. "I request that you yield to me."

The secretary general stopped, her eyes widening in surprise at the interruption.

"Oh, shit," Tolker said, totally out of character for him. "She's going to eat him alive."

Sky looked at her compatriot sitting across the table and nodded. No one crossed the secretary-general unscathed, especially an ambassador from a piddly-ass government like Denton.

To her great surprise, however, the secretary-general, her eyes almost spitting out lightening, nodded and said, "I yield to the ambassador from Denton."

"And I yield to the ambassador from the Brotherhood."

"Holy shit," someone to her right muttered under his breath as Sky wondered what had just happened.

"UAM rules. SOP 1201.3.4410. For an extra plenary meeting, even the secretary general has to yield to whoever called for the assembly. And that person can yield to anyone else."

"And you just happen to have the exact paragraph handy?" she asked her chief-of-staff.

"Given that this is an extra plenary assembly, I thought it prudent to go over all the possibilities."

Sky looked at him, trying to see if there was a rebuke in his eyes, but if there was, he hid it well. He was right, though. It was only reasonable that he look up the rules for such an assembly. She should have, as well. In her mind, Sky was a scientist, first and foremost. As an assistant vice-minister, however, she was a bureaucrat, and if she wanted to succeed, she'd better start acting like one. She gave Keyshon a short nod, the looked back to the projection where the Brotherhood ambassador was walking to the podium.

The secretary-general waited for him, and for a moment after the man reached her, Sky wondered if she would yield to him. It was all for dramatic effect, however. With a sweep of her hand, she ceded her position to him.

The ambassador took his position, and without the dramatic pauses of the secretary-general, immediately said, "The recent attack on Brotherhood host perpetrated by the Federation Marines is an intolerable assault on not only our citizens, but on all mankind. Even more intolerable is the continued alliance with the Klethos."

Sky took a quick glance at the quad. None of the four exhibited any emotion.

"Such an alliance is a threat to humanity's very existence. Until we have shored up our defenses, until we have developed tactics and weaponry that can defeat the Dictymorphs, then to attract them to human space again is beyond foolhardy—it is suicidal. We cannot let the debacle on Purgamentium be repeated on another human world.

"The Brotherhood, along with our allies, will not allow that to happen. As of this moment forward, we will use any and all methods to stop the transit of any ship, military or civilian, beyond the H2S."

There was a murmur and more than a few shouts from the assembly, echoed by those around Sky in the Second Ministry conference room in Pittsburgh. Sky wondered if she heard that correctly. Surely the ambassador couldn't mean that they would physically stop any human attempting to cross the Human 2 Sphere, the practical boundary of human space.

"I repeat. As of this moment, no humans will cross the H2S. From the bottom of my heart, I ask you not to test us on this. You will not like the result.

"Madame Secretary General, I yield back to you," he said, marching off the dais and continuing on to exit the hall.

"Order, order!" the secretary general shouted as voices rose in anger and confusion both.

The Brotherhood ambassador swept up the rest of his delegation in his wake as he left, the smaller delegations of his allies following suit. Within two minutes, they were gone.

"Are we at war now?" Yelcy asked, his normally forceful voice subdued.

Damned good question, Sky thought, as she tried to absorb what had just occurred.

FS TERESA S. GOLDSTEIN

Chapter 3
Hondo

Hondo stared at a spot on the bulkhead over the battalion commander's head as the man seemed to contemplate what he'd just been told.

Just say something!

Hondo was reasonably sure that he'd done what he could during the battle, but his opinion didn't matter much. It was up to the CO. If he thought Hondo had screwed up, his career was over at best, and he could potentially be facing brig time at worst. He'd become the platoon commander with Lieutenant Singh and Staff Sergeant Callen KIA, after all, and that made everything that happened after the lieutenant died his responsibility.

Rumor had it that Lieutenant Wilkes-Jung from Charlie Company was under house arrest in her stateroom for her actions on Krakow. No official word had been passed, and it wasn't as if the non-rates and NCOs could just take a gander into officer territory to check it out, but if the SNCO mafia said it was true, then it probably was.

"XO, do you have any questions?" he asked Major Jespers.

"No, sir. We've watched the recordings, and Sergeant McKeever has validated them."

"You kept your head on your shoulders, Sergeant," the CO said, and Hondo felt the first stirrings of relief. "I couldn't ask for more than that. Before I let you go, though, is there anyone you think deserves a commendation?"

Hondo broke his posture, glancing first at Captain Ariç, his company commander. Recommending awards up the chain was her prerogative, not a squad leader's. The captain gave him an almost imperceptible nod, so he looked back at the CO who was waiting for his response.

"PFC Pickerul, sir. Without her, the Malakh could have taken out more of us."

The CO nodded, saying, "Pickerul it is, then."

He gave a quick glance to the XO, and Hondo realized that he'd already made that decision. The commanding officer was just testing him. Pickerul was an obvious choice, good for a BC Three, at least. Maybe a Bronze Star. But there was somebody else, and Hondo knew the CO didn't know the entire story surrounding that.

"There's someone else, sir," Hondo said as the CO raised his eyebrows.

I knew you weren't expecting me to say that. You thought Pickerul was it.

"And who is that?"

"Gilead Conroy, sir."

"Conroy? From the armory?" he asked, clearly puzzled.

"Yes, sir. Conroy."

The CO looked up at the XO, his brow scrunched up.

He shook his head, then said, "I'm not sure what you're getting at. I know he suited up, which was quite unusual, but I hardly saw him do anything extraordinary. Can you explain yourself, Sergeant?"

"Sir, it isn't that he did something above and beyond what a Marine would do, but he did go above and beyond what a civilian does. He stood alongside Marines in combat, and he did his duty."

"As all of you did."

Shit, he's not getting my point. Focus, Hondo!

He took a breath, then tried another tack. "Sir, you need to know something. Gilead has wanted to be a Marine all his life, only he never made the cut. He was never good enough. Even now, with the draft, he can't enlist because he's in a vital civilian billet. He's stuck working for us, but never being one of us. Never being good enough to be one of us."

"But he's serving a vital billet, as you say. And if he wasn't good enough to make the cut before, then he's serving the Federation the best he can as an armor tech."

"Maybe, sir. But with the draft, he'd make the cut now. More than that, without even going to boot, without ITC, he pulled his weight. He stood by us when the shi . . . uh, when everything was going down, sir. And for my squad and me, that's what counts. He's got what it takes, sir," he said, his voice rising with passion.

The CO took a long, hard look at him.

Oh, fuck. I'm standing here lecturing a lieutenant colonel. You freaking idiot!

"Sergeant Major, what do you think?" the CO asked.

"Well, sir, I be thinking that it's what's in a man's heart that counts. If Conroy's got the drive to be a Marine, and if Sergeant McKeever be vouching for him, then I'd be partial to letting him try."

The CO sat for a moment while he contemplated what had been said before asking Hondo, "How old is he?"

"Twenty-five, sir, well under the cut-off."

"XO, do I even have the authority for that?"

"Technically, no. That would be the director of Manpower. But if you put in the request, it should be a rubber stamp all the way up."

"And Conroy really wants this?" he asked Hondo.

"Yes, sir. He's said it enough times."

"Sergeant Major, get him in to see me. If he tells me he wants it, then let's make it happen. Anything else, Sergeant McKeever? Anyone else you need to champion?"

"No, sir. That's it."

"Thank God for small favors. If that's all, you're dismissed."

Hondo came to attention, did a recruit depot about-face, and marched out of the office. Half a dozen Marines were waiting in the passageway, and they all jumped up as he made his appearance.

"How was it?" Staff Sergeant Anderson from Bravo asked.

"No big thing, Staff Sergeant. He just wanted to get my take on things."

Hondo marched down the passage to the ladder leading out of officer country feeling good. Pickerul deserved an award, and Conroy deserved a chance at becoming a Marine.

That son-of-a-bitch better not have been bullshitting us all this time about wanting it, he told himself as he made his way to berthing to give him the news. *Nah, he does. And if somehow he doesn't, the rest of us will make sure he goes anyway. Ooh-rah, Recruit Conroy!*

AEGIS 2

Chapter 4
Hondo

"Get us another round, Poolee!" Pickerul shouted, already feeling quite good and planning on feeling even more so.

Gilead Conroy, with his orders to report to the recruit depot on Tarawa, jumped up, a huge smile on his face, ready to do her bidding. He didn't care that Pickerul was four years younger than he was, that as a poolee, he was lower than dirt to the three dozen Marines who'd shown up at his farewell party. He also didn't seem to care that he was paying for the open bar. He was going to be a Marine.

Hondo needn't have been concerned about his really wanting to be a Marine. The tech had lit up like the casinos on New Macau when he'd been given the news. Within two weeks, the orders had come in. It was a done deal. Now, he just had to get though boot camp, and he'd be one of the few.

He had his work cut out for him. With only two weeks of poolee training, run by Wolf, there'd been no time to whip him into shape. The Egg's blistering hot temperatures had something to do with that, but still, physical fitness was not Conroy's strong suit.

"Think he'll make it?" Cara Riordan asked Hondo, as she watched Condor run to the keg.

"Yeah, I think he will," he told his fellow squad leader. "He may be a little soft, but he's got some steel in him."

"Steel? I don't think so," she said with a soft laugh.

"No, not physically, but mentally. He might get recycled, but he'll stick with it." He took a sip of his beer, then asked, "So, what scoop do you have on the new lieutenant?"

As the platoon's senior sergeant, she'd been acting platoon sergeant, and she had access to more than Hondo had. That, plus the fact that one of the admin staff at headquarters battalion had a crush on her, gave her an inside leg on getting the intel.

Cara looked around at the others, then leaned in to quietly say, "Not much. Only two years in the trenches, then the Academy. No combat experience. Graduated high in both the Academy and NTC."

Hondo grimaced. The Academy was generally for the hard-chargers, the ones with stars in their eyes. That could be a detriment. If they were so intent on climbing the ladder to the top, then they tended to take risks in order to cover themselves with glory. All of the Academy officers were intelligent, but some were plain stupid as well. The recently departed Lieutenant Wilkes-Jung wasn't a ring-knocker, but he had that succeed-at-all-costs attitude, and that had cost the lives of eight good Marines on Krakow.

"Well, we'll just have to see. Any word on a new platoon sergeant?"

"Nothing yet, so you're still stuck with me."

Hondo just rolled his eyes. It might be better if Cara stayed in the billet. They may be back in garrison, but they'd be back in the mix before long, and having both a new platoon commander and a new platoon sergeant at the same time could pose a problem.

Conroy came back with two pitchers, and Antman called out, "Hey, Poolee, how much do you make as an armor tech?"

Conroy hesitated, then said, "About Fifty kay."

"Do you know how much a recruit gets paid? Four-point-three kay. So, you better have something saved up."

There were hoots and hollers, and Conroy stepped up to bat with, "I've got more than enough saved up, and I'll have plenty of places to spend it on Tarawa, not like you poor sucks here on the Egg."

"Oh, now he's done it," Cara said.

"Oh, you think so? You think Tarawa's going to be a fucking vacation? You're going to boot camp, Poolee. You ain't going out in town in your free time because there's no fucking free time there!"

Several foam cups flew through the air to hit the poolee, two still containing beer.

"Alcohol abuse," someone dutifully shouted as the beer spilled on the deck.

Conroy stared at Antman, then said, "In the one afternoon I'll have off after graduating, there'll be more places to spend my money on within a hundred meters of the main gate than here on the Asshole of the Federation."

"Not a bad burn," Hondo told Cara.

"That's if you make it, Poolee," Antman said, but Hondo could see he knew he'd been beaten. Several of the others pounded Conroy on the back, and Pickerul even stood to bump elbows.

"Not entirely true. Almost, but not entirely," Cara said.

"Close enough for government work."

Aegis 2, "The Egg," had earned the nickname of Asshole of the Federation. A valuable source of rare earths and other minerals, the planet was barely terraformed, had horribly hot weather, and an almost complete lack of social amenities. Other than the mining conglomerates scattered around the planet, the Federation governor's office and the 13th Marines were the major sources of employment here in the capital. There were a few dives and shops clustered around the camp selling 15-credit beer and souvenirs, but most of their time was spent on base where the beer and cider were cold and cost five credits.

"Hey, Corporal Takimora, take note of the poolee. I'll want just as much to drink next week," Sergeant Falt Wiscombe shouted, lifting his now-full cup.

Wolf put his arms around his fellow team leader and said, "Sure you want to take that promotion? Leave us and all that? I'm sure you can still turn down sergeant and stay with us."

"Fucking-A right I'm taking it. Get rid of all you losers," he said, pulling Wolf into a headlock and rubbing his friend's head with his knuckles.

"That's right. You're going to need a new team leader with Taki gone," Cara said to Hondo. "Have they told you who's coming in?"

He shrugged. With Takimora making sergeant and no squad leader openings in the platoon, he was being transferred to Bravo Company's Third Platoon. The corporal had the makings of a good NCO, but Hondo had never bonded with him as he had with Wolf and Ling. First Sergeant Nordstrand had promised him another corporal to take over the team, but as of yet, no one had been designated by name.

Hondo took a moment to gaze out over the Marines. A month ago, they'd been thrust into combat. They'd lost friends, but they'd kicked ass against a prepared opponent. Now they were sending one of their own—Conroy had earned that designation—off to Tarawa. They were happy, he realized. Sitting in the E-Club on the Asshole of the Federation, fighting Grubs on Purgamentium, or simply getting through recruit training on Tarawa, all of it melded into the blood and steel that made up the Corps.

There was little doubt in Hondo's mind that soon, he'd be going into combat with them again, and this time he wanted to be prepared. They had a new lieutenant, and it was the NCO and SNCOs' job to train him. It was Hondo's job to train his squad. They had to be ready for whatever was thrown at them, be it the Grubs or, if things kept going on the way they were, the Brotherhood alliance. That sucked when the Grubs were a real threat, but Hondo had no control over that.

The new lieutenant was arriving the day after tomorrow, and Cara had already turned in the training plan for the week. They were going out into the field to snap him in, and Hondo had a feeling the platoon wasn't going to come up for air for a long, long time.

That left tonight and tomorrow. He emptied his stein, snagged one of Conroy's half-emptied pitchers, and asked Cara, "Buy you a beer, Acting Platoon Sergeant Riordan?"

EARTH

Chapter 5
Skylar

The Klethos warrior rose from the shallow gully and charged the Dictymorph from the flank, managing to drive its pike deep into the creature's side. The massive beast reared up and twisted to face its tormentor, its pseudopods coming together to emit a powerful light tendril that dropped the Klethos to the ground.

By rearing up, however, it exposed its underside, and three soldiers let loose with their flamethrowers, the sticky fuel adhering to it while it burned at close to 1100 C°. More tendrils of light reached out, but incoherently, not targeting Marines nor Klethos as the Dictymorph writhed its death dance.

As if attracted by the soldier's flame throwers, tendrils of light zigzagged and splashed the three Marines, outlining their PICS in a white-blue glow. One soldier managed to bolt to the side, breaking contact, but the other two seemed ensnared while the light broke through their PICS' shielding. It didn't take long. Within a few moments, the Marines were lost.

Sky didn't see the two soldiers die—she turned away at the last second, but the murmurs from the people in the conference room told the story. She'd been glued to her seat for over 12 hours now, not being able to do anything about the disaster on K-932, but unable to leave. That would seem too much like abandoning the Confederation legion that had joined the Klethos in battling the Dictymorphs on the planet.

It wasn't going well. The Klethos had held, despite significant casualties, against the first wave of invaders, and when the legion arrived to reinforce them, the alliance had begun to gain the upper hand. Then another wave of Dictymorphs arrived, turning the tables, and now, the legionnaires were on the run. Fewer than a thousand of them and perhaps a hundred Klethos were left on the planet to oppose an equal number of the enemy.

This was the first time the Dictymorphs had added new fighters, reinforcing a fight, but then again, it seemed that they were revealing something new for every fight. According to their Klethos liaison quad, the Dictymorphs hadn't changed their tactics during their long conflict with them. Enter the humans, with their reliance on tactics, and the Dictymorphs were replying in kind, adjusting to a more coordinated form of warfare.

"Any news on the standoff in IA200?" she asked Commander Throckmorton.

The commander had been awake longer than Sky, and he turned a haggard face to her and said, "Nothing. The task force is dead-in-space, waiting for orders."

"What do you think they're going to do? I mean, those legionnaires won't last much longer."

"I don't have a fucking clue," the exhausted commander said, then added, "Sorry about the language, ma'am."

She could see the commander was dead on his feet, and she didn't care if he threw in a fuck or two. What she did care about was whether the task force, six ships and over 9,000 Marines, would be allowed to proceed and rescue anyone who managed to survive long enough for them to get there.

And that number was rapidly dwindling.

What stood in the way was a Brotherhood task force. The Federation ships were mostly transports, while the Brotherhood task force was formed around a dreadnaught. If it came to a fight, the Federation ships wouldn't stand much of a chance.

She also realized that they couldn't risk those 9,000 Marines to that dreadnaught.

No one knew how many Dictymorphs were out there. What they did know was that there were far fewer Klethos warriors than anyone would have guessed, possibly 50,000 or so. If mankind had known that previously, then things might have gone differently between the two races.

With the Brotherhood's alliance pulling out of the war effort, that left the human force woefully undermanned. The Federation had 816 ships and three million-plus sailors, 260,000 Marines, five million FCDC troops (who were closer to paramilitary forces), and another million militia. The Confederation had two million legionnaires and 430 capital ships. Combined, the remainder of the UAM forces had fewer than a million men and women under arms.

While Sky knew that all military and paramilitary forces would do the best they could, it was taken for granted that the effective forces were the Marine, the Confederation's Batavian Cohort, the New Budapest Rangers, and the Klethos. That was fewer than half a million souls to fight toe-to-toe with the Dictymorphs. The Marines were in surge-mode to increase their numbers, but that would be a long process, one that the Dictymorphs might not allow. Battle-tested Marines were a valuable commodity, and they couldn't let the Brotherhood remove 9,000 of them, along with the six ships and sailors assigned to them.

Hell, Sky, you're getting hard-hearted. "Remove?" *Just say it like it is; it's kill.*

"Remove" or "kill," however, had the same result. There would be that many fewer numbers to face the enemy.

But which enemy? Dictymorph or Brotherhood?

The UAM and the Brotherhood's alliance were not exactly at war . . . yet. There had been the fighting on Krakow, but since then, it had been mostly posturing until yesterday. That was when the Brotherhood Navy had essentially drawn a plane through space, telling the UAM that they would not allow any military vessel to cross that plane and into Klethos space.

Sky wasn't a military expert, but it didn't take one to know that fighting on two fronts would be disastrous. The Brotherhood and its allies were essentially a match for UAM forces. The Dictymorphs looked to be stronger than any of them, even with the Klethos added to the equation.

She had no idea what was going to happen. Her focus was on the Dictymorphs, and she had to put all her energy there. She couldn't ignore, however, the human-against-human conflict that threatened to break out at any minute.

Her head felt like it was filled with cotton. She knew she needed sleep—sleep, not stim—if she was going to be able to function. She was about to leave the room and head back to her condo when the scene over the projection base shifted. Six Klethos stood back-to-back, facing at least a dozen Dictymorphs who were closing in on them.

Sky knew the Klethos didn't stand a chance, and her staying and watching safe and sound from Pittsburgh wasn't going to change anything. She really should leave and rest.

Should and *would* rarely coincided.

Pulling another Joltz out of her bag, she popped the top and guzzled the nasty-tasting liquid, then settled in to watch the inevitable.

AEGIS 2

Chapter 6
Hondo

"Sergeant McKeever, you've got an untenable gap. Fix it now," Second Lieutenant Armando Abrams passed on the P2P.

"Roger that, sir. I'm on it."

"You should have been on it five minutes ago when you emplaced Second Team."

"Yes, sir, I should have."

Shit, Al-Atrash! I'm going to fucking kill you!

Fuming, Hondo ran back to where Second Fire Team had somehow oriented itself at an angle to the other teams, leaving the gap in the lines about which the lieutenant had just reamed him. This week had been a disaster for Hondo. Nothing had gone right, and he was sure the lieutenant thought he was an unsalvageable shitbird. Ninety percent of all the fuck-ups could be attributed to Second Fire Team, and Hondo had had it with Corporal Silas Al-Atrash, his new team leader.

To top it off, the corporal was a "real" Marine, someone who'd enlisted before the Grubs changed the Corps. Only one of the other replacement Marines was a volunteer; the rest were draftees, or in Lance Corporal Hanaburgh's case, a transfer from the FCDC. Hondo had thanked his lucky stars when First Sergeant Nordstrand had told him he was getting

Al-Atrash to replace Takimora. Now he wanted to curse those stars.

Hondo ran past the prone Antman who studiously ignored him and reached the corporal, whose complacent expression changed to one of close to panic when he saw the look on Hondo's face. Hondo grabbed his team leader by his weapons harness and dragged the man to his feet, his helmet slipping off to bounce on the ground.

"What the hell are you doing? I gave you your position! Why did you change it?"

"I didn't change it, Sergeant! I'm right here," the flustered corporal managed to get out.

Technically, he was correct, but Hondo wasn't going to cut him any slack.

"And where are you oriented?"

"Right there," Al-Atrash said, waving his arm to indicate the direction.

Hondo took three deep breaths, then asked, "And why did you choose that?"

"Because that gives us the best fields of fire, Sergeant."

God save me from idiots like him.

"And what is in front of you? Over there?"

"I . . . I don't know."

Hondo let go of the corporal, bent over, and picked up the man's helmet, slamming it down on the bewildered team leader's head so he could pull up his display.

"Just look . . ."

. . . *you complete fucking idiot*, he added in his mind.

The corporal fumbled with the straps, and Hondo lost patience.

"Pickerul, stand up," he passed over the squad net.

Forty meters away, directly in Second Fire Team's line of fire, PFC Pickerul stood. She turned and waved at the two of them.

"So, Corporal, you thought you'd orient so you could light up First Team? Are they the enemy?"

"Oh, no, they're not. I just thought—"

"That's the problem. You didn't think. Now take your team and rotate it to the right and tie into First so you don't kill them while creating a gap big enough for ten Grubs to waltz through."

"Ten Grubs? There not enough room for ten—"

"Can it, Corporal. Ten or one isn't the problem. *You* are my fucking problem! Just do it!"

Hondo spun around and stormed off before he said anything else. He knew he shouldn't have blown up like that, but his frustration level had peaked. Deep inside, he knew he was at fault, too. He'd seen Al-Atrash position his team, and he should have corrected him at the time. He'd been on the corporal's ass for the last two days in the field, and he was simply tired of it. With this being a hasty defense that would probably last ten minutes max before the lieutenant put them on the move again, he'd just let it go.

And got his ass handed to him as a result.

Not that the lieutenant had called him a "fucking problem," Hondo ruefully admitted to himself. No, the lieutenant didn't show much emotion, which made him hard to read. He watched silently, his thoughts hidden, before he spoke out. Hondo didn't know what to make of the man. All he knew was that he was not impressing his new platoon commander, something he vowed he'd change.

He pulled up his own display to check on Al-Atrash, and Second Fire Team was slowly shifting into a better position. They were still in motion when the lieutenant gave the order for the platoon to move out again.

Hondo shook his head.

Five minutes here, just enough time to catch shit.

They had another day in the field, and Hondo vowed that was the last time he'd get corrected by the lieutenant if he had to ride Al-Atrash like a broken-down donkey. The team leader wouldn't be able to fart without Hondo's OK.

EARTH

Chapter 7
Skylar

"How was your gazpacho?" Grigor asked.

"Uh . . . which one was that again?"

"The soup? The cold vegetable soup?"

"Oh, that one?" Sky asked. "I liked it."

"I thought you would, based on what you'd told me."

Sky had liked it, despite her initial misgivings when he'd described it. She didn't recognize most of the food on the menu of the small, out-of-the-way restaurant outside the university and a block away from the Carnegie museums. Unlike Grigor, who evidently was a foodie, she tended to eat whatever the fabricator spat out at her, usually one of her limited dozen or so usual recipes. But she'd gone along with the flow, letting Grigor order the entire meal. She'd given him her major dislikes, then sat back, thankful that for once, she was not making policy-altering decisions. For once, she could let someone else take over, even if only for an hour.

It didn't hurt that Grigor was some serious eye-candy. He was a low-level bureaucrat in the foreign aid division, and Sky had barely known who he was when he approached her this morning to ask her out on a . . .

. . . on a date? she wondered. *Is this a date?*

She'd been about to give him a perfunctory no when something about the twinkle in his eyes caught her attention, and she hesitated. Somehow, within a minute, he'd changed her mind, and she'd said yes.

She'd almost changed her mind again that afternoon as her workload piled up, and she'd been about to call and cancel when she realized she needed the time off. She needed a mental break. She had to eat, and she'd head back to the office after dinner, but for a few precious hours, she could escape.

Grigor picked up the bottle of wine and tipped it slightly over her glass, his eyes questioning her. She started to put her hand over her glass to stop him. One glass was probably enough if she was going to get back to the office, but once again, his eyes stopped her. She took her hand back and nodded. With a satisfied smile, he poured her a second glass.

Look at that expression. This guy knows his way around a woman, and he's a little cocky about it.

Surprisingly, she didn't care. He was pleasant company and damned fine looking, and if he wanted to play the macho man in charge, then she was willing to let the theater play out. This was only a short diversion, so what did it matter?

The waiter rolled out a cart on which a steaming black pan, like a huge wok, sat. Inside was yellow rice with various pieces of seafood mixed in: she could see shrimp, crab claws, black mussels (the shells barely opening), and calamari. Fabricators could shape food to look like anything, but Sky had a feeling this was the real deal. An enticing smell wafted over her as the waiter took her plate and started to spoon her meal onto it.

Sky might not be a foodie, but at least she knew what paella was, even if she'd never tasted it before. The waiter put the plate in front of her, and she couldn't help herself; she leaned forward and took in a deep sniff, letting the aromas fill her senses.

"Do you approve?" Grigor asked, after the waiter left.

Part of her wanted to say no, just to wipe that self-satisfied smirk off his face, but she did approve. The paella smelled wonderful. And it felt good to have someone being so very attentive as to what she might or might not like.

"I'll tell you after we finish," she said, though, with what she hoped was a mysterious-looking smile.

She was enjoying this, but that didn't mean she had to just roll over on him. Let him wait.

"Well, then, a woman who wants to be sure before she commits," he said.

Is he flirting now?

"Then we shouldn't wait. *Bon appetite!*" he said, motioning to her plate.

Sky took a forkful of the rice first, blowing on it as it steamed, then taking a bite. The musty taste of the saffron was interesting—good, but perhaps not quite as good as she'd hoped. She liked it, though.

A huge shrimp stuck out of the rice on her plate, and she stabbed it, wondering if it was fab or natural, not that she thought she could tell one way or the other. She brought it to her mouth just as her PA buzzed. Putting the fork back down, shrimp still impaled, she glanced at the PA.

She was barely aware of Grigor's PA buzzing as the message registered. The Brotherhood dreadnaught *Galilee* had fired upon the *FS Great Bear Lake*. The shot had not been powerful enough to destroy the Federation ship, but there had been casualties—many of them.

Sky rose from her seat, her meal forgotten. Across from her, Grigor rose as well. Without a word, Grigor swiped the payment, and the two left the restaurant to go back down the hill to the ministry headquarters.

The situation had just escalated.

AEGIS 2

Chapter 8
Hondo

"So, where's All Trash now?" BK asked.

"UA."

"Really UA, or just hiding out?"

"This is the Egg. Where's he going to hide out in the Armpit of the Federation?"

"You need to take care of that, Hondo, or it'll bite you in the ass."

She was right, Hondo knew. Newly promoted Sergeant BK Dobbs was one of Hondo's closest friends not just in the Corps, but anywhere. They'd gone through the shit together, and they'd emerged closer than brother and sister. They were ready ears for each other when needed, despite the vast distance that now separated them.

"I will. I've still got time, though."

"Not as much as you think, bro. Shit happens, you know?"

"Yeah, I know."

"So, what about the rest? How's your fuckdick?"

"Hanaburgh? He's OK. The guys call him 'Burger.'"

"I don't want no fuckdicks in my squad. The draftees are bad enough."

"No, really, he's not bad. He was a Spec 5 before he transferred, and I think he'll do fine."

"Did he go to Camp Charles?" she asked, naming the Marine Corps Recruit Training Depot.

"No," he admitted.

"Then he ain't no Marine. Keep your eyes on him."

Hondo understood her point. Lance Corporal Robert Hanaburgh had gone through FCDC boot, and there wasn't a Marine in the galaxy who thought that was as good as Charles. Still, he'd made E5 before he received an interservice transfer to the Corps, accepting a two-rank demotion. Hondo hadn't too much time with the guy yet, but Ling had good things to say about him. Compared to Corporal Al-Atrash, who'd picked up the nickname of "All Trash," Hondo would take Burger any day of the week.

All Trash was going to be the death of him. It wasn't only that he was incompetent as a leader, but he was also a shirker. He was constantly disappearing, for one. He seemed to know just how long he could push it. Yesterday, Hondo had been on the brink of officially reporting him UA to Staff Sergeant Roy Rutledge, the new platoon sergeant, but he was on bad enough terms with the lieutenant that he didn't want Staff Sergeant Rutledge to think he couldn't take care of things.

Hondo took All Trash, along with Ling and Wolf, on a backpack run last night after chow, ten klicks with 50 kilos on their back, and seeing the corporal puke up his dinner after only three klicks had made it all worthwhile. Wolf was royally pissed to share All Trash's punishment, but Hondo didn't care. Maybe he and Ling could whip him into shape.

"Hell, why're we talking about my Marines, anyway?"

"You called me, big guy."

"Well, yeah."

He had called BK, but not to discuss his issues. The problem was opsec. He couldn't really come out and ask anything on the line. The comms AIs would shut him off in a nanosec.

"Well, have you had a talk with Miss Mary-Sue-Ellen-Cheerleader-whatever?" he asked instead.

"You mean Maria? She's old news."

"Old news? Wasn't it last week that you were declaring your everlasting love for her?"

"Ah, that was just lust. Maria was hot as lava but about as smart. No, I gave her her walking papers. I'm with Glenifer, now. She's the one for me."

Hondo shook his head. He had a hard time finding a simple date, but it seemed BK ran through love-interests on a weekly basis.

"She's the one? Every single girl you take to bed is the one, BK."

"No, this time, she really is."

"OK, she's the one, I'm sure now. Then, have you spoken with Jennifer?"

"Glenifer."

"OK, *Glenifer*?"

"Not yet. But I will. Soon."

And that was the crux of his call. BK was in One-One, First Battalion, First Marines, "America's Battalion." Their patron unit is the old US Marines, and they thought they owned the right to be considered the best battalion in the Corps. They were also in the Inner Forces. With the still-limited shooting war started with the Brotherhood alliance, the entire Inner Forces along with three of the four Navy fleets were being deployed to meet that threat.

One-Thirteen, Hondo's battalion, was part of the Outer Forces, and they were business as usual—if you could call anything that was happening now "as usual"—still facing the Grub threat. The entire Fifth Division was ramping up, and they'd take over responsibility as the Alert Division in two short months, relieving the Confederation Legion that now held that position.

Hondo had two months to work out his problems. He'd been worried that BK wouldn't be so lucky, and now, with her comment about talking to her new love interest, he had that worry verified. The brass knew who was going where, of course, but that was rarely promulgated down to the grunts in the field. So now, there were thousands and thousands of Marines and sailors tying up the lines with calls like this, attempting to gather their own intel before the AIs cut them off. It was a fine line that couldn't be crossed, but Hondo had his answer. He didn't know where 1/1 would be going, but he knew it would be leaving Tarawa soon.

"Hey, your time's up. How about letting someone else on the line?" someone shouted from behind him.

Hondo raised his hand and waved. He could have forked out the credit to make a commercial call, but that wouldn't be cheap. The USO, on the other hand, provided lines for free, ostensibly for calls home. With the galaxy coming apart at the seams, those lines were in constant use.

"Look, BK, I've got to go. People are waiting."

"No problem, bro. Thanks for calling."

"Don't get too enraptured by Glenifer, OK? You know how you are."

"Sure, I know."

He was just about to hang up when he added, "Keep your head down!"

That might have been borderline, but he didn't care. The entire galaxy was melting down, and everyone knew it. If he couldn't tell BK to stay safe, then screw it.

"It's all yours," he told the waiting staff sergeant.

BK was a good Marine. She'd be fine. Here on the Egg, he had his own concerns, first of which was to find his wayward corporal. All Trash was not going to be happy once he found him.

Chapter 9
Hondo

"No, sir. I think he's a detriment to the squad and a liability, and I don't want him with us."

"That's a pretty bold statement, Sergeant McKeever," Lieutenant Abrams said. "And you still haven't given me any specifics."

Hondo took a deep breath, trying to calm his nerves. He was trembling, and he desperately hoped that neither the platoon commander nor Staff Sergeant Rutledge could see that.

Come on, McKeever, just spit it out.

Asking for this meeting had been one of the most difficult things Hondo had ever done during his career. Boot camp was nothing, combat was nothing when compared with this. Boot camp was demanding, and combat was stress and fear elevated to intense levels, but neither was admitting defeat, and that was what Hondo was doing now. He was admitting to his commander, the man who would write his fitness reports and have a huge impact on his chances to get promoted, that he was a failure.

He'd gone back and forth over the issue. With BK off facing the Brotherhood along the Second Quadrant's borders, he couldn't confer with her, and for some reason, he didn't want to confess his problems to Cara, so it had been all on him. He didn't want to admit defeat, that he couldn't manage and train a Marine corporal, but in the end, he had to face reality. As he'd just told the lieutenant, Al-Atrash was a liability. If he went into combat with the squad, he'd get others killed. There was no way to get around that. Hondo's pride and hope of getting promoted could not be a factor when Marines' lives were at stake.

"Sir, I've noted all my official counseling sessions, which I've given to Staff Sergeant Rutledge."

"Official?" the lieutenant asked.

The lieutenant had made corporal before going to the Academy. He knew all the unofficial steps that were taken to "correct" weaker links in the Corps. Some technically could result in the NCO taking those steps to subject themselves to a court-martial. Hondo had to focus on not twisting his hand to hide the marks made on the knuckles from the last "counseling session" he administered to All-Trash. If the lieutenant asked him about it, he wasn't going to lie, but he certainly wasn't going to volunteer anything not specifically requested.

"Yes, sir. Official. Since his arrival, Corporal Al-Atrash has shown an almost complete lack of knowledge of military tactics. More than that, he's shown no desire to learn them. He disappears for hours on end, especially when there is work to be done. More importantly, no one in the squad trusts him. No one in his fire team trusts him."

"Why haven't you brought this to Staff Sergeant Rutledge's attention before? Corporal Al-Atrash has been with you for three months now."

"Sir, I thought I could correct him. I mean, he's a real Marine—"

"As opposed to what, Sergeant McKeever?" the lieutenant interrupted, steel suddenly surfacing in his voice. "As opposed to the draftees? As opposed to Lance Corporal Hanaburgh?"

Oh, shit, McKeever. Stupid move!

"Uh . . . no sir. I didn't mean that."

Except that he did, and the lieutenant knew it.

"Let me remind you, Sergeant McKeever. Everyone in this platoon is a real Marine. Corporal Hanaburgh aside, all have gone through Camp Charles, and all wear the uniform. If any of them isn't a real Marines, then I'd say that's your fault. Do you read me?"

"Yes, sir. Sorry, sir."

"So, go on."

"Sir, I thought I could correct him. But we're deploying in a week, and I am positive that he won't change. We're going to be facing Grubs, and if I'm going to be an effective squad leader, I can't be a fire team leader at the same time. It's go time, sir, and I can't afford to take any longer."

"So, you're telling me you failed?"

There was no way to sugarcoat it, so Hondo simply said, "Yes, sir. I failed."

The lieutenant looked at the platoon sergeant and asked, "What do you think, Staff Sergeant Rutledge?"

"Sometimes admitting failure is the first step in fixing a problem."

The lieutenant nodded, then turned back to Hondo, asking, "If we leave Corporal Al-Atrash behind, who do you suggest taking over?"

"Well, sir, if we can't get another corporal, then I'd say Lance Corporal Acevedo."

"He's not your senior lance corporal. Lance Corporal Haus is."

"Yes, sir. That's true. But Antman . . . Lance Corporal Acevedo has been with the fire team, and the other two are used to him."

The lieutenant stared and him for a moment, and Hondo felt the platoon commander was stripping him down to the bare soul.

Finally, he gave an almost imperceptible nod and said, "I want a Form 54 by 1500 today with everything you just told me."

Hondo felt a rush of relief sweep over him.

"Yes, sir. I'll have it to you."

"OK, better get to it," he said, dismissing Hondo. He added, "Don't use the word 'official' for your counseling sessions, Sergeant," as Hondo started out the hatch.

"Aye-aye, sir."

The hatch closed behind him, and Hondo took a moment to lean back against the bulkhead to gather himself. He'd faced Grubs, but facing the lieutenant had been more daunting. But just as he'd survived the Grubs, it looked as if he'd survived this meeting as well, at least temporarily. He wouldn't know for sure until his first fitrep from his platoon commander, but at least now he had time to work on his reputation.

He was just about to leave when through the closed hatch, he heard the lieutenant say, "Well, you were right. Close call, but right."

"Close was good enough. That's why you gave the deadline. Besides, maybe All Trash would have come around. Stranger things have happened."

Hondo knew he shouldn't be eavesdropping, but his feet were rooted in place.

"And McKeever?" the staff sergeant asked.

"He recognized the problem, and when nothing else was possible, he cut it out. He didn't have a choice."

"I hate to say I told you so, sir."

"Bull crap, Staff Sergeant. You love it, so go ahead. McKeever came to us, just like you said he would."

"Yeah, I do love it. So, OK, sir, I told you so."

"Enjoy it. We've still got Wiscombe, and his deadline's twenty-hundred tonight, too."

"We'll see about that. So, do you want me to wait for McKeever's Form 54?"

"No. You've already got it documented. Just send it off now, and then hit up First Sergeant Nordstrand about Corporal Marasco. You said he's good on that?"

"Yes, sir. He's good."

"OK, go take care of that. I need to get down to the armory."

Hondo's feet suddenly took on the wings of Aires as he bolted down the passage before Rutledge could see him. He'd been confused for a moment as he listened in on their conversation. If the two of them knew that All Trash had been a lost cause, then why put him through that? Heck, Rutledge had called him "All Trash" as well. They'd even already asked the first sergeant about Corporal Marasco as a possible replacement.

Then he realized that this wasn't just about All Trash—it was about him as a squad leader. He was being tested. Lieutenant Abrams probably wanted to see if could salvage Al Trash, but from the sounds of it, he also wanted to see if he would address the issue with them. As the lieutenant had said, sometimes you have to cut out a problem.

Feeling far more comfortable than he'd felt all morning, he stepped out of the company headquarters, a bounce in his step.

What was that they were saying about Falt? He's got some sort of problem, too?

Sergeants stick together. That was just the way it was done. All Trash could wait, so he pulled out his PA.

"Hey, Falt, you got some sort of problem with your squad?" he asked when the Third Squad leader answered.

"What do you mean?" he asked, sounding wary, his eyebrows furrowed together.

"I don't know what I mean. I just happened to catch something about the lieutenant having a deadline concerning you, and I think it's tonight. Does that register?"

Hondo could almost see the gears turning in his fellow sergeant's head.

"Maybe," he said grudgingly. "Did you hear anything else?"

"Nope, just that, so I thought I'd give you a head's up.

A look of determination came over Wiscombe's face, and he nodded.

"I think I know what it is, and I'll take care of it."

"OK. I didn't want you to get caught unawares."

"No, I won't. Not now, at least."

Hondo was about to cut the connection, when Wiscombe said, "And thanks, bud. I owe you a big one."

"No, you don't. I know you'd do the same for me, too. We're Marine Corps sergeants, and that's what we do."

He cut the connection, then started whistling as he headed to the squadbay.

SMS Zrínyi

Chapter 10
Hondo

"Come on, Jorgenson. We've gone over this," Corporal Lorenzo Marasco said.

Private Jorgenson was getting flustered as she wracked her brain, trying to pull out the answer.

Hondo kept a straight face, then surreptitiously queried his PA. The anti-personnel round for the PICS WP 2 had 54 pellets, each massing 285 grains. All Hondo knew was that it was a devastating round. Trying to look like he'd known the answer all along, he looked back up at where his new Second Fire Team leader was drilling his three Marines.

Did Diva really need to know the exact specifics of the round? Probably not, Hondo thought. But they were stuck in transit without the large gym and sim-trainers that were aboard a typical Federation troop transport. Military leaders throughout the ages thought that troops left to their own devices degraded by the minute, and the SNCO and officer equivalents of the time devised anything they could to keep the troops occupied. If Marasco wanted to drill them on their PICS' specifications, that was copacetic with him.

Corporal Marasco was fitting in fine. In only two-plus weeks, he'd taken over the team and was working well with Wolf and Ling, to Hondo's relief. When he'd told Lieutenant Abrams that Antman could take over the team, he wasn't exactly lying—it was just that when compared to the dear departed All Trash, anyone would be an improvement.

Life on the *Zrínyi* wasn't optimum from a Marine standpoint. There wasn't room to do much in the way of tactical training, and the so-called gym had room for only ten Marines at a time. First Squad was scheduled for 2030 ship's time that evening, and even then, they'd have to trade off between themselves halfway through their 20 minutes. Of a greater concern to Hondo was that they didn't have easy access to their PICS and weapons. Each Marine had his or her sidearm, but everything else was locked away in one of the holds for the duration of the transit.

At the far side of the berthing space, Ling was taking the improbably named PFC Tony B. Good, Hanaburgh, and Private Radiant Purpose, through molting drill, but without a PICS. Hondo thought they looked somewhat ridiculous as they went through the gyrations, but not actually molting from inside anything.

It was probably a good idea, though. Burger was the second senior Marine in the team, but he'd had no PICS training while in the FCDC. Tony B. Good had a year in PICS, while the super-gung-ho Radiant Purpose had been in the fleet for two months. No amount of training could replicate an emergency combat molt, as Hondo well knew, being one of the few Marines to have done it not only once, but twice. However, the more they practiced, even going through the motions, the easier it would become.

"Ten more minutes, then we're up for chow," he told his three team leaders before stepping out of the space.

Chow was a highlight aboard the ship. The New Budapest Navy had that down pat. With so many Marines crowded aboard, though, feeding them, as well as the ship's crew, was a choreographed ballet.

He made his way down to the sergeant's berthing, stuck his head in, and asked, "Anyone on the next chow shift?"

"We are," Cara said, putting down a reader and swinging her legs out of her rack. "Hold on, I'll go with you.

"I'll be glad to get off this tub," she said as they headed to the galley.

"It's not really a tub. It just isn't made for three hundred Marines," Hondo said.

"I still don't know why we had to split the battalion," she said, something she'd been grousing about ever since boarding.

"They told us. We don't want to attract Brotherhood attention. We'll board the *La Paz* at J-Point."

Hondo sort of agreed with Cara, though. They could put the entire regiment aboard the *FS La Paz*. Take a cruiser as an escort, and blast any Brotherhood ship that tried to interfere. But as the Navy wasn't effective against the Grubs, most of the capital ships were facing off with the Brotherhood alliance navies. The powers that be decided that using non-Federation or Confed ships and splitting up the Marine units was the best strategy for moving the division to J-Point, the empty piece of space that was serving as an assembly area for the next Grub attack.

Alpha and Charlie companies drew the *Zrínyi*, an old New Budapest passenger liner modified with minimal weapons systems for self-defense. With the battalion spread out over three ships, they would reform once they reached J-Point and join the rest of the regiment aboard the *La Paz*. The *Zrínyi* had been given the most roundabout route to J-Point, so Alpha and Charlie would be the last to arrive, but that should still be five days before the turnover with the Confed legion.

Unlike in the large Federation Navy galleys where a sailor or Marine could simply dial up his or her meal on the industrial-sized fabricators, the New Budapest cooks chose up to five main courses for each meal. Hondo had been very hesitant when they'd been briefed on that aspect, but the cooks had put that hesitation to rest. The food had been great so far. Hondo had never heard of hybrid meals, where the raw ingredients were fabricated, then the dishes prepared by the cooks, but he sure appreciated the end result.

The rest of the platoon arrived over the next couple of minutes. They seemed to be in good spirits. The two sergeants held back, waiting for Falt and Staff Sergeant Rutledge. The platoon sergeant arrived, but Falt was nowhere in sight. If he didn't make the platoon's designated slot, he'd have to wait to eat with the ongoing watch section at 1820.

"What're you going to have?" Cara asked as they waited the final few moments until their time slot.

Hondo glanced at the menu board. He didn't recognize two of the dishes, but he understood "grilled ribeye steak with burgundy sauce." His mouth started to water at the thought. If this was his third steak in a row, so be it.

"Oh, come on. Try something new," Cara said when he told her.

"I am. I'm having that Bordoon Swirl Cake for dessert. I don't have a clue what that is."

Cara rolled her eyes, but said nothing. From a nutritional standpoint, there wasn't much difference between ribeye steak and BBQ pork belly—both meats were manufactured by the fabricators from the same raw bases. It was the final touches that made the taste, shape, and texture different.

The clock over the serving line clicked to 1740, and with a surge, the privates pushed forward, followed by the rest of the Marines and corpsmen in order of ascending rank. Hondo, Cara, and Doc Nielsgard-James waited their turn, with only the platoon sergeant behind them.

Hondo kept an eye on the steaks, which seemed to be going fast, feeling more than a little anxious. The cooks would bring out more once they were all taken, but that could take a while, and his stomach was rubbing up against his backbone.

"Just relax, Hondo. You look like a dog begging to be fed," Cara said. "There'll be more of your precious steaks."

"What? I'm not worried," he said, trying to act nonchalant.

Behind him, Staff Sergeant Rutledge choked back a laugh. Hondo didn't give him the satisfaction of turning around.

With one steak left when Wolf hit the line, Hondo tried to will the corporal to leave it. To his relief, Wolf took the Border Stew.

"OK, Doc, we're up."

Doc was an HM5, which was the equivalent of a sergeant, and since she was junior to Hondo, she stepped up to the line before him. She started to reach for the biryani when she diverted and grabbed the last steak, sliding it to her tray.

"Hey, you're a vegetarian," Hondo burst out in surprise.

With a laugh, Doc handed the steak to Hondo, saying, "Sorry, Cara, I couldn't keep it up."

Cara and Staff Sergeant Rutledge were laughing, and Hondo felt his face turn red.

"OK, OK, very funny you guys."

"You should have seen your face, Hondo, like a kid whose parents took back his Christmas presents. Waaaah!" Cara said, rubbing her fists into her eyes.

Hondo rolled his eyes, but he had to admit, they'd gotten him. Payback would be a bitch, though.

He picked up the rest of his food, including the red-swirled cake and joined Second Platoon's sergeants at the table the E5s had staked out as their sovereign territory.

Instead of picking the two empty seats at the end so Cara could sit next to him, he picked the single seat between Gracita Hortense and Lance Orinda and sat down. He wasn't angry—in fact, he had to admit it was pretty funny, but there were forms to be kept in the never-ending game of one-upsmanship.

The steak looked delicious. He bent down, taking in the aroma until it filled his senses, his mouth watering uncontrollably. He looked over to Cara, who was smirking at him, and licked his lips dramatically.

He pointed his fork at her, then turned it over to stab his steak . . . when the ship's alarm went off and a voice came over the 1MC saying, "Condition Alpha, Condition Alpha, I repeat, Condition Alpha. All hands report to your battle stations immediately."

The Marines jumped to their feet, some looking confused as the lights started to flash between yellow and the routine white.

"You heard the man," Staff Sergeant Rutledge yelled out from the small SNCO table in the corner. "Back to berthing, now!"

The Marines were not part of the ship's crew, so their station was the enlisted berthing. With a rush, the Marines pushed toward the galley entrance. Hondo took one quick longing look at the steak sitting there untouched. He was tempted to slip it into his cargo pocket. If he'd been a lance corporal, maybe he would have. Instead, he rushed to the side of the entrance and started directing traffic.

The IMC blared out the condition again while Hondo and Cara pushed and prodded the Marines into an orderly exit. Within 45 seconds, the galley was empty, and Hondo was following the last of the Marines down the passage.

"What do you think's going on? Is this a drill?" Cara asked as she strode beside him.

"I hope so," Hondo said, but some warrior sense told him this was the real deal.

The sergeants had their own berthing space, but during Condition Alpha, the entire platoon, minus the lieutenant, would be in the troop berthing, each squad in its own cubicle.

Falt met them at the hatch, and Staff Sergeant Rutledge asked, "Where the hell were you?"

"I had a . . . an assignation, as they say. What's going on?"

"See me when this is over," the platoon sergeant snarled. "For now, get with your squad."

Shit, Falt. You were hooking up? Now?

Deployed Marines in a combat zone did not have "assignations." Falt was going to have his ass handed to him. That wasn't Hondo's concern now, however.

Two minutes after the ship went into Condition Alpha, the entire squad was in the berthing, sitting on the lower racks.

"Head count," Staff Sergeant Rutledge said, poking his head into the cubicle opening.

"All accounted for," Hondo said.

The platoon sergeant left to get the rest of the headcounts, so he could report to the gunny.

"Are we going to get into it?" Private Zacharias Radiant Purpose asked, his voice rising in excitement.

Hondo wasn't sure he'd ever seen a Marine so gung-ho as RP, as the others called him. That was generally a good thing, if it could be controlled. Hondo wasn't so sure it could be in this case, though.

"We don't know what's happening," Hondo said. "So just sit back and relax. They'll tell us soon enough."

"Soon," however, turned out to be 45 minutes later when the 1MC crackled back on, and the ship's captain said, "This is *Alezerdes* Black. I want to give you an update on

71

what's going on. We've got a Brotherhood frigate closing in on us. They are demanding us to heave to. If not, they've threatened us with a hook."

There were murmurs from some of the Marines.

In the old days, ships in bubble space were essentially untraceable. That wasn't the case anymore. Not only could ships be tracked, but some ships were outfitted with "hooks" that could force a target ship out of bubble space. Unfortunately, the violence of an uncalculated bubble space exit had a tendency to destroy the ship and kill the crew.

"We are not going to heave to under their terms. We have diverted our course to the Lore System where we will exit bubble space and defend ourselves. We anticipate reentering normal space in three hours, twenty-seven minutes. Stand by for further instructions. This is the *alezerdes*, out."

There was dead silence for a moment before the entire compartment broke out into chatter.

Things had just gotten serious.

EARTH

Chapter 11
Skylar

"This development portends increased difficulty to the effort against the Dictymorphs. We are at a loss as how to understand the current situation."

Yes, it does "portend" difficulty, Sky thought as she stared at "Glinda," the head of the Klethos liaison quad.

She stared at the Klethos queen, trying to read into her. Confederation Intel had determined with a 96% probability that Glinda had been a Klethos gladiator thirty years back, registering two victories in the ring. She'd killed two humans, and now she was back as what was essentially the ambassador to the UAM, complete with a somewhat flowery grasp of Standard that seemed at odds with the gladiator Skylar had seen on the recording of her fights.

And now it's my job to appease her . . . all four of them, that is.

There were three others in the quad, of course. Two rarely spoke and the third, the male member, had never spoken a word to a human. Sky had discussed the roles of each of the quad members at length with Harry al Upton, her K-Team leader. Harry was of the school of thought that the other three were window-dressing, but Sky didn't buy that. There had to be more to their relationship. But the fact of the matter was that no one knew for sure how the quad functioned. Everything was conjecture.

Glinda was yet again questioning the split between the human factions. Her predecessor hadn't taken much issue when the Brotherhood-led faction had pulled out of the war effort, but after the killing of Klethos on Krakow, that quad had been recalled, to be replaced by Glinda and her crew. Every day, they made their rounds, pushing their human contacts for a resolution to the problem. Today, it was the Second Ministry's turn, and the minister had pushed the visit off on Sky and her team.

"I can assure you, Ambassador, that we have teams of diplomats negotiating now with those humans who are not contributing to the effort. I have no doubt that we will come to a resolution soon."

Hell, am I becoming that much of a diplomat that I can spew bullshit like that?

"We believe that the current situation has significantly degraded at present, not improved. The fact that the recalcitrant human faction has now detained one of the Marine units planned for the reaction force at the J-Point lends credence to this supposition."

What? Who's doing what to whom?

With a quick subvocalization, she told Keyshon to call Throckmorton and find out if there was some sort of problem with the next alert force.

"I can assure you, Ambassador, that the might of the UAM is dedicated to eliminating the Dictymorph threat, but to humans and Klethos alike. Anything else is just a bump in the road," she said, smiling at the quad leader.

There! she noted as the quad leader moved almost imperceptibly to one of the other Klethos. *She's getting input.*

Sky was sure they could communicate with each other in ways that humans didn't understand yet. Most people agreed that the Klethos had at least one yet-unknown method of communication, and a form of telepathy was the current flavor of the month, but Sky didn't buy that. In some ways, the Klethos seemed so backwards, but in others, their technology far outstripped humans', and Sky was sure this was just another example of that.

"I've got a response from the commander," Keyshon reported back. "The *SMS Zrínyi,* carrying Marines to J-Point for the turnover, was hailed by the Brotherhood frigate *Temperance* and told to heave to. The *Zrínyi's* commander refused, bringing them out of bubble space in the Lore system where the Brotherhood commander is demanding boarding rights. It's a standoff now."

Sky tried to keep a neutral expression as she took it all in, keeping her eyes locked on the Klethos queen. The quad evidently knew what was happening. The question now was what they would do about it.

There were now three camps in the UAM. One camp wanted to enjoin the Klethos to spank the Brotherhood alliance and get them back into the fold. One camp wanted to hold a two-front war, but keeping both separate, while the third advocated pulling back and leaving the Klethos to face the Dictymorphs on their own.

Sky had seen the Dictymorphs with her own eyes. She understood the threat on a visceral level. She'd tasted the sour bile of fear rise in her throat as she saw her death approach. Humans couldn't ignore the threat, or they would face total genocide.

But the UAM could not unleash the Klethos, so to speak, on the Brotherhood and their allies. That would tear humanity apart in total war. Sky thought that those who pushed for that option were in the minority, but they weren't the problem.

Sky thought that the Klethos themselves wanted to become involved. She felt it was a matter of honor to them. The Brotherhood-led alliance had revoked their agreement, after all, and that made them vermin—non-sapients, in their view. It was only the presence of the UAM that stayed their hand, at least for the moment.

As she stared at the queen, she became certain that she was being evaluated, being tested. All of the humans remaining in the alliance were. The Klethos needed humanity, but their sense of honor could lead them to turn on humankind, and not in the gladiatorial ring. Their numbers might not be enough to defeat the human masses, but the destruction would be horrendous.

Sky might be a mid-to-high-level bureaucrat now, but she was uniquely positioned on a razor's edge that she thought was being overlooked. The problem with being on a razor's edge, however, was that not only could you fall to either side, but if you delayed too much, you could sink straight down and be cut in half.

"Well, Ambassador, I thank you for your time. I appreciate the meeting, and I can assure you that we will resolve any differences among us. We are dedicated to the fight against the Dictymorphs.

"But now, I have another meeting, so if I can make my excuses?"

As one, the four Klethos nodded, all four arms on each spread low and wide, their version of a handshake, one which the humans copied with their two arms. She didn't stay to watch them leave but immediately told Captain Throckmorton to meet her in her office. She might not have any input into the standoff in the Lore system—she didn't even know where it was—but she had to keep abreast of developments.

She had a new calling, one that she felt was vital to humanity's very existence. She had to keep the Klethos out of the human conflict long enough for the two human factions to come back together.

And she didn't have a clue as to how she was going to achieve that.

SMS ZRÍNYI

Chapter 12
Hondo

"Hey Burger," Antman said. "Do you know the difference between the Marines, the Navy, and the fuckdicks?"

Lance Corporal Hanaburgh rolled his eyes, but then said, "No, Antman, but I bet you're about to tell me."

"Well, when the Marines are told to secure a building, they go in weapons hot, kill the motherfuckers inside, then kill anyone else who tries to get in."

There was the expected round of "ooh-rahs" and "get some" at that.

"If the Navy is told to secure the building, they get the SPs and put a lock on the door with a sign that says, 'Do Not Enter.'"

"Better than shooting up the place," Doc Leach said.

Antman paused for dramatic effect, then said, "Now the fuckdicks, you tell them to secure the building, and they take out a twelve-month lease with an option to buy."

There was a roar of laughter and one "I don't get it" from Diva while Hanaburgh raised his middle finger in response.

"Hey, why should you always use a fuckdick gym," Pickerul shouted out, then before anyone could answer, "Because the heavy weights are all in unused condition!"

Hondo smiled despite himself. There was, and would always be, a degree of rivalry between the Marines and the much larger FCDC, and Hanaburgh was just going to have to bite the bullet on getting shit upon. Pickerul, all 50kg of her, couldn't lift half of what Hanaburgh could in the gym, but that had no relevance. When you could burn the FCDC, you did, as simple as that.

It was good to hear the laughter, and if some of it sounded forced, that was to be expected. The squad was still in berthing, waiting. Outside in the black, a Brotherhood frigate lurked, and for all they knew, a Sword of God shipkiller could be heading their way as they sat there.

Hondo had faced combat against the Grubs, but this waiting was mind-numbing. He'd considered the Navy before enlisting. His best friend was set on it, but Hondo decided that only the Corps would do for him. He was developing some mad respect now for the sailors; not just the corpsmen like Jay Leach and La'ei Kekoa, of course, who were almost Marines, but the sailors who manned battle stations inside this tin can, not knowing when any moment might be their last.

The *Zrínyi* had popped out of bubble space inside the Lore system two hours before. The Brotherhood frigate had followed 15 minutes later, but outside the outer ring of planets. Hondo had to assume it was maneuvering closer to the out-gunned New Budapest transport. He wondered why they just hadn't run for it, but then again, he knew next to nothing about Navy ships, other than what he saw in the flicks. And if the Navy flicks were as inaccurate as those that depicted the Marine Corps, then he knew squat.

He reached up and ran a finger between the seal of his emergency hood and his neck, where sweat was building. Coming out of bubble space, every Marine had to don a hood, leaving the faceplate open to save O2. That was a sobering moment, letting them know that this was for real. Gunny

Gustav even came in and made them practice slamming the faceplate shut several times.

"Sergeant McKeever," Staff Sergeant Rutledge said, coming into the compartment. "Send a Marine from each fire team to the ship's weapons locker. They'll draw weapons there."

"Buddie weapons? Why can't we get our own, Staff Sergeant?" Ling asked.

"'Cause ours are in the sec-crates in the secured holds, that's why," Rutledge said. "Just be glad we're getting these."

"Antman, Hanaburgh, Haus, that's you," Hondo said. "Get down there and back. No diversions."

For once, Antman didn't crack a joke. He nodded, and the three left the compartment, following three Marines from Second Squad to the weapons locker. Hondo didn't know what the New Budapest Navy carried in their armory, but anything would help. The Marines had their sidearms with them, but Hondo had been feeling decidedly under-armed.

Fifteen minutes later, the three Marines returned, smiles on their faces as they showed off their GE Oxars. The Oxar was a short-muzzled hand cannon that used a magno-ring to "throw" the eight-centimeter-wide "pillow" at the target. It was a close-range weapon, powerful enough to tear an unarmored pirate in two, or defeat most armor at five meters or closer. The power dissipated quickly, however, so it would not be able to punch through a ship's outer hull, making it a favored weapon for ship's defense.

The rest of the Marines crowded around, oohing and aahing over the weapons.

"How long do you think it'll be before we know something," Wolf asked Hondo quietly, while the others' attention was focused on the Oxars.

"Don't know. We just need to be ready for whatever happens."

Wolf fingered the edge of his emergency hood, then asked, "Are we gonna surrender? I mean, I don't think I can do that."

Hondo hadn't considered that the ship's captain might surrender, and he looked at Wolf in surprise.

"Surrender? I don't think so . . . I mean, well . . ."

The thing was, the captain *could* surrender the ship. But would that be binding on the Marines? Hondo didn't know the answer.

"Don't worry about it. We take our orders from Captain Ariç. Whatever she says, we do."

Wolf didn't seem convinced, but he moved over to one of the racks on the other side of the compartment. Now, Hondo had yet one more thing to worry about.

"All hands, don hoods and brace for impact!" the excited voice came over the 1MC.

Hondo jumped up and yelled, "Now, now! Seal your hoods!" before slapping his faceplate shut.

There was a flurry of motion as Marines rushed to comply, then Hondo checked each Marine and Doc Leach to make sure the faceplate was sealed properly and good to go. Staff Sergeant Rutledge, hooded up, stuck his head around the corner and Hondo gave him a thumbs-up.

"Now brace yourselves!" Hondo shouted, his voice sounding tinny through the hood.

The compartment consisted of four racks of three bunks which didn't offer much in the way of bracing, but the Marines did they best they could, jamming themselves in the racks. Hondo made a last check, then started to push himself into the foot of one of the racks when a massive blast shook the ship, a flash of light almost blinding the Marines. Debris flew past the opening to the compartment for a moment before the air started rushing back the other way, a maelstrom that threatened to pull the Marines with it.

Hondo grabbed the vertical support of the rack and hugged it as his feet lifted off the deck. He felt an arm grab him, pulling him back. He risked turning his head to look; debris was flying towards Third Platoon's berthing, closer to the hull of the ship. Like otherworldly mantas, sheets of biopatch fell off the overhead and bulkheads, flattening out as they were sucked to the breach.

There was a second shudder, then a third as the lights and gravity failed. An instant later, emergency lights flickered on, followed by a klaxon that sounded odd in the now-depleted atmosphere.

For a moment, Hondo thought he was out of O2, that his hood had failed, before he realized he was holding his breath. He forced himself to draw in three deep breaths as the grip of the escaping air lessened. There was still no gravity, but he no longer felt that he was going to get sucked out of the ship.

He completed a quick head count—everyone was still there. A few looked dazed, but all had managed to hang on.

"Is everyone OK?" he shouted, his voice loud in his ears, but he wasn't sure if anyone could hear him.

His hood indicator was red: there wasn't enough O2 to breathe. If the berthing space were in a vacuum, the sound wouldn't transmit.

He pulled himself to Wolf, pressed his faceplate to his, and shouted, "Check everyone. Make sure they're OK."

Wolf nodded, and Hondo pulled himself along the racks and out into the berthing passage. At the far end, bulkheads were bent and torn. It looked like something had hit right at the support rib, blowing off the hull, both in the company's berthing and at whatever was on the other side. The sheets of biopatch had done their job, though, sealing what was probably a major breach into the black. As Hondo watched, a body floated into view at the far end, small perfectly spherical globlets of blood trailing behind it.

He pulled himself into the next space where Cara was checking her Marines.

He grabbed her, touched faceplates, and asked, "Everyone make it?"

"Lost Pucini. Got sucked out before we could grab him."

Someone grabbed Hondo from behind and spun him around. Hondo, his nerves on edge, almost lashed out before he recognized the platoon sergeant, who was pulling both sergeants in until their faceplates touched.

"What's the head count?"

"All accounted for," Hondo said.

Cara said, "Pucini's gone. Got sucked out. I need to see if he's still onboard."

"It's . . . uh . . . it's pretty bad down there. Third Platoon's gone, all of them. Second, well, some made it. I've sent Doc Kekoa down to see what he can do. I want Doc Leach and Manuel to see if they can make a difference, too," Staff Sergeant Rutledge told her.

"What about Pucini? Did you see him?" she asked.

"No, and he's probably gone. But we'll check. Right now, I need you two to join with Third Squad down there," he said, jerking a thumb over his shoulder towards the impact area. "We need to secure it."

For some unknown reason, Antman's joke about securing a building came to mind, and he had a huge urge to tell the joke himself. He couldn't believe why that had come to his mind.

Get ahold of yourself.

"Aren't we still in battle stations?" Cara asked.

"Where do we breach ships?" the staff sergeant asked.

Breaching and boarding ships was one of the Marines' missions. Depending on the threat, they could hack a hatch, use a breaching tube to make a new airlock, or simply blast a hole into the side of a ship and use that to enter it.

Like the temporarily-patched rent in the ship's hull at the other side of berthing.

"Got it, Staff Sergeant," Hondo said.

"I'm going to try and contact the lieutenant," Rutledge said. "Get over there and make sure no one comes inside the ship."

"Roger that," Hondo said as he pushed back from the other two.

He pulled himself back to the squad's berthing and grabbed the three team leaders. Using the same method of communicating, he gave his orders.

Why don't these hoods have comms? he wondered. *This isn't the stone ages.*

In a Federation Navy ship, they would all have donned EVA suits, which had full comms and AI capability. But these were the much cheaper emergency hoods that some paramilitary security forces used. Surrounding the head and upper chest, they provided low-pressure, but breathable air. Hondo didn't feel secure in them, but at least he could operate in one, unlike the "walmarts," the cheap, all-encompassing bubbles that commercial liners used to keep civilian passengers alive in case of an atmospheric breach.

They don't keep you warm, though, he thought as he shivered.

It made sense. Ambient heat needed atmosphere, just as sound waves did. He could breathe, but it was getting cold in the ship.

Not as cold as the black, he reminded himself, wondering if Pucini had been sucked out along with the dead and wounded from Third Platoon.

Along the bulkhead, a green light let him know one of the emergency O2 emitters was trying to replenish the atmosphere inside the compartment. Hondo had no idea how long that would take, and he wondered if the Brotherhood soldiers would even give them that time.

"Let's go," he yelled, using his arm to hurry his squad out of their space and towards the hull. Tony B gave him a thumbs-up as he pulled past him, and Hondo wondered if he'd actually heard him. He held his breath for a moment, and he thought he could barely hear the sounds of Marines on the move. He didn't know if that was residual atmosphere that hadn't escaped or if the emitters were having an effect.

When they arrived in the outermost space, not much was left in the twisted remains of the racks and supports. There were a few bloody imprints, but no bodies. Hondo didn't know which two Third Platoon squads had the outermost two spaces, but if they hadn't died in the blast, they'd been sucked out into the black. Even if some of them had somehow survived the blast itself, while the hoods could keep them breathing even in a full vacuum, the cold would kill them within a minute or two.

Staff Sergeant LeMarche, Second Platoon's platoon sergeant, pointed to the upper left corner of the compartment—Hondo was still oriented to "up" and "down," even if the terms were meaningless with no gravity to give them reference. Using hand and arm signals, Hondo got his Marines in place, now oriented in what used to be down. If gravity came back on suddenly, they'd have a nice fall, but they had to cover all angles should the Brotherhood try to breach the ship.

With Doc Leach still working with Second Platoon, Hondo had 13 Marines, including himself. Each Marine was armed with either the Ruger 2mm or Hasert .42. Antman, Hanaburgh, and Haus had managed to hold on to their Oxars.

That wasn't much to face Brotherhood soldiers, who were probably in full battle rattle. As he swept his gaze through the compartment, he realized his squad might be the best armed. Only one of Cara's Marines had her Oxar, and Falt's Third Squad looked to be down two Marines. Hondo doubted if half of Second Platoon was there. They had about fifty lightly-armed Marines to face an unknown-sized force.

It wasn't always the size of the force that mattered, however. Horatius and two others had managed to hold off the entire Clusium army, stopping them at the bridge. If three Romans could hold off an army, then so could they. They were Marines, after all.

"The piss-worm cowards stood off to hit Third Platoon. If they try to breach this ship, we're going to bring a galaxy of shit on their heads," he said to Radiant Purpose, who screamed a loud "ooh-rah."

He went down the line, telling each of his Marines much the same. He could see their posture change. These were no longer the confused men and women who'd just taken a mental blow. They were Marines, ready to extract revenge.

By the time he'd hit each of the Marines and made it back to his position, Hondo almost wished the Brotherhood shits would try and breach the ship. He wanted to lash out and make them pay.

Come on, fuckwads. Let's see how tough you are when you can look us in the eyes.

Chapter 13
Hondo

The light on Hondo's hood turned green. He knew the atmosphere was being replenished because sounds were reaching him, and the circulation fans were beginning to actually push something, but the light let him know they'd reached the Armstrong-Chen Limit, and he could breathe again without the hood.

"Keep your freakin' hoods sealed!" Staff Sergeant Rutledge yelled out through his open faceplate before he shut it again.

Hondo wasn't sure the Brotherhood host was going to attempt to board the ship. Standard Operating Procedure was to board immediately after making a breach before the defending forces could gather themselves and prepare to repel the assaulting force. The Brotherhood had a vaunted military, so if they hadn't tried to assault yet, Hondo thought that it wasn't in their immediate plans.

It didn't hurt to be prepared, though, he had to admit, especially as most of the *Zrínyi's* sensors had been knocked offline and couldn't monitor the Brotherhood frigate as well as desired.

The enemy frigate—the brass had been careful not to call the Brotherhood alliance the enemy, but if they fired on the *Zrínyi,* then what the hell else were they? —had carefully targeted the ship. One missile had hit the ship's weapons pod, which made tactical sense. The other two missiles had targeted the Marines aboard the ship, and that was an overt act of war, as far as Hondo was concerned. The *Zrínyi's* cloaking capabilities were limited, and the Brotherhood man-of-war would have had no problem scanning the ship and locating the largest masses of bodies. One missile had struck the other side of the ship, wiping out Charlie Company. Only 12 Marines had survived the strike.

Only a stroke of luck saved most of Alpha. The missile had hit the ship a few meters too far aft, almost on one of the support ribs, and sent a good portion of the explosion into the engineering spaces. Alpha had lost all but one Marine from Third Platoon, 19 from Second, and four from First.

This had been a surgical strike. Remove the pinchers and stinger from a scorpion, and then you could play with it at your leisure.

Only you didn't get all of the stinger, assholes!

Hondo wished the host would try to breach the ship. He needed to take out his anger on them.

He also knew that was stupid thinking. First, a Marine had to go into combat with a clear head—anger led to mistakes, fatal mistakes. Second, the enemy frigate hadn't been damaged. Her sensors would still be working, and they'd know that over half of Alpha Company was alive and waiting for them.

At least they weren't all in one compartment. Lieutenant Flores, the company XO, had taken what was left of Second Platoon and moved to the other side of the ship, where Charlie Company had been berthed. Hondo had been surprised at first that it had been the XO and not Lieutenant Del Rio, the Second Platoon commander, but the young second lieutenant might be in shock at losing so many of his Marines while he hadn't been there to share the danger.

"Squad leaders, up!" Lieutenant Abrams called out.

Hondo shot across the berthing space, avoiding the jagged pieces of metal and plastic that stuck out at odd angles, and twisted his body around, using his legs to absorb the impact and stopping next to the platoon commander. The lieutenant waited until Falt and Cara joined them.

"The Brotherhood frigate has closed to 800 meters," he said.

Hondo shook his head in surprise. In space terms, 800 meters might as well be chained to each other. Ships just didn't do that in open space, even at ports, without the tractors guiding them. That left only two reasons that he could think of: the enemy thought the *Zrínyi was toothless,* and they wanted to send over a boarding party.

"And we've got movement. We've only got a few sensors still working, but it looks like they got host soldiers in EVAs, ready to cross over.

"If they are coming, we don't know where they'll attempt to board, so be ready for a fluid situation. If they try here, we're as set up as we could be, but if they hit somewhere else, we need to be ready to adjust."

When the lieutenant had arrived inside berthing, he'd quickly set up a basic operations order. It hadn't been much, but Hondo knew what was expected of him and his squad. "Be ready to adjust" did not fill him with confidence. But there was probably no getting around that. If the host tried to breach somewhere else, then he'd just have to follow the lieutenant's lead and trust that training would carry the day.

Hondo went back to the squad and relayed the information. Pickerul and RP looked stoked—he guessed that he wasn't the only one who wanted revenge. Marasco nodded, his face expressionless. And while Diva and Killdeer looked concerned, the rest of his Marines and Doc had expressions of determination on their faces. He knew he could count on them.

"Back to your positions. Be ready," he said.

The squad's position was essentially in a ship's berthing spaces. There wasn't much in the way of cover. But using the wreckage, the Marines did the best they could. Hondo was behind a twisted piece of plastic. It might not even stop a round, and it covered only a swath across his chest, but it was better than nothing.

The clunk from outside the hull caught everyone's attention.

"Get ready," the lieutenant shouted out.

The biopatch shuddered, luminescent lights radiating in waves from a central point. Made from bioengineered algae suspended in a polycero mesh, it was considered "semi-life." When a breach was made in a ship, the escaping air would draw the patch to the hole, where it would mesh with other patches in a colony. It was cheap and effective in making temporary patches, but it offered nothing in the way of armor protection, and it couldn't keep out boarders.

"Secure yourselves," Staff Sergeant Rutledge called out.

A moment later, the section of the biopatch glowed a deep orange, then simply disappeared. Air rushed back out of the compartment, but not nearly as violently as before. The compartment had been kept at the Armstrong-Chen Limit, which was the partial pressure required with O2 at 40% to sustain human activity—about 3.5 PSIA. Lower pressure meant less "air" to evacuate, and the Marines had no problem remaining in place.

The breach was right in front of First Squad and "below" them. The first soldier pulled himself against the diminishing outflow of air, oriented down and slightly to the ship's bow. He never saw Hanaburgh, who took off most of his head above the shoulders with one blast of his Oxar. Blood globules spattered out in a display worthy of Freedom Day fireworks as the body bounced against the bulkhead.

A stream of fire reached out of the breach, rounds ricocheting around the compartment. Marines from Second Squad were in the fields of fire, and they scrambled out of the way.

Haus fired his Oxar into the mouth of the breach. Hondo couldn't see if that had any effect, but he chased the big round with his own 2mm darts. The dead soldier was in a Brotherhood EVA, a maneuverable suit that was probably better than a Federation EVA, but that offered even less ballistic protection.

And something clicked in his brain. Before he quite realized what he was doing, he yelled out "Cover me!" and pushed off the overhead, aiming right for the edge of the breach.

The dead soldier had been carrying a GG-19, a jacketless air-fired slug-thrower. The big 14mm round packed a powerful punch, and the lack of propellant made it very-well suited for shipboard use where fire was always a concern. More relevant, it could defeat the "bones," or the STF—the Shear-Thickening Fluid—armor embedded into the fabric of the Marine's utilities.

Hondo flashed past the opening, spotting a surprised face as he somehow threaded the incoming fire while reaching out and grabbing the Brotherhood rifle, before slamming heavily into the bulkhead and the dead solder. He flailed for an instant, trying to orient himself. Another soldier moved to the edge of the breach to bring Hondo under his aim, and with one arm pushing off, he held out the GG-19 with the other and fired a single shot that hit the soldier in the chest just as he was bringing his GG-19 to bear.

Holy shit, I'm glad I was right, Hondo thought as he pushed back from the breach opening and the Marines were able to open up again.

All Brotherhood weapons were biolocked onto their users. An enemy couldn't just pick one up on the battlefield and use it against them. However, Hondo had read in Defense Monthly that the new EVA suits had some problems with biometrics through the gloves, and the biolocks had been neutralized.

Hondo felt lightheaded as the risk he'd taken hit him. The article he'd read could have been a false flag article, planted by the Brotherhood. It could have been true, but the problem had been fixed by now. Either way, and Hondo would be dead.

There was another explosion over and to the back of him, and he spun around, still hugging the outer bulkhead. Six soldiers came flying into the space through a gaping hole, through which Hondo could see the system's sun. The Brotherhood force had given up on the breaching tube and had simply used brute force to create an opening.

They didn't see him, though. With two carefully aimed shots, he took out two of them before they knew he was there.

And the fog of battle set in.

Hondo's world narrowed. He was aware of more white-suited bodies flowing into the space. He was aware of the heavy volume of Marine fire as the lighter weapons tried to find vulnerabilities in the Brotherhood suits.

Hondo was vulnerable, hanging on the bulkhead like the proverbial fly on the wall. As a round took out a chunk of bulkhead near his head, he blindly kicked off, trusting the big sky, little bullet theory to get him under some cover—only, the "sky" wasn't so big, and the rounds didn't seem so little. Somehow, he managed to reach his initial position unscathed.

Slipping behind his too-small piece of cover, he brought his stolen GG-19 around and started selecting targets. The soldiers seemed focused on Second Squad, and Hondo was able to target three of them, hitting two. One went down hard, while the other, his lower leg a bloody mess, managed to push back out of the ship.

Something hit him high on the shoulder, and he felt the instantaneous hardening of his bones that signaled the armor was working. He didn't know if it was a dart or merely a piece of debris-turned shrapnel, but it wasn't a GG-19 round or something equally as powerful, so he ignored it.

Suddenly, there were no more targets. The dozen or so soldiers left spun almost in unison and shot out the rent in the side of the ship. A Marine from Second Squad rushed forward with an Oxar to engage the fleeing soldiers when a round fired from outside hit him in the forehead. His body kept going forward, where it hit the edge of the opening and went tumbling out of the ship.

Biosheets were already detaching from dispensers and floating towards the openings, but this second one was too big. The biosheets simply floated out into the black.

"Is everybody all right?" Hondo yelled, forgetting for a moment that they were back in a vacuum.

He did a head count as Marines emerged from behind whatever cover they'd managed. He got up to 12, then started again. It was still 12, one short.

Antman caught his attention, waving an arm for him to come forward. With a sinking feeling in the pit of his stomach, Hondo pulled himself to where Corporal Marasco was pulling Diva Jorgenson from under some wrecked bunks. Round red balls of blood, beautiful in their deadly message, rose around her, sent spinning like tiny planets as Marasco pulled her free.

A chunk of Diva's left side was gone with only tatters of flesh remaining. Hondo grabbed Antman, pulled him close faceplate-to-faceplate, and told him to find Doc. He helped Marasco and brought Diva into the open.

Her face, white and serene, gazed unseeing out of her faceplate.

Doc Leach pushed past him, took one look at Diva, then shook his head.

"We've got to get her zombied," Hondo said, pulling him in to speak.

"All the zip-locks are in storage. We'll have to get to her later."

Hondo kept his hold on the Doc for a moment, trying to put his thoughts together.

"I've got to go help with them," Doc said, gently pulling Hondo's hands off of his harness and pointing at the rest of the compartment.

From what had been the upper aft corner, Hondo shifted his gaze across the ruined berthing. He could see six dead Brotherhood soldiers, but his eyes locked on the Marines. With Diva, Hondo counted eleven bodies and four wounded Marines. Four more Marines were positioned at the larger breach, weapons outboard. They'd managed to throw the Brotherhood back, but at a high cost.

The lieutenant raised one hand, then twirled it in a circle, his forefinger and thumb making a C. He wanted the squad leaders.

Hondo pushed off, took a midcourse correction off the bulkhead, and came to a stop beside her.

Cara joined him, and he looked around for Falt. When Corporal Tesseret joined them, realization hit. Falt was KIA or one of the wounded.

He took a deep breath, slowly exhaling as his hood struggled for a moment to scrub the CO_2.

"We're not repressurizing. There's too much damage. Sergeant Riordan, help Staff Sergeant Rutledge and secure the KIA in place, then take the wounded back to the galley.

"Sergeant McKeever, come with me. The Brotherhood has established a foothold on the port side. We're going to see what we can do to stop them."

"What about me, sir?" Corporal Tesseret asked.

"You're coming with us. We move out in one minute."

"Aye, aye, sir," Hondo said, but as he turned, the lieutenant grabbed him by the arm.

"And give that nineteen to someone else. You're a squad leader, not a damned rifleman," he said.

Hondo automatically started to protest. *He'd* been the one who braved the fire to take it, and he'd shot four of the host with it. He was feeling quite good about that in the post-rush of the fight, and now the lieutenant was chewing his ass?

He closed his mouth with a snap, his protest unvoiced. The lieutenant was right, he realized. He was a squad leader, with emphasis on the "leader." His job wasn't to shoot the bad guys, but to lead his Marines so they could work together to kill the bad guys. There was a huge difference between the two.

"Aye, aye, sir," he said.

With a jump, he cleared the open space and rejoined the squad. He handed the GG-19 to Pickerul, whose eyes opened wide, a smile almost cracking her face in two. It hurt a little to let it go, but it was better in her hands than in his.

With hand-and-arm signals (he'd thought they were useless and antiquated when he'd been taught them at Camp Charles, but he was grateful for them now), he gathered his Marines and headed to join the lieutenant and Corporal Tesseret's fire team as they headed for the hatch all the way back near the squad's berthing space.

They may have stopped the host from boarding in their space, but the bastards were aboard the *Zrínyi*, and it was up to them to push them back into the black.

Chapter 14
Hondo

Hondo fell to the deck with a thud, his right arm underneath him. To add insult to injury, Killdeer's leg swung around and hit him on the side of the head.

"I guess we've got gravity again," First Sergeant Nordstrand said, pushing himself up from where he was on top of RP.

It would have been nice to have a warning.

One moment, the Marines were pulling themselves along the 14 corridor, and the next, the artificial gravity kicked back on, painfully giving them an up and down once more. It was for the best, though. Marines worked better with their feet on the ground. They'd all been trained in null G, of course, and they could hold their own, but they were not Navy "nullers," the trained commandoes skilled in null G operations.

Lieutenant Abrams stood and ran his hand across his throat, telling them to shut up. They didn't know exactly where the Brotherhood troops were, and there was no reason to broadcast their own position.

It took a moment to reorient themselves to the pull of gravity, but with First Team leading, they started back down the corridor. Hondo was behind the team, feeling naked with only his Ruger. He still wished he had Pickerul's GG-19, or even Haus' Oxar.

The lieutenant grabbed his shoulder. Hondo turned to see him holding up a single fist to halt, and Hondo grabbed

Killdeer, giving her the same signal. Within a few seconds, the squad-plus had stopped while the lieutenant listened to the voice coming over his earbud. For the hundredth time, Hondo wished the emergency hoods had comms so he could listen in, but only the lieutenant and the first sergeant, who, along with Sergeant Yelci, had joined them, had what were two of the ship's crew's earbuds.

The lieutenant nodded at the unseen voice, then motioned Hondo closer.

"The skipper says the main Brotherhood force is still at the breach site."

The "breach site" was the Charlie Company berthing, where most of the Marines there had been killed by the missile strike.

"She wants us to go back to B-12-6-32 and link up with the XO," he said as the first sergeant joined the two of them. "Let's turn this around get back to the G-ring, then come back down 12."

"We don't need to go all the way back to G," First Sergeant Nordstrand said. "We can go up to seven, then straight across to twelve."

"We can hit seven from here?"

"Yes, sir."

"I don't know that route. Can you lead us?"

A smile came over the first sergeant's face as he said, "No problem, sir. I've got it."

Hondo was a sergeant, still with the squad, but he chafed at not being a "gunfighter" anymore. The first sergeant hadn't been at the point of the spear for much longer, and he had to be welcoming a chance to get back in the thick of things.

"Do it," Lieutenant Abrams said.

The first sergeant made his way back down to Second Team, which had been pulling up Tail End Charlie, and with them now on point, the squad headed back five meters before climbing a ladder and up to the seven corridor. They moved through what looked to be service spaces, then down another ladder to six at space 28, just four spaces from the rest of the Marines.

I guess that's why he's the first sergeant, Hondo thought to himself.

That little shortcut saved them ten minutes at a minimum.

Less than a minute later, he was rapping at the hatch to 32. After a short pause, the hatch opened, and a Marine motioned them inside the space, which was a communal head. Fourteen Marines waited for them, weapons at the ready.

"Where's Lieutenant Flores?" the lieutenant asked, his faceplate flipped open.

Sergeant Nelson, one of the squad leaders, pointed back to the corner of the shower stall where three bloody bodies were laid out side-by-side.

After a quick glance, Lieutenant Abrams said, "Tell me what happened."

Nelson gave the lieutenant the quick down and dirty. Led by the XO, what was left of Second Platoon tried to surprise the 24 host who were in Charlie's berthing. After cutting down several of the enemy in the first few seconds, the Brotherhood's weapons superiority began to make itself felt, and the tide turned. Ten of the Marines were cut down, including the XO and Staff Sergeant Lormander-Norris, and Nelson ordered the rest of them to retreat, bringing the XO and two other Marines' bodies with them. He holed them up in the head until he could figure out what to do next.

Gordy Nelson was a good Marine, but Hondo thought he was very relieved to have Lieutenant Abrams take over.

"I've linked up with Second Platoon," the lieutenant passed to his throat mic. "There's Sergeant Nelson and thirteen others." There was a pause as he listened, then, "One Oxar, ma'am." After yet one more pause as he listened to the skipper, he said, "Roger that. I'm on it."

He turned back to the waiting Marines and said, "A Brotherhood frigate can carry a contingent of fifty-two host. We've accounted for twelve of them, the best we can tell. That leaves forty. There are twenty-one aboard the *Zrínyi* at the moment, and the skipper believes that as per their SOP, they are keeping at least twelve back at their ship. That leaves the seven that retreated from our berthing spaces. The ship has lost track of them, but we have to consider that they can pop up anywhere, and to a lesser extent, so can the remaining dozen.

"Here on the *Zrínyi*, they've got us outgunned, so we need to canalize them to where they can't concentrate their numbers.

"Sergeant Nelson, are your Marines ready?"

"Fucking A yeah, sir," Gordy snarled, his voice full of venom.

"OK, then, I want everyone to gather 'round here so there's no confusion.

Hondo motioned his Marines to crowd in. He wasn't sure how twenty-nine Marines and two ship's crew armed with side arms, four Oxars, and a GG-19 were going to evict 21 entrenched and well-armed enemy, but if the lieutenant had a plan, he was eager to hear it.

Chapter 15

Hondo

This is eliminating confusion? Hondo wondered.

The lieutenant had gone over his plan in detail, saying he wanted to eliminate any confusion, but Hondo wasn't sure that had been successful. He knew what he was supposed to do, but he didn't have a clue if the entire thing was going to come together or not.

He looked over at the first sergeant, waiting for the word to go. With only the lieutenant and first sergeant having ear buds, Hondo was blind, and the lieutenant's plan relied on synchronizing the two groups.

Splitting the Marines had been a tough decision, particularly as they were already outgunned, but as the lieutenant had pointed out, they were relying on constrained spaces anyway, so it didn't matter as much as it could have.

First Squad was packed inside C-22-4-24, which had the advantage of two hatches, one leading into 4 and the other to 6. Pickerul, Antman, and Hanaburgh were crouched by the main hatch, weapons ready. Haus had given up his Oxar to Gordy Nelson's squad, so he was back to his Hastert.

This isn't going to work, he told himself again.

With the entire ship to roam, the host should be heading straight to the bridge to try to take it over. They should not be enticed to go rushing down inconsequential corridors.

"Stand by," First Sergeant Nordstrand said. "Our rabbit may have caught the attention of the foxes, and they're heading our way."

Maybe this will work after all, Hondo thought, lifting his eyebrows in surprise.

The "rabbit" was one of the two sailors who'd linked up with the Marines. She'd volunteered to be bait, and once she proved she knew her way around an Oxar, the lieutenant agreed, saying that the host might be more inclined to chase down a sailor than a Marine. She'd been led to where the Brotherhood force was moving, fired a couple of rounds from her Oxar, then ran towards the space where the other Marines were lying in wait. The host hadn't followed, so she bypassed them and fired from another position. This time, the host took chase, and now it looked like she was leading them down the 4 corridor.

That switched the missions between the two teams of Marines. Hondo hoped that the lieutenant had his team moving, as they now were the maneuver element.

"It's a go," the first sergeant said.

The muffled report of an Oxar sounded from right outside the hatch. MA3 Nikolaidis had made it that far, at least.

There were still too many things that could go wrong. If the host could pick up the waiting Marines, and the damaged *Zrínyi's* countermeasures weren't able to spoof the frigate's surveillance, then they'd know exactly where Hondo and his Marines were positioned. Almost as bad, if they'd split up and sent only a few host after Nikolaidis, then this would have been a wasted exercise in futility.

"It looks like it's all of them," the first sergeant said, his voice low in a whisper. "And they're hot on her trail."

Stupid, Hondo thought. *How can they be that dumb?*

That didn't mean Hondo planned on cutting them any slack. It was their grave they were digging, after all.

Unless they're playing us somehow.

Hanaburgh, Pickerul, and Antman were crouch by the hatch, looking back at him for the order to go. Antman's hands were rhythmically squeezing the Oxar's stock, and Pickerul had a wry smile on her face that frankly gave him the creeps. All three were ready to jump into the fire, just waiting for his word.

He hoped they wouldn't regret it.

"Now," the first sergeant told him.

Hondo flipped the manual lock and recessed the hatch. As one, the three Marines stepped out, Pickerul kneeling, Hanaburgh crouching over her, and Antman standing. All three opened up, firing three rounds before ducking back.

"I got the sucker!" Pickerul shouted as a series of rounds dinged along the corridor in response.

"Two," Hanaburgh told Hondo. "I'm pretty sure of it."

"Now!" the first sergeant yelled, and Hondo slammed the hatch shut.

The first sergeant ran back to the hatch leading to the 6 corridor and held it open as Second and Third Teams ducked through and disappeared toward midships. Corporal Wolf and First Team held back at the hatch.

"You ready, McKeever?" the first sergeant asked.

Hondo nodded, then at the first sergeant's order, he undogged the hatch and gave it a tiny push as if it hadn't been properly dogged and was swinging open a few centimeters on its own. He immediately bolted to the other hatch and got behind First Team while the first sergeant left them to join the rest of the squad.

The four Marines crouched in the corridor, peering into the compartment, waiting to see if anyone was going to try and follow. After a minute or so, the hatch to the 4 corridor slid open, and something was thrown in. Haus pulled their hatch closed and held it until it was rocked by an explosion. He immediately pushed it back open, and when two figures burst in, firing their weapons, Pickerul opened up, dropping one of them before the second was able to dive back out of the space and into the safety of the 4 corridor.

"Get that weapon," Hondo told Haus, who scrambled in, sidestepping the growing pool of blood and grabbed it, then rushed to get back out.

"Well, one isn't bad," Hondo said, looking at the body.

"I should've got them both," Pickerul said. "Sorry."

"You did good, Tammy," Hondo said, putting his hand on the younger Marine's shoulder. "You'll have more chances."

The far hatch was now open to 45 degrees. If Hondo and First Team left their present position, that would be an obvious access point for any host to cross over and come up the squad's rear.

If he were on the other side of the hatch, he'd have someone poised beside it, ready to toss in another grenade the moment someone else entered. It was an obvious course of action, so the host leader in the 4 corridor had to have thought of it, too.

This was where "eliminating confusion" was making things more confusing. Hondo knew that he should rejoin the rest of the squad, but that would leave a big security gap. If he had comms, he could simply ask the lieutenant for orders. Without comms, he had to figure out what the lieutenant would want him to do.

"Give them a few minutes. If they don't try again, we're going to dog that hatch and move on."

Then he realized that comms weren't just made with Marine Corps equipment.

"Private Killdeer, I've got a mission for you. Run up the corridor and find the first sergeant. Tell him the hatch to the 4 corridor isn't secured and ask him to find out what the lieutenant wants me to do: secure or bypass it. Tell him I think there might be more host on the other side."

Killdeer nodded, then took off towards midships. It shouldn't take her more than a couple of minutes to get back with an answer.

Something, maybe the slightest of sounds, caught Hondo's attention. He stepped back in the middle of the corridor and looked around, trying to figure out what it was. Try as he might, he couldn't hear anything else.

It's nerves, McKeever.

Still, something didn't seem right.

"Did you hear anything?" he asked Wolf.

"Nope. Nothing."

Hondo looked back down the passage towards the hull. The sterile passage showed no signs of anything.

Wolf, Pickerul, and Haus were focused on the compartment. That was almost overkill, three Marines with two solid weapons between them in such a confined space.

"Haus, come with me," Hondo said.

"Where're you going?" Wolf asked.

"Just checking something out. You watch that hatch. Anything comes flying in, and you shut this hatch."

"Roger that."

"What's up, Sergeant?" Haus asked as the two slowly advanced down the corridor.

"Probably nothing. But better be safe. This corridor hasn't been cleared."

The two Marines advanced to the second hatch, and nothing seemed out of the ordinary. Hondo paused, peering over Haus' shoulder, wondering if they should go any farther, but aware of the fact that he didn't want to get separated.

"OK, let's get back, he said.

For no particular reason, he gave the hatch next to him a shove, and it opened into a darkened compartment. The Federation Navy was death on open compartments, and he thought the New Budapest Navy had to be the same, so he reached inside to pull it shut.

The upswung rifle butt caught Hondo by surprise. He ducked back, but it glanced off his chest, tearing his hood and bunching it up in front of his face. Acting more on instinct, he reached out and grabbed his assailant as the barrel of the rifle slammed into his shoulder, firing twice into the bulkhead behind him. If the soldier got separation, Hondo would be finished. With his hood bunched up, Hondo couldn't see much, but he didn't need to. He slid his left arm around the man's neck, and hugged him tight, bringing up his Ruger with his right. With the barrel of the Ruger flush on the base of the soldier's throat, he fired, hoping to panic the man.

The soldier didn't panic but simply slumped in his armlock. Wary about a feint, Hondo pushed his hood off so he could see, and his opponent's face, gasping as blood welled from his mouth, was centimeters from his. He almost recoiled as the soldier seemed to try to ask him something before the light faded from his eyes.

Hondo was confused. EVA suits were not armored in the classical sense, but they used a ceromesh to ward off micrometeors, and a D-layer to protect from ultraviolet radiation. The ceromesh should have been able to repel his little 2mm darts, but at the base of his neck, he could see a line of holes, right at the joint where he'd placed the muzzle of his handgun.

He was surprised, but the results were plain. He dropped the soldier as a second charged him from inside the compartment, his face scrunched in unholy anger. EVA suits were made to protect people in the vacuum of space. They were not made for hand-to-hand combat. The soldier should have stood off and shot Hondo, but anger had overcome him, and he was closing in, bringing his G-19 around to bear.

Hondo, clad in only his utilities, was far more maneuverable. He dropped to the deck just as the soldier fired and dove forward, hitting the man in the knees and sending him tumbling. He reversed himself, diving to tackle the man in the back as he tried to struggle to his feet. That was all the time Hondo needed. He grabbed his first attacker's 19 and drove the barrel into the base of the second soldier's back as he fumbled with the trigger. As with the first GG-19 he'd taken, this one had the biolocks bypassed, and Hondo put two rounds through the man. A fountain of blood and guts sprayed the bulkhead as the man collapsed.

Breathing hard, Hondo looked back down the passage, weapon ready, but there wasn't anyone else coming.

"Haus! Why didn't you help?" he snapped as he tried to get a hold of his breathing.

He turned to see the Marine on his back, almost cut in two. Even the weapon he'd taken was broken, blasted into a hunk of mangled plastic. Hondo looked at him in disbelief.

"How . . .?"

The first soldier had fired twice when Hondo had pushed his rifle aside. Those rounds had hit Haus, he realized, who was trying to come to his aid.

"Oh, hell, Went," he said.

Wolf and Pickerul charged back down the corridor with Wolf sliding to a stop when he saw Haus' body. He slowly knelt and tried to push the two sections back together.

"Not now, Wolf," Hondo told him. "We'll come back and get him zombied."

As bad as it looked, Haus' head was untouched, and if they got him in stasis, there would be a good chance at a resurrection and a successful, if long, regen.

Pickerul grabbed Wolf by the shoulder and helped him up, saying, "Let's go, Corporal. We've got to get the bastards that did this."

"Looks like Sergeant McKeever already did that," Wolf said, pointing to the two host.

"There're still more of the fuckers, and I want me some of them."

She picked up the second 19 and handed it to him. He snapped it out of her hand, checked the action, and nodded. Hondo knew he was back in the game.

There was the sound of firing from up ahead, and Hondo took off at a run, his ruined hood forgotten. He'd be toast if the ship lost atmosphere again, but now he had full visibility, and he felt reenergized.

He reached the intersection with the C-ring and turned left.

"Coming up your rear!" Hondo shouted as the three reached the back of the squad.

Relief flowed over Killdeer's face, and she swung back around to look forward. Not that she could fire—the way was blocked by the rest of the squad. Hondo couldn't even see Hanaburgh and Antman, but he could hear the steady reports of the Oxars.

"Cover our six," he told Wolf, then with his second stolen GG-19, started working his way forward.

He wasn't sure if there was anyone left behind him, but he had thought that direction was clear before.

At the side of the corridor, the first sergeant was sitting while Doc Leach applied a pressure sleeve to his left upper arm. Blood dripped off his fingers to pool on the deck.

"What's the situation?" he asked the first sergeant, kneeling beside Doc.

"Your lieutenant's engaged up ahead. Hanaburgh and Acevedo don't have targets, but they're pumping out rounds to remind the host that this way is a no-go for them."

Hondo could see the two Marines now, one on each side of the passage, taking turns firing rounds.

"Antman, how many rounds do you have left?" he yelled.

The lance corporal glanced down at his readout and shouted back, "Twenty-two."

"I'm at twenty-eight," Hanaburgh added. "But I've got one more mag."

Hondo shook his head. Both knew better than to ignore fire discipline. If they ran out of ammo, their Oxars would be useless.

"Pickerul, up!" he shouted back.

"Take Antman's place," he told her. "And give Hanaburgh this," he said, handing her the GG-19 he'd just taken. "I want Hanaburgh's Oxar, though."

She grabbed the 19, ran forward to hand it to Hanaburgh, and immediately fired ten rounds down the corridor.

"Fire discipline, Tammy! Sustained fire."

Antman came back, carrying Hanaburgh's Oxar, which he gave to Hondo.

"Just sit tight. I don't want you firing unless you have a target."

He turned around to the first sergeant, who was looking pale.

"You OK, First Sergeant?" he asked.

"I was fucking shot, McKeever. No, I'm not OK."

Right. Pretty obvious. Of course, he's not OK.

"How did you get hit? A seeing-eye round?"

He managed to look sheepish despite the pale pallor. "I sort of went forward to see if I could get eyes on what was happening. One of them got me.

"The bones worked, though, right Doc?" he asked the corpsman.

"I told you, the round didn't penetrate, but it snapped your humerus, and that tore through the skin. You'll heal up fine," Doc said.

"Still, hurts like a bi—" he started before he went quiet, raising his left hand to the side of his hood. "They're bolting to 24. The lieutenant wants you to get your asses up there to stop them."

Hondo jumped up and said, "Everyone, move out now!"

He ran forward to Pickerul and Hanaburgh, grabbed each of them by the shoulder, and said, "The bros are bolting up a deck. We need to stop them, but pick your targets. The lieutenant's up there, and we don't need any friendly fire fuck-ups. No blind firing."

With both Marines abreast of him, he ran forward, all senses on the alert as they ran down the curving C-ring. Within 20 meters, they were on the enemy, a last EVA-suited host climbing through an access hatch in the ceiling. All three Marines fired, and the soldier tumbled to the deck, bouncing once, then laying still.

A stream of darts peppered the bulkhead around them, and Hondo screamed out, "Cease fire, cease fire! We're First Squad."

He felt a hornet's sting on his left ear before the incoming darts ceased.

"Son-of-a-bitch," he shouted, raising his hand to the ear, which came down bloody.

"Cease fucking fire, I said."

He reached up and explored his ear. It hurt like hell, but it didn't feel like it had gotten much. A couple of millimeters to his right, and he'd be down for the count, though.

Corporal Tesseret and his fire team of Marines hesitantly advanced into sight. Tesseret grimaced when he saw Hondo.

"You OK?"

He wanted to shout *You fucking shot me!* but the attention had to be on the host and what they were doing.

"They went up there," he said instead, pointing to the still-open hatch in the overhead. "And secure that guy," he added, pointing to the soldier on the deck, who had weakly raised one hand in surrender.

PFC John gave his weapon to Tesseret and patted down the wounded soldier while Lance Corporal Western started up the access ladder to the hatch. Western stuck his Oxar up through the hatch and fired three rounds, only to drop his weapon as it was hit by return fire. The Oxar almost hit the John and the soldier, and Tesseret stepped in to kick it out of the way. A chagrined Western climbed back down to retrieve the weapon, checking it over for damage.

Lieutenant Abrams came into view. Hondo could see that he was talking over the ship's comms as he peered up into the hatch.

Suddenly, he turned to Hondo and yelled out, "They're heading back towards berthing. Get your squad back down the six corridor and cut them off."

Hondo wheeled around and started running, pulling the rest of the squad in his wake, trying to picture where the six would lead him.

"McKeever, take this," the first sergeant said as he passed, tossing up the headset. Hondo snagged it in mid-air and fumbled it onto his ear. He could hear Captain Ariç giving a running position check on the fleeing host.

Not the entire host. One soldier stayed behind, guarding the access hatch they'd used to get out of the C-ring.

"Bypass him, Armando," the skipper told the lieutenant. "We need to stop the host and keep them aboard."

Why? If they are giving up, let them, Hondo thought for a moment before what she'd said registered.

She knew that if the Marines could capture a significant number of Brotherhood host, they would be human shields, protecting the *Zrínyi* from being blown into her component atoms—and the Marines and Navy crew along with her.

That was probably why the host was booking, if what it looked like was true. They still had a weapons advantage over the Marines, but with the Marines' stiff resistance, what they probably hoped would be an easy ship takedown was getting harder and not worth the effort.

"Skipper, is anyone closing in on our corridor?" he asked over the comms.

"Who is this?" she asked.

That's right, this is a ship's portable comms system, and it can't identify me.

"Sergeant McKeever. We're in pursuit along the six corridor."

"That's a negative, Sergeant. I'll let you know if I see anything closing in on you."

"Pick it up!" he yelled to Wolf and First Team, who were now point again.

Wolf was advancing according to SOP, which meant clearing every intersection. With the skipper on angel watch, they could speed up in the hopes of cutting the host off before they reached Charlie Company's berthing spaces.

Wolf turned around, a confused look on his face.

"It's clear ahead. Just go for it."

He gave a tiny shrug, then broke into a run.

"You're behind them, McKeever," the skipper said, "and falling behind."

Hondo sprinted ahead, pulling alongside of Wolf. The corporal was huffing and puffing as he ran, the hood's faceplate fogging up. Hondo, without a hood, was having no problem.

"Faceplates up!" he shouted.

Killdeer gave a "Thank God" as she flipped up her hood, her face red with exertion.

The lieutenant had given the order for the hoods to be closed up, but sergeants were paid the big NCO credits to have initiative. He should have ordered that when they started off in pursuit.

"Sergeant McKeever, the first host have reached the outer ring, and I don't think Lieutenant Abrams is going to get there in time to stop them. You've got to push it."

The *Zrínyi* was an older ship with evacuateable compartments. With the berthing space now open to the black, the ship's emergency system would not allow an inside hatch to be opened unless that space had its atmosphere evacuated. Any adjoining space could be used as an ad hoc airlock. If the soldiers had something to blow the hatch, they were in EVA suits and could survive unless the suits were damaged by the ragged junk inside berthing. If they couldn't or wouldn't blow the hatch, they had to wait until the space was in a vacuum.

First Team ran into the last secure space and turned around at the door, waiting for the rest to crowd inside. Hondo pushed forward and stood, motioning with his arm for the rest to hurry when Wolf tapped him on the arm.

"What?" Hondo snapped.

Wolf pointed at his own hood, then at Hondo's naked head.

"Shit!"

He wasn't good at breathing vacuum.

He looked around, and there was an emergency chest close to the far door. He pushed back to it and opened the lid, sighing with relief at the five hoods, still in their packs.

"Close it," he ordered Marasco, motioning to the round wheel that would seal the door.

Unlike a hatch, with a simple lever to lock it in place, the doors used wheels that could be either be spun shut under power or by hand. Power was still good, so it took only a moment for the space to become an airlock.

"Start evacuation," Hondo yelled out as he pulled the hood out of its pack.

Marasco hesitated a moment, looking at Hondo, who yelled, "Just do it. I'm fine."

Only he wasn't fine. He was surprised at how quickly the air was evacuated, and he was feeling hypoxia as he slammed the hood over his head and hit the seals. A moment later, blessed breathable air filled the hood.

"What's your status? The host is entering berthing," the company commander asked.

"Almost there, ma'am.

"First, right, Third, left, Second, right up the middle. We need to stop them, and if possible, alive."

Sounds were already getting tinny, and he hoped his Marines heard him.

The wait was almost unbearable as the evacuation system struggled with the last vestiges of atmosphere. Finally, the red light by the outer door switched to green. Hondo rotated his arm in a big circle. That may not have been one of the standard hand and arm signals taught at Charles, but it got the point across. Wolf hit the switch, and the wheel spun open. He pushed on the door, and it opened into berthing.

Halfway through the door, Killdeer spun around, grabbing her chest as she fell to the deck. Tony B stepped over her and into the space, firing his Hasert .42.

There was no sound of weapons firing, but the flashes of light told the story of a fierce little firefight. Hondo vaulted Killdeer into the compartment, looking for a target. Three soldiers were standing shoulder-to-shoulder at the edge of the gaping hole in the ship's bulkhead, firing back at them. Six Marines were through and firing, but the soldiers weren't hit.

Fuck that, Hondo thought as he stopped, then deliberately brought up Hanaburgh's Oxar, calming his mind as if he was on the rifle range back on the Egg. He wasn't going to miss.

Before he could get his sight picture, though, the three soldiers wheeled and dove out of the ship. There was a mad rush of Marines to the torn edge, but the three soldiers had doubled back around the hull of the *Zrínyi* and were almost out of sight as they hugged the hull.

Almost didn't mean *completely* out of sight, however. Hanaburgh fired two shots at the retreating figures, sending one of them pinwheeling into the hull, where he bounced and tumbled. One of the other soldiers doubled back, threw a grappling line around his buddy, and reeled him in. Hondo thought the wounded soldier was hit one more time, but his rescuer pulled him out of the Marine's line of sight.

"Skipper, they all got away," Hondo reported, hating having to give her the news.

Of course, she already knew that. The ship's still-working sensors would have told her there were no remaining host in berthing.

"Bring your Marines back to the main galley. I want you and the lieutenant to see me in CIC."

There was some backslapping among his Marines. They'd just defended the ship from a better-armed Brotherhood unit, after all.

It was probably a Pyrrhic victory, however, one that could have signaled their doom.

EARTH

Chapter 16
Skylar

"So, what are you saying?" Sky asked Glinda.

"My words are my words, Vice-Minister," the head of the Klethos quad said. "They have no meaning other than what they have."

But yes, they do, and just what are you telling me?

Sky, Dr. Affoue Kouassi from Greater France, and Dr. Norelco Pavoni from the Confederation headed the gathered team that was sent by the secretary-general to try and make sense of the increasingly cryptic remarks coming out of the liaison quad. The meeting was taking place in the ancient Place des Ducs de Bourgogne in Dijon, far enough away from the pressure and prying eyes of Brussels, yet only a half-hour away for everyone except Sky.

She took a moment to look out the window where the morning sun played through the leaves of some of the huge honey locusts that surrounded the city hall. It was still dark in Pittsburgh, where one moment the evening before she was following the emergency on the *SMS Zrínyi,* and then the next minute found herself on a shuttle to DC to catch the diplomatic hop to Paris. Despite getting no sleep on the way over, she didn't feel the least bit tired. Something very important was being *not-said*, and she had to figure it out.

"Words have meaning, Ambassador, but what the speaker intends to convey is not always received as such. Differences in culture, for example, can act as a filter."

"Words have meaning," the Klethos said again, revealing nothing more.

"So, when you say honor must be restored, whose honor?"

Foue nudged Sky's foot with hers, unseen under the heavy table.

"Any honor, all honor. That is the way with all *d'lato*."

"And are we humans *d'lato*?" Sky asked, repeating the Klethos word for which they referred to themselves, not specifically as Klethos but as a class of being, the best human linguists could tell.

"*D'lato* are *d'lato*. It comes from within."

"Let me ask, Ambassador," Foue said. "We believe we are *d'lato*, just as you. We've honored the fighting ring for over 100 of our years. All humans have honored the ring. Is this a sign of *d'lato*?"

"All *d'lato* honor the ring," "Gerly," the nickname they used for one of the other Klethos, said, only the fourth or fifth time Sky had ever heard her speak.

Glinda stared at the humans impassively.

"So, even the Brotherhood, who had provided Gladiators for the ring, they are *d'lato*?" Foue asked.

"*D'lato* is not a permanent state of being. It is the now and when."

When?

Sky felt she was at the cusp of a breakthrough, and with just one or two more pieces of information, everything would fall into place. One thing was evident to her, however. "*D'lato*" gave a being status. The Trinoculars and all the species the Klethos had exterminated were not *d'lato*, and so they had been beneath notice, "sub-human" in human thinking. By understanding the Klethos honor and agreeing to the terms of gladiatorial combat, humanity had elevated itself to *d'lato* status.

But now she was sure that the term wasn't a description such as human, Klethos, or even sentient; it was something that had to be maintained, and those in the Brotherhood alliance had somehow lost that status. The big question was how that would affect the relationship between the Klethos and the UAM alliance.

No, it isn't, she suddenly realized. The *big question is how that affects the Klethos and the Brotherhood alliance.*

The more she thought about it, the more she was certain. Foue had been on to something, asking about the Brotherhood.

"So, please forgive the question, as I know it is obvious, but for clarity's sake, what happens when honor is forfeit?"

Sky was sure she saw a quick flick of Gloria's nictitating membrane.

"When honor is forfeit, those with honor must remediate the situation to bring honor into balance again."

"So, if a Klethos warrior lost honor, it would be her fellow warriors who would remediate and bring honor back into balance."

"Your words are words," Glinda said, speaking once again.

Meaning what I say is true, and so my words are real words.

She was sure that the Klethos was telling her that the Brotherhood alliance had lost honor, that they were no longer *d'lato.* More importantly, it was up to the rest of humanity to restore the balance in honor.

"And if we don't?" Dr. Pavoni asked.

Sky kept her face straight. Pavoni understood where the conversation was going, but evidently, he didn't believe in diplomacy.

"Honor must be remediated or there is no honor."

And with that, we're no longer d'lato. They're getting their asses kicked by the Grubs. Would they really jeopardize our help for a matter of obscure honor?

Looking at the four Klethos, Sky was suddenly sure that they would. They would cripple their effort if it meant keeping their honor intact.

"It is acceptable for those in need to request help from other *d'lato* to remediate honor," Gary said. "It would be mandatory for another *d'lato* to render such aid, whether it was asked for or not."

Sky's mouth opened in shock. This was the first time any male Klethos had spoken to a human. Some specialists had conjectured that they couldn't speak at all. Not only had he spoken, but he'd been clear in his meaning.

She exchanged a quick glance with Foue, wondering if they'd both come to the same conclusion. The UAM forces had better deal with the Brotherhood alliance to restore humanity's honor. If they didn't, the Klethos were going to step in and "remediate" the situation themselves.

SMS ZRÍNYI

Chapter 16

Hondo

"OK, that's enough for now," Doc Leach shouted up to Tony B, who was crouched above the container of zip-locks.

The *Zrínyi* was a hybrid, neither a real man-of-war nor a transport, and that meant it did neither well. The container carrying the medical supplies had been packed among a myriad of other containers that made normal access impossible. One of the ship's engineers had to cut open the top just to give the Marines access to it.

And access was needed. The two companies' corpsman had each carried two zip-locks in their personal kits. Only three zip-locks that had been carried by the Charlie corpsmen had been recovered in usable condition, so that left the zip-locks carried by Doc Leach and the other surviving Alpha Company corpsmen, twelve zip-locks in all.

There were twenty-two Marines, one corpsman, and five Brotherhood host KIA on the ship who had a chance at resurrection, and they needed to be put into stasis. Captain Ariç had given First Squad the task of recovering more zip-locks and breaking into the weapons containers, while Second Squad collected the dead.

All told, Hondo was glad that he was in the cargo hold and Cara was moving the KIA into the ship's galley.

Hondo had been glad to leave the CIC. Tension had been high, as the two captains didn't seem to be on the same page. The skipper was angry, but it was a collected anger, as she tried to develop a course of action with the ship's CO. Captain Warrant, the Charlie Company commander, was mad enough to take action himself if he could, and he even told the ship's CO to get the impulse engines online and ram the Brotherhood frigate.

The two captains looked about to come to blows when the four sergeants had been dismissed and given their tasks. Hondo wasted no time in beating feet out of there.

He understood Captain Warrant's anger. As the senior Marine onboard, he was the commander of troops, and he'd been in CIC when the frigate had attacked. He's lost almost his entire company while he'd been in the safest part of the ship. It was no wonder he wanted to take it to the Brotherhood.

But the question was how. The *Zrínyi's* weapons were offline or destroyed. The ammo locker was even off-limits. One of the larger pieces of ordnance had been cracked, and radiation had flooded the space. The ship had no propulsion power and could not get underway, which was probably a good thing with Captain Warrant wanting to play Roman galley and ram the frigate. They didn't have EVA suits other than the eight, brightly-colored Navy EVA suits used for external repairs.

What they *did* have was one ship-to-shore shuttle, a cargo sled, and their personal escape pods, and it was looking more and more like those pods might be their last hope if the frigate's captain decided to fire on the *Zrínyi* again. With the ship being inside the Lore system, the pods wouldn't have any trouble making it down to the system's lone inhabitable planet.

They also had the five resurrectable Brotherhood KIA and three EPWs, all wounded. As per the Harbin Accords, the names of the three prisoners and the KIA were being sent to the frigate, so the captain would know that action taken against the *Zrínyi* would be action taken against their own personnel.

As Tony B climbed down from on top of the containers, Hondo looked at the long line of them that filled the cargo hold. Inside those containers were over two hundred PICS, armed and ready for battle. They represented a very significant force, but they weren't much use in the confines of a ship. Even if they'd been accessible during the fight, they wouldn't have done much good; they were simply too big. One of them hunched over in a passage would have been a pretty serious obstacle, but it would have been more of a pillbox than a maneuverable asset.

The thought of beaming a squad of PICS Marines inside of the frigate to wrack havoc gave him a temporary smile, but beaming was a figment of the scifi flicks and books, not real life. A PICS Marine would have to shuttle over, or even use their putt-putt, the tiny impulse pack that could be strapped on to maneuver a PICS in the vacuum of space.

The thought of the putt-putts perked Hondo up for a moment.

What if we . . .

He dropped that line of thought almost before it began. The putt-putts could move a PICS at possibly five klicks an hour, even if they had 200 of them onboard, which was extremely doubtful. They would advance so slowly that a gunner on the frigate could use visual sighting to blast each Marine on the transit over. Even if the frigate was still 800 meters off, that would mean it would take ten long minutes for a PICS Marine to cross that distance. It would make more sense to use the container jockey to throw the Marines across that distance.

He laughed at the mental image of Marines being shot across like so many containers, ready to be caught by the appropriate distribution rails. Wal-Tesco might have developed the system to get its myriad of products to the customer, so why not Marines?

Then he stopped short.

Why not Marines? Could it work?

He looked over at the five container jockeys locked into the rails in the overhead. This was an extremely stupid idea, but at the moment, he couldn't think of an obvious reason why a jockey couldn't handle the job. They handled just about everything Wal-Tesco sold.

I've got to talk to the lieutenant.

Человека

EARTH

Chapter 17
Skylar

"I've got to talk to the minister," Sky told Keyshon as she took the maglev back to Paris.

She'd just left the meeting and was sitting with Foue in a secured government compartment, thanks to her Greater France counterpart. Sky had only met Affoue Kouassi once before, two months ago, but she'd taken an immediate liking to the tall scientist. Liking her or not, though, did not matter as much as the fact that she'd read the same thing into the meeting that Sky had. The Klethos had been giving them a warning: either take care of the Brotherhood alliance, or they would.

Given the relatively small numbers of Klethos warriors, Sky wasn't sure if they could actually defeat half of humanity in an all-out war, even given their better technology. No matter what, however, such a war would be devastating. The Klethos had to be convinced not to let honor take both species down.

"The minister left for Brussels two hours ago," her assistant told her.

Foue looked at her with raised eyebrows from her seat across from her.

"Change my schedule. I'm going to Brussels. I'm arriving in Paris in . . ."

"Eight minutes," Foue told her.

" . . . in eight minutes. Get me to Brussels as quickly as possible."

"Will do. I'll have it up to you in two minutes."

"Is that related?" Foue asked in her lilting accent.

Greater France and the Federation had somewhat of a love-hate relationship, going back to France's decision not to join the Federation upon its inception. They'd been allies, and they'd been at war with each other. High-level officials from each government were not prone to sharing certain information.

Well, luckily, I'm a scientist, not a bureaucrat, and we're allies in this.

"I don't think so. The minister was supposed to meet with the chairman this morning, so something big is up, but as far as I know, you and I are the first to discover this issue."

"And Pavoni," Foue said.

"He's Confed through-and-through. He'll be reporting back to the counsel himself, most likely, before he makes a move."

"I've downloaded my initial report," Foue told her.

Sky wrinkled her forehead. She had an initial report ready to upload, but she'd wanted to speak to the minister face-to-face, to make sure he understood exactly how she felt. Bulleted notes on an eDoc couldn't convey the same urgency. She didn't know why the minister was on his way to Brussels, but he hated leaving Pittsburgh, even to go to DC.

Her PA softly chimed, and she glanced down to see she had a maglev to Brussels in 23 minutes, leaving off track 23 at Gare du Nord. She'd be in Brussels by 11:54.

The minister needed to know now. With a sigh, she sent the report, with a request to meet him in his UAM office at 12:30. She stared at her PA for forty-five seconds before he responded confirming the meeting.

She held up her PA for Foue to read, then asked, "When's your meeting?"

"One," she said. "If you're still in Brussels at three, give me a call. If your minister approves, I'd like to compare notes with you."

"Will do," Sky said without hesitation, as the first buildings of the Paris metroplex came into view.

SMS ZRÍNYI

Chapter 18
Hondo

"It would be suicide," Captain Ariç said. "Anyone would still be picked off before they got halfway there."

"Some might be, but not all," Captain Warrant said. "Hell, I'll lead the wave over myself."

Hondo, trying to fade into the bulkhead in the back, raised his eyebrows at that. Marine captains were not known to be lead-from-the-back officers, but to volunteer to lead what probably would be a suicide mission gave the man cred, and he had to give him props.

Hondo had been surprised when Lieutenant Abrams had thought his crazy idea had merit. He hadn't been pleased, however, when the lieutenant had dragged him into CIC to tell the skipper.

Captain Warrant had immediately seized on the idea and championed it, allowing Hondo to retreat into the background. The ship's commander, *Alezerdes* Black, had called the cargo chief to CIC to ask if using the container jockeys would be possible.

He looked up at the overhead as if searching for an answer there, then shrugged and said, "*Igen*, sir, it could be done."

Captain Warrant fist-pumped the air in triumph before Captain Ariç asked, "One, how accurate would it be, and two, how . . . well . . . fast would it shoot someone?"

"Well, ma'am, extremely accurate. It don't make no difference in a vacuum as to size and shape. If you shoot it, it will go where you want it. Some of the big commercial pod liners, they send containers nigh on four klicks to get into the right distribution system. As to speed, well, up to 48 meters per second."

Shit, that's . . . he had to stop to do the calculation in his head . . . *over 170 KPH.*

Hitting a ship at that speed would mess up a PICS, and more so the Marine inside.

Captain Ariç could do the math herself.

"Could you slow that to about ten meters per second?"

"Aye-ah, Captain. It's just an adjustment on the actuator ring."

"See, Tess? A PICS can withstand a 35 KPH hit," Captain Warrant said. "It can take a 50 KPH hit."

Probably. Not a good idea, though, especially if we've got to stop on a ship's hull, Hondo thought.

"OK, say 15 meters a second, then. That's still a minute to get from the *Zrínyi* to the frigate. That's a long, long time to be a target. Think of it, a minute."

Hondo hadn't considered that, and his tempered enthusiasm dropped a few levels. Almost every weapon a frigate had would make mincemeat of a Marine in PICS.

"No one would be a target for a full minute. A frigate like that has cutouts for anything close in."

Hondo knew what a cutout was in a Marine tank. The main guns could not be lowered so far as to fire and hit itself. But tanks also had close-in anti-personnel weapons, too, to take care of infantry who got in too close. A frigate might have the same kind of cutouts for her main weapons, but he couldn't imagine an expensive investment like that wouldn't have many ways to repel boarders.

"It's still too long," Captain Ariç said. "One sweep with the Borring Gun, and every Marine would be cooked."

"That gun takes time to aim."

One of the Navy officers said, "About thirty seconds for a one-eighty shift."

"Which would be enough time to get in close," Captain Warrant said, pouncing on the statement like a cat on a mouse.

"You're assuming that the gun is already pointed at a one-eighty away from the ship, and I'm betting its crosshairs are locked onto us right now."

The Buddie captain sat quiet during most of this interchange. The New Budapest Navy and the Marines were not technically in the same chain of command, but as the master of the ship, no action would be taken against the Brotherhood frigate without his say-so. Hondo tried to read into the man's expression, but he was a blank slate.

"What if we drew the gun away from the ship?" Lieutenant Abrams asked, the first words he uttered after Hondo and Cara had given their reports.

"What do you mean?" another of the Navy officers asked.

"*Alezerdes,* you still have a cargo sled, right?"

"Yes, but it doesn't have any offensive capability," the cargo chief answered for the ship's captain.

"None that are built in, but what if it looked like it was a threat?" the lieutenant said, but still looking at the ship's CO. "There's also one of your bombs in the magazine, leaking radiation."

"Yeah, one of the HR-40s. Leaking bad."

"So, what if we loaded it aboard the sled and sent it out?"

"Won't do nothin'. The forty can't just be carried over there to detonate. It don't work that way."

"It doesn't have to," the lieutenant said, looking right at the New Budapest commander. If we strap your HR-40 into the sled, trailing a stream of radiation and send it looping around, then what's that Brotherhood commander going to do? Ignore it? He doesn't have time to analyze the thing. He's got to assume it's a threat, and he'll have to take action."

For the first time, Hondo saw the CO break his stony demeanor. The man seemed to be considering it. All hands in the CIC waited silently for him to say something.

"Can we do that?" he asked the chief.

"Technically? Yes, sir."

"And if we can get you Marines to the frigate, is there anything they can do against the ship?"

Captain Warrant's eager expression faded. Getting the Marines to the ship was one thing, but as powerful as a PICS was, it was nothing against a Navy man-of-war.

"I might think of something," the ship's weapons officer said.

Captain Warrant looked up with renewed hope in his eyes.

The *alezerdes* stood up and said, "Twenty minutes. Get back to me with a plan. We'll run it through the AI, and if we've got a 33% chance or better of success, it's a go."

EARTH

Chapter 19
Skylar

At 12:37, the minister blew into his office like a tornado, trailing the vice-minister and three underlings. Sky jumped to her feet, and the minister held up a hand, palm out, to stop her.

"Set up a meeting with Archbishop Tallyman in twenty minutes in the Vault," he told his EA.

Grace Jordache, who'd been the EA for no fewer than eight second-ministers, said, "He's not going to agree to that."

"He will if he thinks I can get the first minister to stand down."

"Can you?"

"I don't know," the minister said, suddenly looking weary. "But we have to try. We can't let the Lore incident pull us into a shooting war, and if we both send in tasks forces, that's what's going to happen."

"Yes, sir. I'll get him there," Grace said, leaving the office.

Sky had almost forgotten the crisis out at the Lore system. Just ten hours earlier, it had taken all of her attention, and now it had been pushed to the side in lieu of something much bigger.

He turned to Sky, and without civil pleasantries, asked, "How sure are you of this?"

This is it. Time to step up.

She was certain to her very core that what she said now could not only affect the Federation, but all of humanity. If she was wrong, the consequences could be simply too dire to even imagine.

"I'm positive, sir. I'm staking my professional career on it."

"Your career means jack shit, Skylar. As much as I like you, I'd fire you in a second if I thought it would serve the Federation."

"Right, sir. Then to be blunt, I'm staking my life on it. And in this case, it isn't the Federation I'm worried about. It's mankind."

"I've read your report, Skylar. It's just . . . well, it's a lot to absorb. Jerry?" he asked, turning to the vice-minister.

Vice-Minister Jerome Lucient and Skylar were not on the best of terms, and the vice-minister had blocked Sky before. Sky steeled her face to listen to what Lucient said, readying her counter-attack.

"I hate to say it, sir, but I can't find fault with it. I'm not ready to vouch for it to the chairman, but Ybarra could be right. I think we need to run it through some others and run some sims, though."

Sky was surprised at Lucient's response. She'd been expecting pushback. Instead, he seemed to offer a tentative agreement. His suggestion to run the sims was even welcomed. That would be a huge relief, she realized, taking the heavy load of full responsibility off her shoulders. She should have suggested that in the beginning, but she'd been too focused on getting the minister to initiate action.

"How much time do we have?" the minister asked.

That question took her by surprise. It shouldn't have, but once again, she'd had blinders on in her efforts to let the minister know the threat. She had to think for a moment, but she didn't have much to go on. The Klethos were hard to fathom sometimes, and their sense of time seemed to be far different from that of homo sapiens.

"I . . . I can't honestly say right now," she admitted.

This was too important to simply try and make a SWAG just to save face.

"Ten minutes? Ten hours? Ten days? Give me something, Skylar."

"Not ten minutes. Days, maybe? Weeks?"

The minister looked at her with his famous piercing stare, as if he could read into her very soul. It took an effort of will for Sky to stare back, unflinching.

"Jerry, I want the Bravo group in the conference room at sixteen hundred. Get Knowles from First and Bue from Third to join us. I want this hashed out, and then start sims by this evening.

"Skylar, go check into the Metropole. You're staying here for the duration. And get a nap if you can. I want you rested and ready at sixteen hundred.

"And now, I've got to go deal with the arch-bishop. I thought we were only trying to keep humanity from breaking out into war, but now we've got to worry about the Klethos, too."

"Are you going to tell the arch-bishop about this?" Lucient asked him.

"I don't know. If I have to. If it comes down to the Klethos attacking them . . ." he said, leaving the sentence unfinished.

If it comes down to the Klethos attacking the Brotherhood, the Federation will have to support their fellow humans, she finished the thought.

She supposed she knew that, but it was sobering to have the minister refer to it.

Despite that, Sky felt a huge wave of relief sweep over her. Holding what she'd learned at the meeting with the quad had been a huge burden. Now, the minister was on it, and she no longer felt she had to save the galaxy alone.

SMS ZRÍNYI

Chapter 20
Hondo

"Up-check!" Hondo passed over the net. "I want to hear your greens."

It felt good to be back in his PICS after fighting in what was essentially a plastic bag over his head. The fact that the official projection gave them a 42% chance of success didn't dampen his mood. They were finally taking the fight to the enemy instead of waiting for them to strike first.

Four hours before, he'd taken his idea to the lieutenant; now he was in the assault force.

His plan had not survived the officers, both Buddie Navy and Federation Marine. He wasn't surprised. "Simple" and "straightforward" were often foreign words to the Os, as if they had to make sure their fingerprints were all over everything.

For Hondo, at least, the mission was pretty clear, and he could ignore the other working parts. Those parts were what pushed the chance of success over the ship commander's 33%, but none of them were in his control, so he didn't have to concern himself with them.

"Make sure you're on Null-G weapons settings," he passed again.

It should be obvious, but it never hurt to check. A PICS' weapons systems worked whether in the vacuum of space or on a planet. The targeting systems had to be adjusted, however. A kinetic round had a different trajectory under 1.2

Earth Normal than it did at .5 Earth Normal than it did in Null-G. Even energy weapons had different characteristics.

"Captain, are your weapons on Null-G?"

Hondo could see Captain Warrant mouth "shit," but he said, "Don't worry about me, Sergeant. I've done this before."

Hondo wasn't happy to have the captain along. He'd given the man his props in CIC for saying he'd lead the assault, but in reality, the man was probably going to be a liability. Hondo didn't know him, and he certainly hadn't worked with him.

To make matters worse, since the Charlie Company commander had interjected himself into the assault element, that meant Lieutenant Abrams had to come along, too. Hondo was surprised that Captain Ariç hadn't joined the party, but there was no way she was going to let Captain Warrant go with Hondo without someone to run interference for him.

Hondo didn't mind the lieutenant joining him. They'd worked together enough times, and they were a pretty good team, he thought. However, with only ten putt-putts aboard the ship, that meant ten Marines were going to make the crossing. That meant he had to drop a fire team, and with only two Marines left in First, that was Wolf and Pickerul.

Wolf was still glowering as he helped the rest of the Marines get ready. He'd tried to get Hondo to change his mind and leave behind someone else, but this made the most sense. Pickerul was even more pissed off, if that was even possible. She was assisting the Navy weapons tech in attaching the "package" to Hanaburgh, but her body language screamed anger.

His PICS ready to go, Hondo walked over the Hanaburgh to check the progress. The weapons officer was standing in front of the Marine, going over the deployment of the weapon for what had to be the tenth time.

Hondo looked at the contraption warily. It looked like it was put together by a crazed scientist, but the weapons officer promised it would work—if it was emplaced properly. There were only a few locations on the frigate's hull where it could be effective, and even then, unless the thing was kicked off correctly, it would all be for naught.

He didn't like the fact that they had only one of the bombs. If Hanaburgh was picked off in the transit, they had nothing but their own PICS weapons, and while they could help blind the ship, or at least degrade her sensor suite, they couldn't do much to the ship as a whole.

"OK, Burger, you're ready!" Pickerul said, slapping him on the chest carapace.

"Hooah!" Hanaburgh shouted.

"Fucking A, Burger, it's 'ooh-rah,' now, none of the fuckdick shit."

Hanaburgh was prone to revert back to the FCDC "hooah" instead of the Marine "ooh-rah," and he took a ration of shit from the others every time he did so. Hondo thought he might be doing it on purpose, though, to push back against the grief he took for being an FCDC transfer.

"OK, all non-essentials, out of the hold!" the deck officer shouted.

"You and Pickerul, get into your PICS and hook up with Sergeant Riordan. I'll see you on the flip side," Hondo told Wolf as most of the Navy crew started to leave the hold.

"Kick some ass for me, OK?"

"You got it."

Within moments, the cargo hold was empty except for the cargo sled, the ten Marines, and four red-suited sailors. The ten Marines moved into position at the container jockeys. The first five—Hondo, Hanaburgh, Ling, Tony B, and RP—stepped forward so the force clamps could adjust to their shape and mass. There'd been some concern that Hanaburgh, carrying the bomb, might be better off going in the second wave, but Hondo insisted that he be with the first. The first wave had a better shot at making it across before they could be brought under fire, so unless there was a nasty surprise waiting for them at the frigate, this was their best shot.

The next five—Marasco, Joseph, Antman, the lieutenant, and the captain—took a position right behind the first five. As soon as the first wave was sent, they would take a step forward and the force clamps would grab them as well. The cargo chief said that it would take seven seconds to cycle.

Hondo turned and looked into the control booth where the chief and one of his cargo handlers waited. He gave them a thumbs-up, then waited for the weapons techs.

He didn't like this part of the plan. The bomb—the sailors got upset when he called it that, but it was supposed to go boom, so it was a bomb, right?—was about to be taken out of the magazine. The red-suited sailors were going to cloak it in an attempt to contain any spewing radiation, but the cargo hold was going to be contaminated. And that meant the ten Marines would be, too. Their PICS would keep them safe, but that meant they would have to go through decon before they molted.

An alarm sounded inside the hold, the red light flashing. All ten Marines turned to watch the four techs enter, pulling a gravmule on which the bomb was packed. Almost immediately, Hondo's PICS registered the rise in radiation. The techs guided the mule to the cargo sled where an arm descended from the overhead to pick up the bomb and place it on the sled. Two of the techs secured it while the other two headed for the decon station at the far end of the hold.

"This is it," Hondo passed. "Let's get it done."

One of the two techs jumped off the sled and headed to the decon station. The lone tech stood there, looking up at the control booth. Hondo raised a gauntlet in salute. The guy had balls the size of watermelons; there was a good chance that he couldn't get back in time, but the lieutenant told Hondo that the sailor had volunteered for the mission.

There was the slightest sideways pull, and outside the curtain, Hondo could see the stars start to spin. The hold doors were on the opposite side of the ship from the frigate, and while that posed no problem for the sled, it did for the PICS Marines being "shot" at it. They had to get a line-of-sight view. It was going to be a long twenty seconds before the maneuvering jet pods could turn the ship around enough for the Marines to be launched.

The tech on the sled whipped off the cloak, then bolted for the decon station. The sled lifted off and moved through the curtain, a ripple of distortion marking its entry into the black. Around the ship, Hondo knew that the escape pods were being ejected, full of the surviving crew, the zombied personnel, the EPWs, and all the remaining Marines other than Staff Sergeant Rutledge and Cara's squad, packed inside the shuttle.

Up in the control tower, the chief gave them a thumbs-up, and suddenly, Hondo was being pushed along the overhead rails. He half-expected the G-force to knock him silly, but it barely registered.

And then he was out of the ship and into the black. Up ahead, bright in the reflected light of the system's sun, the Brotherhood ship lay silent in space, menacing.

Hondo's faceshield highlighted two spots on the ship, two of the three target areas. Luckily, one of them was their first choice, and his AI calculated that they were exactly on target.

Around him, escape pods filled the void, red emergency lights flashing. Hondo hoped that the four Marines were lost in the confusion of what had to look to the Brotherhood crew as if they were all abandoning ship—which they were, of course.

Hondo looked to his left just as a flash lit up the two ships. The frigate had just taken the sled out of action. They'd taken the bait. The two waves of Marines now had twenty seconds before the gun could engage them.

The frigate was getting huge quickly, and for a moment, Hondo worried that there'd been a malfunction, that they were coming in too fast. His AI assured him that it was OK. He'd be able to handle the shock of landing.

And then there were inside the cutout.

Hondo opened the net and said, "We're in. Target number one."

He still couldn't see what made their target spot any different—it certainly looked like any other patch of hull to him, but every sim indicated this would give them the best chance of success. If they were trying to cripple the ship, Hondo thought that the big thrust cones would be the most logical place to attack the ship. At least he could see them. But the Navy braintrust said that the cones would be almost impervious to the small bomb Hanaburgh carried. They had to cripple the ship *before* the impulse stream reached the cones.

A hundred meters out, Hondo flexed his legs to handle the impact, but before hitting the frigate, the ship began to move. Hondo looked over at the thruster cones, expecting to see flames shooting out. That was Hollybolly, though, not the real world where the impulse was invisible to human eyes. But there was no doubt, the ship was slowly moving.

Too late, though. The four Marines landed just meters from the target point, their bootplates locking onto the hull.

"Place it!"

Tony B did the exaggerated hull walk to Hanaburgh and helped release the device from his back, a leash keeping it attached to him. Together, the two placed the bomb on the designated spot as the next four Marines came in. Three landed around the first four, while one hit hard and glanced off to rebound into space.

Hondo started to move when the lieutenant passed, "The captain's dead. Got hit right before we made the cut-out. Form your perimeter."

Hondo regretted any bad thoughts he'd been having about the captain. He hadn't needed to come on this mission, but he did, even at the cost of his own life. He gave the body, now fifty meters away, one last look before focusing on the front.

It was going to take a minute or so to set up the device, then another minute before it would begin to have an effect. The nine Marines had to make sure it was undisturbed until then.

Hanaburgh, with Tony B assisting, twisted the locking ring in place. It was designed to keep the device steady while the little torch inside did its job. Tony B gave it a few kicks, almost losing himself in the process as his other foot came free and he had to give his putt-putt a tiny burst to return.

"Watch it, Tony," Hondo said needlessly.

Hanaburgh hit the test, and a series of lights flashed before settling on a steady green.

"I'm turning it on," he said.

Hondo should have been watching outboard, but he couldn't. He had to see if the thing would work.

Hanaburgh bent over and threw the large red switch. A horrendously bright light suddenly appeared through the edges of the locking ring.

It was working!

Whether it would have any effect was another matter, but at least it had touched off. Now, only time would tell.

"I've got something," Corporal Marasco passed over the net.

Hondo was about to reply when the lieutenant asked, "How many?"

"Three so far. Standard EVA suits."

Hondo turned to look, but the curve of the frigates hull blocked his view.

"Acevedo, shift right, and you two engage as they head towards us. Everyone else, stay in position."

Hondo wanted to reorient the squad, but what the lieutenant said made sense. Three soldiers or sailors in EVAs would be far more maneuverable than the Marines, but not nearly so lethal. The Marines wouldn't be maneuvering anyway. Their place was right there with the device as its photon torch cut through the hull.

"Above" him, the *Zrínyi* no longer had any sign of activity as the distance between the two ships started to lengthen. Hondo wondered if the tech who'd sat with the bait-bomb had made it off. As he watched, there were several flashes, and the slow process of the ship's destruction began as it collapsed in on itself, each section slagging into a molten mass.

His alarm shocked him out of his trance.

Shit, I'm hit!

He turned towards Marasco, but he and Antman were engaged across the curve. He spun back, almost losing his grip, and two EVA-clad enemy were advancing, firing small hand beamers. His shields were still solid, but he couldn't let them get closer. He lowered his left arm and fired a burst of his M90, sending 80 6mm darts that easily pierced the Brotherhood suits. The two bodies floated backwards, feet still attached to the hull.

"Got them. Four in total," Marasco passed.

"We're through the hull!" Hanaburgh shouted. "Hooah!"

"That doesn't mean anything," the lieutenant passed. "Keep your positions."

Breaching the hull might have been the most difficult part of the assault. The next stage was the one not even the Navy knew if it would work, so just getting there didn't mean success. They had to be on the right spot, which was based on Intel, and then if they were, the proton torch had to be able to cut far enough to breach the impulse tubes.

Hondo couldn't see anyone in front of him except for the two dead men. He risked one more glance up. The *Zrínyi* was noticeably smaller, and not just because of the distance opening up between them. She was collapsing, each ring being pulled in before the next one was. Flares of light and the weird balls of flame, driven by molecular diffusion, blazed from the ship as she consumed herself.

"Hanaburgh, Good, get back," the lieutenant shouted over the net.

"It's not—" Tony B started before Hanaburgh grabbed him, pulling him backwards away from the device, Tony's bootplates still holding him fast.

There was an explosion of light and plasma, and the device blew right off the hull of the ship. Tony B released his bootplates and tumbled ass -ver-heels in his attempt to get out of the way.

"Lift off now!" the lieutenant shouted.

Ah, shit, here it goes, Hondo thought, as he gathered his legs and jumped with all his strength.

He started putting distance between himself and the hull, while below him, the blind energy that moved the frigate inside normal space escaped from its colloidal prison and out into space unfiltered and unfocused. Hondo caught sight of the two men he'd killed, now flopping around like the used-

143

hover dummies that caught customers' attention as the huge frigate began to twist away from the rent in its side.

All around him, nine Marines were desperately trying to gain distance as the ship twisted. It looked so slow, but it massed so much more than a Marine in a PICS that it would crush them like a fly if it hit.

That wasn't the main threat, though. While real space impulse drives were invisible coming out the cones, pre-filtered, they were a roiling stream of white and gold. That stream was shooting into space, eating away at the hull as it burned.

"Antman!" Hondo yelled reflexively as the Marine tried to escape upwards instead of to the side. "Right angle!"

Hondo never knew if Antman heard him. The flare of energy passed over him as the ship spun, and Lance Corporal Andrew Acevedo, Antman, was gone.

"Watch the fucking flare!" Hondo screamed over the net, his eyes tearing up.

Hondo kept out and away, his putt-putt at max impulse, a wary eye on the flare as the ship spun. His focus was almost his downfall. As the ship spun, the far side came around, looking lumberous and slow, but it was huge and packed a powerful punch. Instead of moving laterally and away from the flare, he reoriented and climbed away from the ship. Everything looked to be in slow motion as the eight Marines tried to gain separation.

Hondo wasn't sure he was going to make it, but as the ship came around, it missed him by less than 40 meters. To his surprise, he had a clear view of a sailor in the observation port, who simply returned his stare.

The ship kept spinning off-kilter, and the next pass of the flare wasn't going to be close. From the ship, escape pods started to pop off as the crew started to abandon ship.

Hondo was in shock. Somehow, unarmed with ship-killer weapons, it looked like they'd taken out a Brotherhood man-of-war with what was essentially a shipyard tool.

It just wasn't possible.

"On me," the lieutenant passed on the net.

Where?

All eight surviving Marines were scattered, and Hondo had to pull up his display to pick out the platoon commander, then translate the 2-D display to 3-D space. Eventually, he identified him and started slowly moving that direction.

It took twenty minutes before RP made it, the last one. The lieutenant ordered them all to hook safety lines to each other.

"What now, sir?" Hondo asked.

They were alone in the black, with a two-days' supply of air. They had their little putt-putts, but nowhere to go. Lore took up a good portion of the sky, and they could aim at it, but it would take them six months to get that far, and it would only be their desiccated corpses that would create a flash in the sky as they burned up in the atmosphere.

"Now, we wait."

THE LORE SYSTEM

Chapter 21
Hondo

"With Pa gone and the debt collectors looking, the FCDC was my only option," Hanaburgh said.

"But that was your dad's debt, not yours," Ling said. "That's not on your back."

"It is on Emerson."

"Emerson's still part of the Federation," Marasco said, "and debts don't pass to the children."

"Some governments have more autonomy. It depends on their charter," Lieutenant Abrams said.

The eight Marines had been tethered together, floating in the black, for almost two days: 46 hours, 12 minutes, to be more exact. O2 levels were down to 6% for Ling and up to 13% for Tony B. They had a few more hours until they'd start to asphyxiate, something Hondo was not looking forward to. Sure, they would have a good chance at resurrection—if they were ever recovered. No one knew what had happened to the crew and the rest of the Marines, who had been heading to Lore. They'd also watched escape pods erupt out of the Brotherhood frigate, and they'd be heading to the planet's surface as well.

The waiting was getting to all of them. Private Radiant Purpose, maybe the most gung-ho of all of them, couldn't take it. His PICS had drugged him into a happy daze 30 hours before.

For the first two hours, the Marines had a mission to keep themselves occupied. Corporal Ling had seen the first one, a tiny spot of white in the distance. At full magnification, the spot turned out to be a body. Under putt-putt power, the eight Marines had moved together, closing in on the body and corralling it with a line. No one recognized the sailor, but he was obviously *Zrínyi* crew. He didn't have his emergency hood on, and his face was covered with white ice crystals. Those didn't hide his gaping mouth nor wide-open eyes, however.

Hondo had shuddered at the sight, knowing that could be their fate as well, dying out in the black.

They managed to find two more, including Lance Corporal Kyle India from Third Platoon—or rather, most of him. His legs were gone at the thigh, rose-tinted crystals this time forming on the stumps.

They kept searching, but couldn't find anyone else. The black was just too big, and there'd been too much time for bodies to travel.

After that, there wasn't much else to do. Initially lost in their own thoughts, gradually, they came together, telling their life stories. Perhaps with their fate hanging over them, perhaps with the relative anonymity their PICS provided, they opened up. Hondo had even told about his life on Paradhiso, and how he'd always felt like an outsider.

Most of the time, though, Hondo listened. He'd thought he'd known his Marines, but he realized now that he'd barely scratched the surface. Marasco had been bullied as a kid, Joseph had been sexually assaulted as a child. Ling came from a repressive society where his sexual preferences were considered a sin. Tony B had dreamed of becoming a beat-beat singer, and he'd given them all in impromptu concert with the black as a stage. He was surprisingly good. Even the lieutenant told his story. He'd given up a career as a professional etherball player to become a Marine.

Hanaburgh's story, though, was probably the most revealing. Hondo had wondered why he'd given up his sergeant's rank in the FCDC to become a Marine, but he'd never bothered to ask. The lance corporal had always dreamed of being a Marine, and he'd intended to pursue that upon graduation, but when his father had been murdered in the random violence of the ghettos of Emerson, he and his sister had become liable for the debt, and he had to drop out of school and find a job. Without a secondary school degree, he was not eligible for the Marines, so when he became of age, he took the FCDC waiver. The FCDC was still Federation service, so that wiped out his debt, even on Emerson. While serving, he took night courses to complete his certificate, and once his minimum time served was reached, he opted for the interservice transfer.

"I'm glad you made the transfer, Robert," Hondo said, moved by the story. "You're a good Marine."

There was a soft chorus of ooh-rahs from the others, and Hanaburgh said, "Thank you Sergeant. I appreciate that."

Silence settled over the group. Hondo checked his O2: he was at 8%. Looking over where RP was in happy-land, he wondered if he should join him. At least then he wouldn't mind drifting off, and if they were never recovered, it wouldn't matter to him anyway.

"How long can we be dead and still resurrected?" Tony B asked quietly, something that had been gnawing at Hondo's mind as well.

They all turned as one to the lieutenant.

"For stasis? About fifty years has been the maximum so far, although the length of time shouldn't matter," he said. "From being frozen out in space? I'm not sure. There was the crew of that Confederation pinnacle that was recovered after thirty years. All except for one made it, if I remember right."

That's right. It's not just the O2. That will get us first, and then, after the power gives out, the cold will take over.

He checked his power level. They weren't expending much energy, and his PICS was at 52%.

So, it's asphyxiation, not freezing for me.

"They'll find us," Hondo said with a certainty he wasn't sure he actually felt.

"I'd just as soon they find us before I run out of air, Sergeant, not after," Tony B said.

For some reason, everyone found that funny. Hondo laughed along with the rest, although he wasn't quite sure why.

"Shit, Tony, don't make me laugh. I think I dropped another percent of O-two," Corporal Ling said, which brought out another round of laughter.

They slowly settled back into silence. Hondo decided he wasn't going to pull up his gauge on his display again. It was what it was.

Less than five minutes later, he checked his O2: 7%.

OK, now I'm really not going to check again.

He started humming "Gold Lock," the song with which Tony B had serenaded them.

His voice sucked, he knew, and he was about to ask Tony to give them another, when the lieutenant said, "I think I saw something."

Another body? Hondo wondered as he followed the platoon commander's pointing arm.

He scanned the black, looking for something that didn't belong when Hanaburgh said, "I think it's a ship!"

Hondo's heart jumped to his throat as he slaved off of the lance corporal's PICS. There was something there, and it was moving. It was still too far to make out, but there was definitely something out there.

"Check your beacons," the lieutenant said.

They'd gone through this fifty times if it was once, but Hondo ran a check again. His beacon was steady and strong.

In complete silence, the eight Marines watched, afraid to say something to jinx it. Hondo tried to will whatever it was into a rescue.

If it had been a tank, personnel carrier, or almost any atmospheric aircraft known to man, his PICS AI could identify what it was long before he could, but nothing popped up on his display. That made him nervous. It could be their salvation, but it could also be a piece of wreckage or even ancient space junk.

"There's a light flashing," Tony B said.

Hondo tried to see the light, but he couldn't make out anything.

"It's a vessel, then. Ours or theirs"? Lieutenant Abrams asked.

"I can't tell. It doesn't look like our shuttle."

If it was a Brotherhood vessel of some sort, there wasn't much any of them could do if it arrived with ill will. And if it demanded their surrender, Hondo didn't know what the lieutenant would say. Hondo certainly didn't want to be taken prisoner, but the thought of choking out his last breaths in the cold emptiness of the black wasn't very appealing, either.

"It's them," Tony B said, at last.

"Are you sure?" the lieutenant asked him.

"Yes, sir. I can see it. It's upside down to us."

"He's right," Marasco said. "I can see it now."

Hondo let out a huge breath of air in relief. If their younger eyes thought it was the shuttle, then that was good enough for him. Five minutes later, he could see it himself. His mind had wanted to see it on the same aspect as he was.

With no up or down in space, however, the *Zrínyi's* shuttle was "tilted" about 150 degrees to the side. With his mind oriented now, it was pretty obvious.

He pulled back his magnification, and the shuttle disappeared from sight.

"How far away is it?" he asked.

"I can't ping it, but maybe fifty klicks?" the lieutenant said. "I'm trying to raise them now."

"Fifty klicks? They see us, right?" Joseph asked.

"They're coming right at us," Hondo told them. "They see us."

I hope.

The shuttle and PICS didn't share comms, but there had to be a workaround. The comms freq remained silent, however.

The shuttle could cross 50 kicks in seconds, but it had to be able to come to a stop near them, so it was advancing much more slowly. Time seemed to drag on forever, but his AI timer indicated that only a few minutes had passed before the shuttle, clearly visible now, was a klick off and creeping closer.

"Drop your buddy lines," the lieutenant ordered. "Keep the KIA attached to each other, though."

The shuttle slowly turned around, still "upside-down" to the Marines. There was a flash of light as the back ramp opened.

"Good, Hanaburgh, you two take the dead first," the platoon commander ordered. "Just give them a shove inside. PFC Joseph, you help Radiant Purpose."

Two sailors in their red EVA suits came out of the shuttle. One raised a voice-activated light gun, which sent light waves that could strike hard surfaces and then be transmitted into sound.

Sounding somewhat weird, but still identifiable as Wolf, the "sailor" said, "You all looking for a ride?"

Hondo hooted a wordless shout in response.

Tony B and Hanaburgh gently pushed the three KIA forward. Wolf and who had to be Pickerul, caught the buddy lines and pulled them back into the hold. Hondo hung back as Joseph assisted RP—who was barely cognizant of what was going on—into the shuttle. Quickly, the others boarded the shuttle until it was only Hondo and the lieutenant left. Hondo motioned for his platoon commander, but he nodded, one hand out and pointing to the hold. Hondo nodded and flew forward, twisting around so that his "up" and the shuttle's "up" matched. He held his breath until he crossed into the shuttle.

Oh, mother of God, I've made it.

There were at least 20 bodies strapped to the forward bulkhead of the hold, and Wolf and Pickerul were adding the three that the Marines had recovered to the group. With the bodies, the eight PICS Marines almost filled the hold. As the back hatch started to close, Pickerul pulled out a pressure hose with the universal coupling and pointed to them, miming hooking the hose to their PICS.

Air! Hondo thought, checking his reading, which was at 6%. *Heck, who needs rescue? I still have a couple of hours left.*

EARTH

Chapter 22
Skylar

"They recovered them," Keyshon said, looking at his PA.

"Recovered who?" Sky asked, her mind preoccupied as they walked down Rue Lysander to the Swiss embassy.

"The Marines. The ones who took out the *Temperance*."

It took a moment for what he was saying to register. The *Temperance* was the Brotherhood frigate that had attacked the *Zrínyi*. The fate of the Marines who'd somehow managed to cripple the ship had been unknown for the last two days, something that had had taken over the undernet in a viral wave.

Sky had been preoccupied with her new mission, and had barely followed the story. Even now, after being told, she didn't feel a sense of relief, only wondered how the news would affect the upcoming meeting.

What's wrong with me? Those were incredibly brave Marines, Federation citizens.

She should feel something more, but to her, the stakes were higher than ten Marines. She had to focus on the overall situation.

Still, her lack of compassion bothered her. She briefly wondered where the Skylar she'd known all her life had gone.

"Do we know how many of them were killed? The Brotherhood?" she asked Keyshon, glad he'd arrived from Pittsburgh yesterday to assist.

"From the ship being lost? Not many, by all accounts. It looks like most of the crew and the reaming soldiers were able to evacuate. They lost more in trying to take the *Zrínyi*."

The actual damage to the *Temperance* had seemed minimal to her as a civilian. Although spinning out of control, it had remained intact for ten hours, according to the briefing she'd received yesterday, before the stress of the unconstrained propulsion broke the ship apart. It still boggled her mind that a military ship could be destroyed by a simple fusion torch.

"What's been the buzz from the Brotherhood nets?"

"As you could expect. The ten Marines were saboteurs, nothing more, who killed peace-loving Brotherhood citizens."

"Peace-loving my ass," Sky said bitterly. "They're the sons of slime fired on the *Zrínyi*."

"Ma'am . . ." Keyshon said in an almost-but-not-quite-scolding tone.

Sky raised her hand to forestall any more and said, "I know, I know. I've got to play nice. No accusation, no incriminations. I can't mention the Lore system."

Keyshon nodded, and the two kept walking. Sky shouldn't bring up the attack on the *Zrínyi*, unless the bishop mentioned it, and even if he did, she had to move beyond that to the larger issue. Somehow, she had to convince the bishop that the Klethos threat was real and not a political ploy. The inherent problem with that was that if she convinced them that the Klethos were a threat, then that would buttress their claim that the UAM was playing with fire by cooperating with the Klethos in the first place.

She'd spent the morning with the best minds in the Federation, trying to come up with the best tack to take. At one point, the First Ministry vice-minister had threatened to take over, but this was a Second Ministry responsibility, one that the minister was not going to simply hand over to the First.

Part of Sky wished that the First Ministry—or anyone else, for that matter—would take over. She was feeling the pressure mount. She wasn't even convinced that this should be a Federation effort, but the professional diplomats adamantly insisted that since the Brotherhood alliance was completely controlled by the Brotherhood itself, then the Federation had to act on an equal-basis.

Sky would have welcomed Confederation, French, or any other assistance, if for nothing else than to give the threat credence. That was out of her hands, though.

They turned left on Rue de la Loi and walked the half-block to the ancient white-brick embassy. There were no guards standing post, unlike most embassies, and Keyshon rang the bell. A moment later, the twin doors swung open, and an officious-looking young lady in an oh-so-proper gray suit, welcomed them and asked that they follow her.

The meeting with the bishop had been set up through numerous channels, with the Swiss Ambassador as the official host. This was to be low-key, without the pomp and formality of most such meetings. Sky and Keyshon would meet the bishop and his assistant. No one else. Sky was going to calmly lay out the situation to the best of her knowledge and then hope that the bishop would pass it on up their chain. It would be nice if she could convince the bishop, but as long as he passed it up, that would suffice.

Sky didn't even know who she'd be meeting, only that he was of bishop rank. The political division had briefed her on the six most likely choices, based on who was in Brussels at the time.

"Dr. Ybarra, if you will. The bishop is already here," the young woman said, opening up two doors, then stepping aside.

Sky pulled herself up and strode into the room, trying to look confident . . . and almost faltered.

Bishop Grandice van Meter stood up at her entrance, his face cold and hard. The political team had made van Meter the fifth most likely choice, given his antipathy towards the Federation and what bordered on hate for the Klethos. The fact that he was sent to the meeting had to reflect on the Brotherhood's willingness to listen to what she had to say.

Sky plastered a slight smile on her face and strode up to the table, hand out to shake, saying, "Bishop van Meter, thank you for taking the time to meet me. I'm Assistant Vice-Minister—"

"I know who you are."

Sky kept the smile, but she nodded and sat down.

This isn't going to be easy, Sky, but just make it work.

LORE

Chapter 23
Hondo

Hondo took one last breath of fresh air, then grabbed the donning handles and twisted his body up, making the circus-worthy contortion needed to get into his PICS. He'd been out of it for seven hours, cleaning himself, getting some chow, and taking a quick nap. He'd thought their fight was over.

Thinking had a habit of getting him into trouble.

Now, he was going back out with the 17 other PICS Marines, led by the lieutenant. Sixty klicks away, the Brotherhood force was making its presence known, the ship's commander demanding that the Federation Marines and Buddie sailors lay down their arms. He promised *Alezerdes* Black that no one would be hurt, but given their unprovoked attack on the *Zrínyi*, neither the ship's commanding officer nor Captain Ariç were inclined to believe the man.

They refused the demand, with the CO quoting Harbin Accord rules for shipwrecked passengers. The Brotherhood commander refused to acknowledge those rules, and said that the Marines and sailors would suffer the consequences of that decision.

If the Brotherhood was planning anything, the UAM force had to find out, so the PICS Marines were going to go take a look. Sixty klicks were nothing when compared to the size of Lore, but it would be quite a hike for those Marines on foot.

Hondo ran through his diagnostics. With a new powerpack, everything was green. He was good to go. Switching over to the rest of his squad, he ran their numbers, and they checked out as well.

"Five minutes," Staff Sergeant Rutledge passed on the net.

"How's Bunyansarn?" Hondo asked Wolf on the P2P.

"I don't know," Wolf said. "It's not like I've had any time to get to know her, you know."

After their assault on the frigate, the squad was down to ten, including Hondo and Doc Leach. With eight in the teams, he was going to go down to two four-man teams, with Wolf and Ling as the team leaders, but PFC Nok Bunyansarn, one of the Charlie Company survivors, had managed to get her PICS aboard the shuttle with Cara. The skipper, now the senior Marine with Captain Warrant KIA, assigned her to Hondo's squad.

That left him with nine trigger pullers, so he went to three three-man teams, moving Tony B to First Team.

"You watch her. I heard Pickerul calling her the DMS. We don't need that."

"Tammy didn't mean anything," Wolf protested.

"Yeah, she did, and you know it."

"That's just Tammy being Tammy, Sergeant."

"Which is fine if the other person knows her. Bunyansarn doesn't know Pickerul."

"DMS" was the acronym for "Dead Man's Slot," (sometimes called a "redshirt" for reasons lost to time) given to a newbie who was a replacement to a KIA. In Hollybolly tradition, which had since gravitated to real Marines, the DMS was always the next to die. Bunyansarn wasn't actually a newbie, having served with Charlie Company, and she'd been one of only 12 survivors of the company when the ship had been hit. If anything, she had lady luck looking down over her shoulder.

"Just watch her," Hondo told Wolf. "And make sure she isn't in hero-mode."

That actually concerned Hondo more than Pickerul's teasing. Bunyansarn had lost almost all of her friends, and she might be looking for revenge.

"Let's go," Staff Sergeant Rutledge passed. "Limited comms from here on out."

Hondo thought that might be overkill. The Brotherhood forces had evacuated their ship pretty quickly, and he doubted they had much in the way of sophisticated surveillance. The comms shielding on a modern PICS was excellent, so Hondo felt the risk of comms being not only intercepted but cracked was small. It wasn't his call, though.

First Squad moved out in a squad wedge, Second Team at the point, First Team on the left, and Third Team on the right, with Hondo and Doc in trace of Second. The lieutenant was on his ass, and the staff sergeant, Cara, and her depleted squad pulled up the rear. At their ground-eating jog, they could cover the 60 klicks in a couple of hours, but the Brotherhood Saul XBs had pretty good shielding themselves, and the lieutenant didn't want to jog into an ambush. They conducted the advance to contact at a much slower 20 KPH for an hour, then down to 15 KPH, the wedge formation flat and covering almost 500 meters of frontage.

With only nine trigger pullers, Hondo would have liked to tighten that up some, but the lieutenant wanted to cover as much ground as possible while still keeping reasonable security and the ability for the Marines to support each other should something go down. Still, given the terrain, a battalion of the host could be heading to the UAM camp without being spotted, two fighting forces passing in the night, so to speak.

It won't be a battalion of them, though, at least we know that.

At best, no Sauls had made it to the surface. At worst, maybe 40. Some of the host had been killed on during the fight, and others almost certainly had to have died when their ship went out of control. If Hondo was a betting man, then he'd guess the armor was about even, while the Marines had an advantage in straight infantry.

To his right, Third was beginning to bunch up slightly. Hondo wanted to tell Ling to keep his dispersion, but the lieutenant wanted limited comms.

Does this count as limited?

He peered through the scrub, trying to catch sight of the corporal, who was crossing a dry creek bed. After a moment, Ling came into view, and Hondo waved his gauntlet, trying to get his attention.

It took a moment, but Ling waved back, and Hondo put both gauntlets together, palm-to-palm, then spread them out. Ling raised one gauntlet in acknowledgment and turned to Hanaburgh just as there was a flash, then an instant later, a huge explosion rocked the corporal, his PICS almost blowing apart.

"Second, assault right, First, provide a base of fire," Hondo shouted before everything had completely registered. "Arrays on max!"

There was a second flash that lit up the scrub, but no resultant explosion.

"Second Squad, envelope right," the lieutenant passed, as arrows appeared on Hondo's display.

A moment later, Cara's squad broke their formation to begin a quick movement around a piece of high ground.

Hondo broke into a run, his combat AI determining the POO, or Point of Origin, of whatever had hit Ling. He fired his M44 at the position, five of the 60mm grenades arching up to land at the spot, gouts of dirt and vegetation shooting upwards, but no confirmation of a kill.

Hanaburgh, who'd been off of Ling's flank, fired his Chimera, the missile whooshing into the vegetation. This time, there was a flash of light as the missile struck true, and Hondo's AI was now able to pick up the wreckage of the Saul.

Rounds were flying, the traces crisscrossing Hondo's display as his AI struggled to catch them all. A PICS' AI worked best in conjunction with other surveillance sources, but with no Navy ship overhead nor drones in the air, the AI network had to rely on the organic sensors on each combat suit.

A PICS' prime counter-surveillance was the use of the Variable Fractured Array, a much-improved version of the original FA. A random number generator in each PICS both boosted and cloaked the combat suit's emissions in alternate waves, essentially simulating a PICS jerking back and forth every microsecond. Incoming weapons had extreme difficulty determining the exact location of a PICS, and they couldn't adjust quick enough for a hit once they were close enough to break through the array.

The Brotherhood Sauls, however, relied on cloaking, "hiding" the combat suit in plain sight. The Marine's PICS were having difficulty finding the Sauls in order to target them, but the Sauls were having an equally hard time simply hitting the PICS.

Something clanged off of Hondo's leg. Ordnance did not have the Sauls' ghosting capability, and with a direct hit, his AI identified the POO, the Point of Origin. Hondo shifted his direction and charged, firing a string of grenades before launching a salvo of three shoulder rockets at a blank spot ahead. The dust from the grenades seemed to coalesce around a large, man-like figure for an instant before at least two of the rockets struck home. The Saul immediately became visible as it was blown over backward.

Two more Sauls were destroyed, and the incoming fire began to slacken, finally coming to a halt. Hondo stopped, taking stock of his squad.

Corporal Ling was KIA, but no one else was out of commission. RP had expended too much power, and was at 76%, but that was still well within combat parameters. His AI identified four downed Sauls.

"Sir, I think we've broken the ambush. One friendly KIA and four enemy."

He knew the lieutenant, who was only 43 meters to his left, according to his display, could see that, but it wouldn't hurt to make sure.

"Form a perimeter oriented to 330 while we wait for Second Squad," the lieutenant replied.

"Aye-aye, sir."

Hondo's instinct was to push forward. The squad hadn't cleared the ambush site yet, and someone could still be out there. The lieutenant has seemed a little withdrawn since the fight on the ship, and Hondo wondered if something was eating at him—not just the normal feeling of loss, but something deeper.

Forget it McKeever. He's just being prudent. Better to wait for Cara.

"Doc, how's Ling?" he asked.

"Not much hope. I'm putting him into stasis."

Shit, shit, shit!

"OK, do what you can. After you're done, take Tony B and check the Brotherhood KIA. If they can be resurrected, zip-lock them."

"And then what do we do with them?"

"Upload their coordinates to the Red Cross, you know that. Then it's out of our hands."

Hondo positioned the rest of his Marines looking forward, checking each position for their fields of observation.

"How do we see if anyone is out there, Sergeant McKeever?" Bunyansarn asked, as he checked her position.

"Just look where there isn't anything," he said, immediately realizing that didn't make any sense. "What I mean is that their ghosting hides whatever is behind them, too. Just look for a spot that is a little blurry, OK? And keep an eye on your displays. Our AIs aren't that great all alone like this, but they can sometimes pick up something."

"OK, Sergeant. Thanks."

"How did Bunyansarn do?" he asked Wolf on the P2P.

He could pull up her track, but he didn't want to take the time.

"No problem, Sergeant. She was fine. Don't worry about her," the team leader responded.

"Well, here comes Second Squad, so get ready to move out."

"Rodger, dodger," Wolf said, ever flippant.

"Sergeant McKeever, to me," the lieutenant ordered.

Hondo pulled his platoon commander up, located him, then jogged over to where they were joined a minute later by Cara.

"Listen up. We know the host are here, and they know we are, too. The skipper still wants us to advance, so we are going to change to a bounding overwatch."

Hondo shrugged. It made sense. A bounding overwatch was a leap-frogging-type movement where one element set up a base of fire and provided covering support for the other element as they advanced. The lead element would then set up their own base of fire so that the trailing element could advance past the lead element of fire and set up a new base of fire. This way, only one unit was moving at any given time, and that unit was always covered by the other. It made for slower going, but it provided far greater security.

"Sergeant McKeever, your squad is taking the lead. I don't want you more than 500 meters before you assume the support mission. Sergeant Riordan, you don't move until I say so, and that isn't going to happen until First Squad is set."

"Where are you going to be, sir?" Cara asked.

"I will always be with whichever one of you is the forward-most element at the time. Don't worry about me, you just lead your squads. Any questions?"

"Arrays on?" Hondo asked.

The major problem with the arrays was that they pulled an inordinate amount of power.

The lieutenant mulled that over for a moment before he said, "No, we can't. We'll never make it over and back if we do."

"What about Corporal Ling?" Hondo asked.

"Doc got him zip-locked?"

"Yes, sir. And one of the soldiers."

"Mark him. Both of them. We'll retrieve Corporal Ling on the way back. Anything else?"

"No, sir," the two chorused.

"Then let's move it. Keep on the alert."

Hondo returned to his squad, got the teams ready to move out, and did a quick terrain study while he waited for Second Squad to get into position. From where he was, the terrain descended in a gentle slope dotted with acacia bushes, each about five meters tall. Acacias were commonly used in terraforming due to their hardy nature and easy propagation, but they offered plenty of cover for opposing forces. At about 400 meters, the slope reversed, climbing to a low hump at 575 meters, according to his display. That was a little farther than the lieutenant wanted, but it offered the only reasonable location on which to set up the next base of fire so that Cara and her squad could displace forward.

"Move out, First," the lieutenant passed.

Back in their wedge, the Marines stepped off. Hondo felt blind without better surveillance, but it did feel good knowing that Cara and her Marines were behind him providing support.

He strode past one of the dead Brotherhood soldiers, the one Hanaburgh had taken out. The remains were a mangled mess, and not much of what had been a human body inside the wreckage was recognizable as such. Doc Leach hadn't bothered wasting a zip lock on that poor soul.

"Watch your dispersion, McKeever," the lieutenant passed.

The squad looked pretty good to him, but Hondo repeated the platoon commander's orders.

As they advanced, Hondo's display showed flickers of activity, but nothing solid. Flickers could come from small animals, feedback from his own Marines, abandoned objects, or a host of other things—including a cloaked enemy. His AI ran through huge amounts of computing power separating the wheat from the chaff, analyzing the slightest emission before eliminating it as a threat.

Hondo hadn't spotted anyplace that would serve as an effective overwatch position by the time Second Fire Team reached the upslope, so he sent the lieutenant the location he'd previously selected, another 150 meters ahead. The lieutenant approved, and Hondo told Corporal Marasco to reach the brow of the slope and stop. As Hondo approached, he could see over the brow, and 350 meters ahead and slightly to the right, was a small knoll that looked like it offered excellent fields of observation and fire that would serve Cara and Second Squad well.

"Cara, I'm flagging your potential position," he passed just as a flicker of light appeared on the knoll.

"Oh, crap!" he said, cutting Cara off as rounds started impacting around him.

Someone else thought it would be a good position as well.

A huge explosion erupted from Second Team's position, and Hondo caught a glimpse of a PICS rising in the air before falling back down. Marasco's avatar flipped to the light blue of a WIA.

"Fall back and take cover!" Hondo shouted.

Something hit him hard in the chest, making his PICS ring, but he was still functional.

The slight brow in the hill didn't provide any cover for an upright PICS, but a Marine could override a PICS' gyros and go prone.

It was a tricky maneuver, but Hondo had done this so often in training that he could do it in his sleep. He was on the ground, focusing on his display.

PFC Bunyansarn, however, was either confused, or she was not as adept. Still standing to Hondo's left, she'd just started to bend when a missile slammed into her.

"Dead Man's Slot," Hondo muttered, despite not believing that garbage.

Behind him, the lieutenant rushed forward while Cara's second squad was firing, peppering the knoll.

"Get down, sir!" Hondo shouted, as a flash flew off the lieutenant's shoulder, indicating he'd been hit.

It didn't seem to faze the man, nor the glow of an energy beam that briefly flashed an orange corona around him, before he dropped prone beside, but slightly farther forward, to Hondo. With his head just over the brow, he could see across to the knoll.

If the lieutenant was going to do that . . .

Hondo eased forward until he could see the knoll as well. It was under intense fire, but it was dishing out as well as taking it in, with most of the fire aimed back at Cara.

"We've got a tank," Tony B shouted.

Impossible! No way they could have gotten one down from their ship. We'd have seen it!

But something had just appeared on his display. Hondo raised his head, and a Mouse burst through an acacia bush not 30 meters from Second Team.

The Mouse was sort of a joke among the Federation Marines. It was a tiny armored vehicle, barely a meter high, which could be airdropped or even shot out of a long-range launcher. It was remote controlled or could go full AI mode, and it could carry an array of modular weapons.

It might be a joke, but the wide-bore cannon staring Hondo down looked plenty big to him. The gun belched out a round, which Hondo heard as it whizzed over his head on its way to Second Squad before the tube started traversing down towards the First Squad Marines. Grenades started slamming into it as his Marines took it under fire, but without effect. This wasn't a PICS which had to have room inside for the Marine. This was a slab of armor carrying a weapon and powerpack, nothing more.

"Watch for the corporal!" PFC Joseph shouted.

Marasco, still alive, was prone as the Mouse advanced, the ricocheting grenades posed a threat to him. The Mouse, though, posed a threat to everyone else.

And then Marasco moved, rolling his broken body over as the Mouse passed. He raised his M56 as it passed, and at point-blank range, fired into the powerpack. The Mouse disappeared in a tremendous explosion, and Corporal Marasco's avatar changed to the red of a KIA. Joseph's change to WIA.

Pieces of Marasco's PICS were scattered, part of his poleyn bouncing to a stop a meter from Hondo. To his right, the lieutenant stood, looking back towards Second Squad, waving his arms. Hondo wasn't on that net, so he couldn't hear what the platoon commander was telling Cara.

As he watched, something else hit the lieutenant, staggering him forward a step until his gyros kicked in.

Forward? To the enemy?

No, there're more behind us, he realized.

Hondo stood, and to the east, a small crevice snaked its way north and south. It didn't look like much, but his AI was picking up incoming, and the position was in defilade to Second Squad. Even if they weren't engaged with the knoll, they couldn't provide cover.

"First and Third, with me!" he shouted, forwarding a big huge green flag on their displays.

Within a heartbeat, the four Marines were racing after him as he charged forward, trying to cover the 350 meters as fast as humanly possible—correction, as fast as possible for a Marine in a PICS.

One hundred, two hundred meters, and he was barely aware of straight-leg infantry scrambling back before their onslaught. With a grin, Hondo switched his magazine to darts just as his PICS howled out its warning siren. He was under fire from a beam weapon, and his shields were failing.

"Mother fuck, another Mouse!" he shouted out as the armored gun poked its projector over the edge of the wash.

Hondo tried to juke to the left, but his reflexes could not match that of the Mouse's AI, and the beam was locked on. His shields were down to 20% and failing fast.

A Chimera fired, hitting the Mouse's projector, and the beam fell off of him.

"Mother of God," Hondo whispered.

His shield was at 17%, and his power was at 27%.

But the Mouse was damaged, not taken out. Hanaburgh had fired his Chimera, and the AI brain now identified him as the major threat. The projector, damaged, but still functional, locked onto the Marine and fired, the beam far more dispersed, but still strong enough to take down a PICS.

"Support Burger!" Hondo shouted as he fired his darts, clanging them off the Mouse in a flurry of sparks.

Hanaburgh was down to one missile, not that it made much difference. He had to break the lock. But he didn't dodge, he didn't juke. He picked up his armored legs and charged the Mouse, his Chimera in the launch sleeve. He couldn't even fire because the beam would destroy the missile at that range.

He's trying to close the range!

Hondo pulled up Hanaburgh's stats, and his shields were failing, down to 50, then 40, then 30 as he closed the gap.

"Now, Burger, now!" Hondo shouted out.

At 8% and 20 meters away, Hanaburgh fired his missile and juked to his right. It streaked forward, a plume of disintegrating casing sloughing off, before it hit.

There wasn't a dramatic explosion, and Hondo held his breath. The meson beam sputtered on and off, but the projector no longer tracked Hanaburgh. Pickerul raced forward to the side of it, placed her foot at the top of the mouse, and pushed, knocking it upside down. The projector kept sputtering as it fired into the dirt, soil evaporating under the power of the beam.

"Hooah, Burger, fucking hooah!" she shouted over her externals.

"Hooah!" Hondo joined in with the FCDC battle cry.

Five Brotherhood soldiers stood up from where they were hiding at the back of the wash, hands in the air.

"If you're done hollering, we're surrendering," one of them, an officer of some type, said.

"All of you, on them," Hondo passed to four Marines, breaking the exultation.

"You, sit down, hands on your heads," he said over his externals, pointing his M90 in emphasis.

It was only then that he noticed that the duel between Second Squad and the soldiers on the knoll was over. He checked his display. One of the Second Squad Marines was KIA, but the rest, along with the lieutenant, Doc Leach, and Tony B, were fine. Joseph was still WIA, and Doc was already on him.

"Sir, we've got five EPWs. One looks like an officer."

"Secure them. I'll be right there."

The SOP for handling EPWs did not include PICS, but Hondo was not going to tell anyone to molt to secure them. He was just going to keep them sitting for the moment.

"Johnson, Pickerul, watch them," he ordered.

He turned and went to Hanaburgh, pulling up the Marines stats. His shield was almost gone, and his power was at 22%.

"You OK?" he asked.

"Never better," the lance corporal answered.

"That was some shit, there."

It was pretty much impossible to shrug in a PICS, but he tilted his head slightly to the right in the PICS version of one.

Hondo didn't know what to add to that, so he checked out the Mouse, which was still sputtering away, beaming a hole in the dirt. The stupid thing had almost killed him. It would have, had it not been for Hanaburgh. He gave it a kick, and it let out a satisfying string of sparks.

The lieutenant arrived, went right up to the EPWs and said, "I'm Second Lieutenant Armando Abrams, United Federation Marine Corps. Who are you?"

The officer-looking guy—Hondo was not up on Brotherhood insignia—said, "Captain Merit Longfellow, from the Host of the Brotherhood of Servants. I offer you our surrender."

"I accept your surrender. I want your assurances that you will not try to prosecute the ongoing fight."

"Certainly," the captain said with a smirk on his face. "For as long as it lasts. As we speak, our own forces are closing in on your camp while your battle suits are here with this token and mostly automated force."

Hell, I knew it, Hondo thought, as he took a step forward to stand beside the lieutenant.

"Yes, we five stopped you in your tracks," the officer said. "And I am sure you will receive orders to surrender to us soon."

Not just five. We killed three of you in your pathetic attempt at an ambush.

"Orders to surrender? I'm surprised at you, Captain. Sun Tzu said know your enemy, and you obviously don't know our procedures. Should a commander ever surrender, then other forces, such as my platoon, are free to do as they will. If our commander does surrender, that has no bearing on my platoon."

A flicker of doubt crossed the captain's face.

"And if your Sauls are being used to attack our camp, which given the distance, is likely, then we have an open path to your camp. I might add, even if you kept some back, that should pose us no problems, just as the three Sauls that tried to ambush us posed no problems to our PICS."

This time, the look of concern on the man's face was plain.

"I suggest that you call whoever you want. Ask your commander to check the Federation UCMJ, Paragraph 2.02.14. We'll give you time. After all, we can cover eight klicks in ten minutes."

At this, the man's face went white. If Hondo understood the lieutenant's meaning, then the Brotherhood camp was eight klicks away. How the platoon commander knew that was a mystery to him, however.

The captain pointed to his belt, and once given permission, put an earbud in his ear and a mic on his throat.

"Lieutenant, how did you know where their camp is?" Hondo asked on the P2P, as the captain consulted with his commander.

"I don't know."

"But I saw his reaction."

"I guessed. They walked here, so that limited their range. If I looked around, there were only two logical places for it to be."

"So, how did you pick the one?"

"I didn't. They were both about the same distance, so I left it at that. Let him think I knew which one."

Hondo laughed, then said, "Ooh-rah, Lieutenant."

Thirty minutes later, the lieutenant got the call from Captain Ariç. He walked up to the captain, who was sweating as he sat in the dirt.

"You are free to go," he told him.

The man looked up, surprise all over his face.

"So, you mean you surrender?" he asked hopefully.

"Are you high, sir? We're Marines. Of course, we don't surrender."

Hondo could picture the lieutenant scowling inside his PICS at the question.

"Then . . . then, what's going on?"

"Our commanders have spoken, and let's say that they've reached an agreement that our little fight is over. Your force is on its way back, and we'll return to our camp to await extract. We have given the coordinates of your dead, so you can recover them."

The Brotherhood captain gaped at the lieutenant, so he added, "I would suggest you move, Captain. As EPWs your freedom was not a foregone conclusion, and that could still change."

At those words, two of the other soldiers jumped up, one with a "Fuck that shit," and started walking off. The other three, including the captain, immediately followed.

EARTH

Chapter 24
Skylar

"If the Klethos do decide to intervene," Sky said, using the term instead of "attack," as her political handlers insisted, ". . .then no one comes out ahead."

"I'm glad you are coming around to our side," Bishop van Meter said. "The Klethos are an abomination and a threat to humanity. We cannot work them."

You are misconstruing my words, as you well know.

This was their second meeting, and it was just as mired in the mud as the last one. Sky had given a full report to the minister, telling him that they needed someone more experienced in diplomacy to handle the contact, but he assured her that she'd done well and that she was still the point-person. He'd said the choice of van Meter to represent the Brotherhood was unfortunate, but as Sky was a scientist first, she provided a better face forward than a career diplomat.

"We are allied with them, Bishop van Meter. This has happened, and there's no use to litigate the past. We are now approaching a crisis point, and how we both proceed can have drastic consequences to humanity's very future."

"As will continued subservience to the Klethos when your actions draw the Dictymorphs into human space again."

Sky kept a straight face. The Brotherhood claim about human cooperation—not subservience, as the bishop put it—with the Klethos had almost certainly drawn the Dictymorphs into the attack on Purgamentium. But she was equally certain that it had merely hastened the process. The Dictymorphs were slowly but surely heading their way. The one base truth that had to be acknowledged was that humanity's best chance at defeating the Dictymorph threat was to ally themselves with the Klethos. It boggled her mind that any rational person or government couldn't understand that.

"They are coming again, whether we like it or not."

"Which is your fault."

"Whether we like it or not," she repeated. "So, we can quibble about blame, or we can look to the future and what we can do about it. And the first step is to ensure that the Klethos do not intervene in our family squabble."

The bishop said nothing, so Sky continued, "If the Klethos do intervene, surely that is not something your alliance wants."

"The Klethos are not nearly as numerous as we once thought. It is our belief that we can defeat them."

Sky had to keep from rolling her eyes. Yes, the Federation's own analysts had come to the same conclusion, but there would be huge casualties, possibly into the hundreds of billions.

"At a significant cost, which would cripple us in the fight with the Dictymorphs."

"Which wouldn't happen with the Klethos gone. There would be no conflict with the Dictymorphs."

Do you believe that claptrap, or is this some sort of diplomatic game?

"If you believe the Dictymorphs are not coming, then you are sadly mistaken," she said, unable to keep the note of scorn out of her voice.

The corner of the bishop's mouth broke into the tiniest of smiles, as if he'd scored a point. If he had, Sky had no idea what it was, nor did she particularly care.

"Vice-minister, let me ask you," the bishop said, a predatory gleam in his eye. "If the Klethos do decide to attack us, fellow humans with whom your Federation has shared centuries of peace and mutual defense, what will you do? Will the UAM come to our defense?"

Skylar didn't need to be a diplomat, she didn't need to see Keyshon stiffen in his seat beside her, to know she was treading on dangerous ground. Scientist or not, she was an official representative from the Federation if not the UAM.

"I am here to make sure we maintain the peace between us, Bishop."

"You didn't answer the question, Vice-Minister."

Nor will I.

"I'll repeat, I am here to maintain the peace."

Sky wasn't sure, but it looked like he was disappointed. Maybe he was hoping to take advantage of her inexperience. She gave him a steady stare, trying to keep her face expressionless.

He seemed about to answer when he stopped, and his face took on the look of somebody listening to a conversation—which was against the agreed-upon rules of the meeting. There were to be no recording devices nor communications to the outside world.

His face slowly hardened, and he turned to her, his voice low but full of menace, as he said, "If you are here to keep the peace, why are your Marines attacking our shipwrecked crew on Lore? Answer me that, Vice-Minister."

Hell, Lore again? What's going on there?

Sky didn't understand why the two sides just didn't go in and pick up their survivors and be done with it. She knew both the Federation and Brotherhood had ships standing by, waiting for the details to be worked out to affect the rescue.

"I'm sorry, I don't know what you are talking about. I've honored the rules for these meetings, and I have no communications with my embassy."

He didn't even pretend to look guilty but instead stared at her with an iron gaze.

"Mr. DeAngelo, if you would please step outside our host's embassy and find out to what the bishop is referring?" she asked.

Keyshon left the room, and Sky and the two Brotherhood reps stared at each other for a few moments until the bishop got another message.

He turned to his assistant, whispered in the man's ear, and the two of them stood up.

"This meeting is over," he said. "It's up to the first brother and your chairman now to sort things out."

He seemed about to say something else, but he evidently thought the better of it. He left the room. Their Swiss minder asked him something that Sky missed, and a moment later, she stuck her head into the room.

"Is there anything I can do for you, Vice-Minister?"

"Yeah, can you stop a war?"

"Pardon me, Vice-Minister?"

"Nothing. And no, I'll be leaving now."

I don't know what happened on Lore, but it's clear I've blown this part of the mission. Now I've got to convince the Klethos not to remediate their honor.

LORE

Chapter 25
Hondo

"That's the last of them, sir. We're next," Hondo said.

The lieutenant nodded, then went back to his PA. He'd been quiet since the truce, somewhat withdrawn. Hondo wanted to say something to him, to tell him that he respected the man. That *all* his Marines did.

"Leave him be, Hondo," Staff Sergeant Rutledge said.

"But he saved our asses."

"True that. But he blames himself for those we lost, and not just here on the planet."

Hondo could understand that. All day, his thoughts had drifted to his losses. To Marasco, Antman, Ling. To Diva, Killdeer, Haus, Nok. Some of them would be resurrected, but others were lost for good.

The lieutenant had lost all of those, but also most of Third Squad and half of Second. That had to be a heavy burden.

He nodded, then strode over to where Hanaburgh and Tony B were manning the approach. It was all well and good to have a truce with the host, but until each and every one of them had boarded the Swenson liner and left the system, the skipper was not going to let down her guard.

"Anything?" he asked, more to fill up the silence than because he wanted to know.

"Quieter than a mute mouse in a tempest," Tony B said.

"Well, the next shuttle's ours. Be ready to fall back."

"We'll be ready, Sergeant. I don't want to spend any longer on this fucking dirtball than we have to."

"It's not that bad," Hanaburgh said. "Look at it. All this room. A man could stretch out here."

Hondo looked at Hanaburgh in surprise. He agreed with Tony B; he just wanted to leave. He shifted his gaze for a moment to take in the view. Lore really was a pretty planet, when you got down to it. As a Class 1 terraformed world, it was lush and green. There was plenty of room for humanity to expand on this continent. Not that Hondo ever planned on coming back, but as a child of the Emerson slums, he could understand why Hanaburgh might be intrigued.

"Sergeant McKeever, the shuttle's inbound. Get your people to the LZ," Gunny Gustav passed.

"Roger that, Gunny," he passed, then "That's it, then. The shuttle's on its way."

The three Marines took one last look towards the north, then turned and started back to the cleared area that had acted as the LZ. Two of the Buddie Navy cargo handlers were standing by the last of the cargo, while Wolf, Pickerul, and RP were donning their PICS.

The familiar scream of the shuttle's ion engines reached them as the shuttle swooped in from the south, hugging the terrain before it flared to a perfect landing. This was a civilian shuttle, with the passenger hatch on the side. Pickerul and RP moved up to help the sailors, using their PICS' strength to hand up the cargo.

"OK, go ahead and board," the gunny said.

Hondo motioned for his Marines to board, and they clambered up the ladder, barely fitting their bulk inside the hatch.

"I'm getting the lieutenant, Gunny," Hondo said, walking back to where he'd left him.

Lieutenant Abrams had already donned his PICS, but he wasn't moving.

"Sir? It's time to go."

"I'm coming, Sergeant McKeever," he said after a long wait.

Without another word, he stepped off, heading to the shuttle where Staff Sergeant Rutledge, the gunny, and the skipper waited. Hondo reached them, then as the staff sergeant climbed the ladder, he turned, searching for any sign of movement, any sign that the Brotherhood was breaking the truce. The countryside was deserted.

"Get aboard, Sergeant," the skipper said.

Hondo nodded, then climbed up into the shuttle. Inside, the seats had been retracted, but he still had to crouch to avoid hitting his helmet on the overhead. He did a headcount, then told the gunny that all of his Marines were onboard. Behind him, Captain Ariç climbed up, paused in the hatch, and took a moment to look back.

"That's it, then. Let's blow this place."

The hatch whispered closed, and the shuttle smoothly took off, leaving Lore behind them.

EARTH

Chapter 26
Skylar

"That's that, then. The last of the Marines and the *Zrínyi's* crew are off of the planet," Keyshon said.

"No glitches? No last-minute changes of their demands?"

"No ma'am. It looks like the planet's back in the hands of Horsinger, Inc."

Thank God for small favors.

The last two days had been tense, to say the least. A truce had been called and relayed to the two sides on the ground. But twice, it looked like war was going to break out again, all while Sky and her team tried to keep the Klethos along the sidelines and the more seasoned diplomats dealt with the Brotherhood to try to avert an escalation. Neither side had wanted to allow the other side's warships that lurked outside the system to affect a rescue, and all the while, the planetary government—read, Horsinger, Inc—was screaming bloody murder about their sovereignty being violated.

Finally, cooler heads prevailed, and two civilian liners were hired to take the UAM and Brotherhood forces off the planet and transport them to military vessels outside the system.

Nothing was over. There were lawsuits and official protests in the works, but for the moment, it looked like a shooting war had at least been postponed.

And that left her with the Quad. She couldn't put it off any longer. They'd been requesting a meeting, which the Secretary-General himself had quashed, but now it was time.

"You ready?" she asked Foue and Dr. Pavoni.

They both nodded. Sky was glad that both were there. Dealing with the bishop alone had been stressful, but with the Klethos, the powers that be felt that it was better to show a united front to the Klethos, to remind them that most of humanity had kept honor in their relationships. Sky agreed with that line of thinking, but she was also simply grateful that she wouldn't be alone.

The three led their teams into the meeting room, then stood waiting for the Quad to arrive. Two minutes later, the four Klethos strode in. Sky tried to catch the eye of Gary, the male, but he wouldn't do it.

"Was your confrontation *lassor*?" Glinda asked, without civil niceties.

Sky was ready for the question. *Lassor* meant an attempt to remediate honor, something between a punishment and a salve, as far as the best human linguists could determine. It would have been foolish to assume that the Klethos were unaware of what had happened on Lore, and it was logical, given their last meetings, that the Klethos would assume that the UAM was attempting punish the Brotherhood for their lack of honor.

"When some are without honor, it is up to *d'lato* to remediate," she answered.

Which was not an answer, she knew.

Glinda stared at her, and it took an effort of will for Sky to stare back into the piercing eyes.

"Was this *lassor*?" Glinda asked again.

Sky was ready for that, if Glinda didn't accept the swivel.

"This was the first step of *lassor*. We wanted to remind the Brotherhood of what honor means."

"*D'lessu* will never understand," Gloria interjected, her neck frill rising to its full glory before settling back down.

"They were *d'lato* for many years. We believe that honor can be restored. This was a reminder for them."

"Yet you left them alive," Glinda said.

"We destroyed their ship. We killed their soldiers. We were not merciful."

That was a pretty severe slant to what happened, but not technically a lie.

"And we have a reminder for you. If you cannot remediate honor, then you are not *d'lato*, and *lassor* is in your future as well."

Without another word, the four rose and stalked out of the room.

The meeting had lasted just over a minute, but the message was clear: the UAM had better do something to restore honor, or the Klethos were not only going after the Brotherhood alliance, but the UAM as well.

FS FIRTH OF CLYDE

Chapter 27

Hondo

"There was damage to your cuirass. What do you remember of that?" the civilian asked.

Hondo tried to think back. He'd take a pretty hard blow to his chest, but he hadn't paid much attention to it when it happened. His armor had held, and he'd been rather preoccupied at the time.

"I can't really say, sir. I think it was when we were in the thick of it."

"By 'in the thick of it,' I am assuming this was when your squad was engaged after you overran the initial ambush. We've got you at between two and four hundred meters from the Brotherhood forces at the time. Does that sound right?"

"Yes, sir, I guess so."

"And what was your aspect to the Brotherhood soldiers?"

"Sir?"

"Were you facing them? Did you have a side aspect?"

"Uh, sir. I was in combat at the time. I can't tell you where I was facing at any given moment."

"Sergeant, it's vital information. I wouldn't be spending my time here if it wasn't," the man said, sounding a little peeved.

Hondo was about to snap off a retort when the lieutenant colonel said, "Sergeant McKeever, we all know you were worrying about keeping your Marines alive and dealing with the enemy, and no one is besmirching what you did. Far from it. You made the Corps proud. But Dr. Silverton's questions are important, too. This was the first time in history that PICS went up against Sauls, and we need to analyze what happened, so we can prepare for a future engagement. You understand, don't you, son?"

The civilian might be some high muckety-muck, but Hondo was about fed up with him. The lieutenant colonel, though, he was a different story. Hell, that was the same rank as the battalion CO, and he might as well be a god as far as Hondo was concerned. If he were telling Hondo to try and dredge his memory, then he would.

He looked up at the overhead, trying to replay the fight in his mind. The problem was that it was like a kaleidoscope, whirling fragments that fit together to make the whole. He thought that he'd been advancing when he was hit, but was that before or after he'd fired to the left? Could that have turned him around?

"I'm sorry, sir. I just can't remember. Can't we look at my combat footage? Wouldn't that tell you?"

"We have looked at it, son. That's why we're asking you. It wasn't clear."

"The R16?" the civilian asked the lieutenant colonel.

The lieutenant colonel took a deep breath, then said, "Sergeant McKeever, Dr. Silverton would like to put you under for a memory mine."

Hondo blanched and jerked backwards. He'd heard about memory mining. How could he not have? They were a staple of flicks and holos, and those going under usually had either crippling mental issues, became vegetables, or had personal information revealed.

"Sir?"

"It's OK. Sergeant. Think of it as an assisted hypnosis. Completely harmless."

"I . . . I don't want my brain fried."

"Oh, good God," the civilian said, rolling his eyes.

"It's nothing like that, son. No one can see inside your head, and you'll be completely awake. R16 simply helps you remember better."

"Do I have to, sir?" Hondo asked.

"No, you don't," the lieutenant colonel admitted. "No one can force you. But I can tell you this. What you and your fellow Marines tell us can save lives in the future. That's important, right?"

"Uh . . . is anyone else doing this? Lieutenant Abrams?"

"Yes, Lieutenant Abrams has agreed. So has Staff Sergeant Rutledge."

Hondo felt his heart pound and sweat was forming on his brow. This was worse than facing the Brotherhood. His brain was *him*, who he was, and they wanted to mess with it. Maybe it was for the good, but still . . .

Ah, hell. If the lieutenant's doing it, I've got to.

There was really only one decision he could make if it could keep Marines alive.

"Sir, OK. I'll do it."

The civilian muttered something under his breath that sounded like "about time," and Hondo was tempted to tell the man he'd changed his mind. But this was about making the PICS better, and that could save lives, so he really had no choice.

"Are you going to do it now?" he asked, steeling himself.

"Oh, no. We don't have the ability here. We'll do it once we arrive at J-Point."

Hondo let out a sigh of relief. He still had time.

"Do you have anything else for the sergeant, sir?" the officer asked the civilian.

That rubbed Hondo the wrong way. The civilian was maybe a few years older than Hondo, but the lieutenant colonel was calling him sir? It didn't seem right.

"No, you can dismiss him. Who's next?"

"That would be Corporal Curtis Johnson," he said, then added, "Sergeant McKeever, please sent him in."

Hondo got up, happy to be leaving. Outside, the office, Wolf and Pickerul were waiting.

"How was it?" Wolf asked.

"They want to mine our brains," Hondo said.

"Fuck that shit," Pickerul said, her eyes wide.

"They say it's safe," Hondo said.

"Yeah, like they said we were just getting transported to J-Point, and we saw how that worked out."

Pickerul's logic was flawed, but he could appreciate what she'd just said.

"Look, just try and remember everything you can. They've got our combat footage and our analytics, but they want more. So, go, they're waiting."

Wolf shrugged, then opened the hatch.

"Were they tough?" Pickerul asked, for once, the bluster gone, giving hints of the little girl she had to have been once.

"Hell, nothing scares you, and neither should this. They just want to know what happened."

"Are we in some sort of trouble?"

The question took Hondo by surprise. He looked up, and Pickerul had scrunched up her eyebrows, her face worried.

"No, what gave you that idea?"

She just pointed to the closed hatch.

"No, don't worry. You know this was the first time we've fought Sauls, and they want to analyze things down to a T. They want to make the PICS better, so we can kick ass when we meet again. Not everyone's as good as First Squad, so we've got to give those other sorry-ass saps all the help we can."

"We did good, right, Sergeant?"

"Damned right we did, Tammy."

He reached over to give her a clap on the shoulder, and somehow, she melted into him for a hug.

"I miss them," she whispered.

Me, too, Tammy. Me, too.

He held her tight for a few moments before she shoved him back, the tough-as-nails Marine again.

"Sorry about that, Sergeant. It won't happen again."

"No problem. Well, I'd better get back. Staff Sergeant Rutledge probably has got a to-do list a klick long for me to do."

"Thanks, Sergeant," Pickerul said as he walked away. "For everything."

His step perked up, and he made his way to the senior enlisted berthing and rapped on Staff Sergeant Rutledge's space. There was no answer, so he poked his head inside.

Wonder where he is?

He wandered down to the troops' compartment where Hanaburgh, Tony P, and RP were lounging.

"Are we up?" Hanaburgh asked.

"Yeah, head on down. Wolf's in there now," he said. "Has anyone seen the staff sergeant?"

"He came looking for you. Said he's going to see the lieutenant and for you to come," Hanaburgh said, as he handed Hondo his PA.

He'd been instructed to leave it before his interview, and Hanaburgh had been entrusted with its security. He glanced at it, and the meeting icon was flashing. Making his way to officer's country, he knocked on the hedge of the lieutenant's open hatch.

"Enter," Lieutenant Abrams said.

Normally, the lieutenant would be sharing the stateroom with three other lieutenants, but as the *Clyde* had been dispatched specifically to rescue them, there was plenty of room.

"Plenty of room" was all relative. The small stateroom was still crowded with Cara and Staff Sergeant Rutledge in there.

"Tale a seat, Sergeant," the lieutenant said, pointing at the lower rack across from him.

Hondo sat by Cara, who seemed amped.

"What's up, sir?"

"These two already know. We're not going to J-Point."

"Really, sir?" Hondo asked surprised.

He felt . . . disappointed? It wasn't surprising that they might not be sent back to J-Point. They'd suffered some heavy casualties, but still, their mission was the Grubs. Surely there were enough Marines at J-Point to flesh them out again.

"We're going to Destiny," the lieutenant told him.

It took him a moment to process that.

"Destiny, sir? Isn't that a Brotherhood world?"

"Yes, it is."

"So, why are we . . . shit, sir, we're invading the Brotherhood?"

"Not exactly," the lieutenant said, looking at the other two Marines before continuing. "We're going to meet up with the rest of the battalion en route, then we're going there to defend it."

"Sir?"

"The Grubs have invaded Destiny, and we're going to kick them back off the planet."

EARTH

Chapter 28
Skylar

"The threat affects all of humanity. We cannot ignore it."

"They are not *d'lato*," Glinda said, with the slight hiss that indicated Klethos scorn. "You would sully yourselves?"

This isn't going well.

Sky glanced up at the small cam that was broadcasting the meeting to probably thousands.

Once again, Sky wondered why she was there. She may be one of the foremost experts on the Klethos, but she had next to no experience as a diplomat, something Norelco Pavoni had brought up yet again.

She happened to agree with the Confederation representative, but she didn't accept his reasoning. She and Foue were both much younger than him, and Sky didn't think that he appreciated the fact that she was the team lead. As an older man, he thought he was entitled to the position. What he was forgetting was that the Klethos were a female-oriented society, and they didn't seem to give the same respect to males, whether Klethos or human. Call it a cultural bias.

Still, Sky could use some help here, no matter the source.

"We are not reacting to save the Brotherhood, Ambassador. We have citizens on Destiny. The Saint Peter Canisius Monastery is also on the planet. The Jesuit brothers there are independent, and they've provided much of the scientific insight for the new weapons we use to fight the Dictymorphs, weapons your own warriors use."

The quad leader froze for a moment, and for once, Sky thought she'd surprised her. She knew that the various factions within humanity perplexed the more homogenous Klethos-lee. The idea that the monastery was an independent enclave on a Brotherhood world probably blew their raptor-like minds.

Several of her staff thought that piece of information might sway the Klethos not just to stand down from their threat to take on the Brotherhood, but to actually enlist their help on Destiny. At the moment, the Klethos fighting force with the humans was still on J-Point while the human task force was en route to the planet. They could make a huge impact if they would join the effort.

"They are not *d'lato*, and only *d'lessu* would commune with them," Glinda said, squashing that theory.

Time for number two, she told herself.

She wasn't too confident that this one was going to work either, but the groupthink was that it was the next best option.

"Ambassador, our own honor is at stake here. We will address *lassor*, but after the Dictymorph threat has been eliminated. As our allies, as fellow *d'lato*, we simply ask that you hold back. Do not take any action concerning honor while we fight the Dictymorph. When we have won, we can re-open negotiations."

Glinda rose up from the special chair that had been made for her, her neck frill fully displayed.

"You think we are negotiating with you? There is no negotiation with honor," she shouted, every word underscored by hissing. "We may have been mistaken to believe you are *d'lato,* and that is to our shame."

She stepped away from the table as the other three scrambled to their feet. Without another word, she strode past the assembled humans and pushed open the double doors. And then they were gone.

"That went well, I'd say," Dr. Pavoni said, breaking the stunned silence. "Nice choice of words, Skylar."

Sky hadn't thought that tack was going to work, but she hadn't foreseen Glinda's reaction.

She looked back up to the cam, knowing that the Minister was watching. Pavoni could be somewhat of a jerk, but he was right. No one had given her the word "negotiation" to use. It had just slipped out.

What have I done?

DESTINY

Chapter 29
Hondo

"This sucks," Cara said, as she and Hondo watched their Marines check IDs.

That's an understatement, Hondo thought.

He was just as unhappy with the situation as she was. They'd arrived on the planet ten hours ago, ready to join their battalion—only the battalion had been essentially disbanded. The two intact line companies had been attached to other battalions while the *Zrínyi* survivors had formed a conditional company and been assigned to security duty.

Hondo had faced the Grubs before, and it wasn't high on his list of fun things to do, but while he was safe and sound on one side of the planet, the Grubs were tearing through the main continent on the other side.

And so far, they were letting the Grubs do what they wanted. The local Brotherhood forces hadn't been able to put up much resistance.

Hondo knew they had to build up the forces in order to prosecute the defense, and they couldn't use naval assets to soften up the Grubs, but still, it hurt to let them establish a beachhead on the planet. More could come and reinforce those already here, making it even harder to defeat them when the real battle commenced.

Even being on Destiny was surreal. The platoon had just fought the Brotherhood, had killed and died on Lore, yet now they were on a Brotherhood planet defending the bastards.

Yeah, bastards!

Hondo didn't have it in him to simply forget that the Brotherhood was the enemy. He'd lost too many of his Marines to them to make such a drastic 180. The brass evidently felt the same, otherwise the platoon wouldn't be set up on the road under a huge monastery with orders to keep all Brotherhood citizens away from the UAM buildup. This might be their planet, but they weren't going to get into the assembly area.

Down the hill and into the plain, Hondo could see the activity associated with military operations. Aircraft flew on short hops, and vehicles kicked up dust. Marines in PICS would be out there, rehearsing, and Hondo wished he was with them.

"Do you wish you were down there?" he asked Cara.

"Hell no! Go out there and fight the Grubs? We've got it made here, sitting with our thumbs up our asses. I mean, I didn't join the Corps to fight now, right?"

Hondo was quiet for a moment, then said, "Yeah, I wish I was down there, too."

EARTH

Chater 30
Skylar

"And while your forces sit in Grayson, we've lost most of Canaan!" the arch-bishop shouted, his face florid with anger, spittle coming out of his mouth.

Ambassador Hortense, keeping her voice low, but as if lecturing a small child, said, "We cannot engage until all our forces are ready."

"It's your fault, you and the entire UAM," he said, pausing to shift his gaze from the Federation ambassador to sweep over the entire assembly. "If you hadn't provoked the Dictymorphs, they would still be hundreds of parsecs away from human space. You brought them here, first to Purgamentium, and now to Destiny."

"He's right," Yelcy said. "We did get their attention."

"Which is said and done," Sky said. "And it would have been only a matter of time before they reached us anyway."

She turned back to the holo to watch as the Brotherhood ambassador railed against what he saw as a delay. Brotherhood forces that had been in the UAM Dictymorph task force were arriving on the planet and getting routed, all the time while the UAM task force built up their forces.

Sky had to wonder if the delay was not, in fact, a military necessity, but rather a political move. She wouldn't put it past the members of the task force to be doing their own *lassor*, punishing the Brotherhood while imparting on them the importance for all humankind to actively fight the invaders. If it weren't for Saint Peter Canisius, Sky wondered if the UAM would let the planet fall, but the Jesuit brothers were still a major source of Dictymorph research, one too valuable to lose.

Was it coincidence that the Dictymorphs had invaded Destiny, of all places? There were a thousand human worlds, but only a few were hubs of Dictymorph research.

Too many people, Sky included, tended to think of the Dictymorphs as big, mindless worms, or Grubs, as the masses called them. But they'd shown to be able to adjust to meet new threats. Sky didn't know if they'd targeted Destiny for a reason, and they'd landed on the opposite side of the world from the monastery, but she suspected that the choice of a target was deliberate.

Back in Brussels, the Dentonian ambassador had the floor. As an ally of the Brotherhood withdrawal from the task force, tiny Denton was merely a Brotherhood mouthpiece. The wizened old man, with his flowing white locks, might have seemed frail, but he had a surprisingly robust voice as he called out the UAM for letting Brotherhood soldiers and police die while the Marines were "flipping their widgets." Sky had never heard that particular phrase before, but its meaning was clear from both his context and tone.

Sky's PA vibrated. She frowned while she picked it up. She'd given Jack strict instructions that unless the chairman herself called, she was not to be bothered while they watched what was going on in Brussels.

"Ma'am, you have a visitor waiting in your office. I think you need to see him," Jack said, his voice subdued.

"I don't have anyone on my schedule. You can tell whoever it is to make an appointment."

"I really don't think that's a good idea, ma'am. You're going to want to see this visitor."

"Who is this vaunted visitor that you insist I see?" Sky asked curtly.

Jack lowered his voice and said, "It's Gary."

"Gary? Gary who?"

"You know, that Gary. The Klethos Gary."

Sky pulled down her PA and looked at it in shock, no more surprised than she would have been had it turned into a cobra in her hand and started singing *Carmen*.

She brought it back up and asked, "Are you sure? Gary? In my office?"

"It's not something I could be mistaken on. They don't really blend in with the crowd."

Sky looked around at the rest of the team. No one seemed to have noticed that she took the call.

"OK, I'll be there in two minutes," she told Jack, then buzzed Keyshon.

Meet me in my office now. We've got an unusual visitor.

Keyshon looked up in surprise and caught her eye. She nodded, stood up as casually as she could, and then walked out as if going to the restroom. She had no idea why she was trying to keep the Klethos' presence a secret, but she wanted to find out just what the heck was going on before she informed anyone else.

Keyshon came out of the conference room and asked, "What's up, ma'am?"

"We have a visitor, a very VIP one. I want you with me when I meet him. Make sure every recording device is running."

He raised one eyebrow in a question, and she said, "It's Gary. The Klethos Gary."

"Holy shit!" Keyshon said, the first time that Sky had ever heard him resort to crude language. "Does the ministry know he's here?"

"I doubt it. If they did know, I think they would have given us a heads-up. Confirm that all of this is being recorded, then come in with me."

"This will just take a second," he said, pulling out his PA. A moment later, he added, "Done. Visuals and analytics."

"Then let's not keep our visitor waiting."

Jack was standing in the outer office as the two entered, wringing his hands.

"I'm sorry, ma'am. He just waltzed in. I didn't know what to do, so I put him in your office. Is that OK?"

Normally, Sky's office was off-limits if she wasn't in it, but this was an exception.

"That was a smart move, Jack. For now, make sure no one bothers us. No one comes in unless I OK it."

The two entered the office. Gary was standing alongside the far wall, looking at a signed print of a Dvorak. It wasn't worth much, but Sky liked the play of color in the forest, colors that had never existed in nature.

"This is . . . unusual," Gary said, not turning around. "I will conjecture that it is a representation, not an accurate rendition?"

"That is true, Ambassador."

No one really knew what to call the other three members of the quad, so by mutual agreement, all four were given the ambassador honorific.

"But it is no less real for being in the artist's mind."

"I guess you are correct."

Why are you here, Gary? Not to chat about human art, that's for sure.

Gary turned around, gave a slight nod of his head and the elbow twitch that Klethos sometimes performed when meeting someone.

"Uh . . . Ambassador, I have to admit that this is unusual. We have never met with you alone. May I ask why you are here?"

"Yes, this is unusual. This is the first time I have done this on Earth."

"Are you here in an official capacity?"

"Words do not always mean what they mean," he said. *That's not what Glinda told me.*

"It is known I am here meeting with you by some, but my quad is unaware of my present location."

Sky's mouth almost dropped open in amazement. He seemed to take what he'd said as a matter of course. His neck frill remained flat. If he was under any sort of pressure or stress, if he was doing anything wrong, he wasn't showing it.

"So, if I can ask, why are you here?"

"To teach you about us. There is a word, *d'lamma.* I believe you do not know this?"

"No, I don't," Sky asked, suppressing the urge to call it up on her PA.

"It is not one we use often. The concept does not coincide with some of our beliefs. *D'lamma* is somewhat like *d'lammo,* our young, who are not *d'lato,* but who are also not *d'lessu.*"

Sky had to concentrate. There were too many d'whatevers being thrown around.

"I ask you, are your young held to the same standards as your adults?" he asked.

"No, of course not. They need to learn right and wrong."

"And so it is with honor as well?"

"Yes, a child does not understand honor yet," Sky answered, wondering where Gary was going with it.

"This is the way of the universe. But I ask you, cannot someone, an adult, not understand right and wrong, not understand honor?"

"I suppose so."

"To simplify what I am saying, the *d'lamma* are these. Ones who are not *d'lato*, but because they do not understand."

Sky's mind was churning. Gary wasn't just giving her a language lesson—he was telling her something important, something she could almost grasp.

Gary stood there silent, as if waiting for her to say something. Sky was grasping at straws, not knowing what to say, so she said the first thing that came to her mind in order to buy time.

"So, what do you do with these *d'lamma*?"

She could have sworn Gary's posture relaxed a fraction, as if in relief, as he said, "You teach them. You allow them to ascend into *d'lato*."

It was almost there for her, and she knew she had to understand what he was telling her.

"So, if someone is without honor, they can be brought into honor?" she asked.

"This is so."

Something clicked into place, and she asked, "Without the need for *lassor*?"

This time she was sure Gary showed a degree of relief.

"Without the need for *lassor*. *Lassor* is for those who refuse honor, not those who do not understand it."

"So, let me ask you this, Ambassador. If people, if *d'lessu* reject honor, they are subject to *lassor*. But if someone doesn't understand honor, like a child or a *d'lamma*, they can be taught."

"Again, this is so."

"So, I ask you, how is someone, well, *designated*," she said, not knowing what term to use, "as *d'lessu* or *d'lamma*?"

"It is invoked."

Just like that? It can't be that easy.

"So I understand it, if I, for example, invoked *d'lamma* status on someone, then it's done?"

"It is so."

"And what if someone disagrees?"

"If you, as *d'lato*, invoke it, honor demands that all recognize it."

"And then, if I'm correct, *lassor* cannot be conducted."

"It is so."

"And would honor demand that all act to assist, to protect *d'lamma* from a threat?

"Honor would demand it, particularly if she who invoked it were taking action herself. Honor would require assistance."

Sky felt a surge of excitement. Gary, for whatever reason, had handed her what might be a solution to the terrible situation they were in.

"And this is iron-bound? No one can block it?"

There was slight twitch to Gary's neck frill, then he said, "Honor demands all recognize it, if she who invokes it is *d'lato*. But if the invocation is without honor, she who invokes it is no longer *d'lato*."

Her sense of euphoria suddenly deflated. If she was reading him right, trying to get the Brotherhood this *d'lamma* status could result in the UAM itself losing their *d'lato* status.

That would be catastrophic, something almost too terrible to comprehend. Mankind could suddenly be facing two enemies. Its very existence would be at risk. This had to go up the chain, not only to the Federation and UAM, but to the Brotherhood and the rest of their alliance as well.

There was a long moment of silence. Sky tried to let what she'd heard sink in. She'd go over the recordings after the meeting before she forwarded them to see what she might have missed. Gary had, in fact, offered them a golden ticket, but like all golden tickets, this one had risks.

"I will take my leave now, Vice-Minister," Gary said, breaking the silence.

Sky gave a quick glance at Keyshon, then stepped over to stop the Klethos.

"Please, can I ask you? Why did you tell me this?"

"You are the human expert on the Klethos-lee, correct? Should you not know more about us?"

"I don't mean that. The rest of your quad doesn't know you're here. And unless I'm completely mistaken, I don't think the ambassador, uh . . ."

"Glinda?" he asked, then when he saw Sky's face, added, "Yes, we know you have taken to name us."

"Uh, right. So, then, I don't think Glinda would approve of you telling me that. She does not seem to be too, shall we say, *forgiving*, of the Brotherhood?"

Gary stared at her for a long moment, and Sky wondered if she'd overstepped her bounds.

Finally, he said, "Glinda was a *d'relle*, and her hold on honor is without parallel."

"And yours isn't?" Sky asked, before thinking about how that could be taken as an insult.

"I am male, Vice-Minister."

"And?"

"The Klethos-lee are strong on traditions, traditions that have allowed us to survive longer than you have been out of the trees and walking upright. We rely on our females to protect us from our enemies, both within and without. They have been bred for aggression, both physically and emotionally. Without honor, without *fassonay*," he said, using a term Sky had never heard, "their aggression would have destroyed us, a fate that almost occurred twice in our past."

He waited as if trying to formulate his thoughts, then said, "We males, we've been the glue that provides for our very future. We set on our eggs, we raise the *d'lammo* to provide the next generation. We may be the weaker of the genders, and we are not as wedded to tradition and honor as our females. But we will do whatever is required to make sure our *d'lammo* survive."

"To include making sure that the Klethos do not get into a destructive war with humans when the Dictymorphs are the true threat," Sky said quietly.

"It is so, Skylar."

Gary brushed by the unresisting Sky and out the door.

"Holy shit," Keyshon said, the second time in ten minutes that he'd let his language slip.

"What do you think?" she asked her EA.

"He seemed to be on the level," Keyshon answered. "What about you?"

"I think we need to get all the recordings and analytics up to the minister. The rules of the game have just changed."

DESTINY

Chapter 31
Hondo

Hondo stood at their checkpoint on the road beneath the monastery. Below him, the bulk of the Marines were finally getting underway. They were displacing to the other continent where the Grubs had taken everything in their path. Hondo was not privy to the top-level plans, of course, but he knew that the intent was to stop the Grubs on that side of the planet and not let them expand their footprint to the more populous western hemisphere.

"What happens when the Grubs attack more than one world at a time?" Wolf asked him. "I mean, they all look good down there," he said, pointing at the Marines. "But that's a third of our force, all for one Brotherhood planet."

Wolf wasn't completely accurate. The force below was a third of the Marines, but not the UAM. The Confederation and the rest of the governments in the fight had two times the strength of the Marines, and the FCDC was even larger. But Wolf's point was a good one. So far, the Grubs had attacked one planet at a time. If they attacked more concurrently, then humankind and Klethos would be hard-pressed to withstand that.

And the Klethos were not even here on Destiny. The Klethos force at J-Point hadn't even left. It sort of made sense to Hondo. The Brotherhood had abandoned the war effort, so he could understand the Klethos not wanting to help. Hell, he didn't want to be there. Right now, he pretty much hated the Brotherhood and everything they stood for.

"Let's just hope they never do that," Hondo said, which was pretty much BS.

Marines didn't rely on hope—they took charge of their destinies and made sure they could meet any contingency.

"Maybe they will, maybe they won't," Wolf said. "Meanwhile, we get stuck here babysitting refugees."

That wasn't true, either. Tens of thousands of refugees from the eastern hemisphere had been brought to the valley, Q-huts springing up like mushrooms after a rain to house them all. But they were being managed by the Brotherhood civilian administrative police, not the Marines. What was left of Alpha Company was augmenting the small Marine security force being left behind to guard the rear area camp. Their secondary mission was to assist in the security of the big monastery on the hill.

No one in the company knew why the monastery was important. Hondo thought that the monks or priests or whatever could just evacuate like anyone else. And why would the citizens of Destiny be a threat to their own monastery?

He was just a grunt sergeant, though. What he thought didn't matter one whit in the grand scheme of things, so if First Squad was tasked with manning a checkpoint on the highway leading into camp, then that was what they were going to do.

EARTH

Chater 32
Skylar

Skylar felt faint. Her heart was racing, her palms sweating. She still couldn't believe that she, a mere assistant vice-minister for the Federation, was being put in this position.

Not everyone wanted her in the position, and she agreed with them. But Gary had chosen to inform her, not anyone else, for reasons unknown. But "unknown" didn't mean "unimportant." The powers that be had decided that they'd better error on the side of caution. Now, after six hours of extensive preparation, Sky, flanked by Foue and Pavoni, was as ready as she would ever be.

They marched three abreast, heading for the triumphal arch. Sky wasn't sure why the UAM had set up the meeting in the Parc du Cinquanteraire in the city's European Quarter. Foue thought the arch would be a show of strength, but that assumed the Klethos knew what the arc represented. Sky didn't even know that. There were so many triumphal arches scattered around human space that this one could commemorate a basketball championship, for all she knew.

Pavoni had a more pessimistic viewpoint. If Sky failed, the three of them could be abandoned by the UAM as rouge players in the game of thrones. It would be harder to do that should they meet inside the UAM complex.

As they approached, Sky could see the quad was already there. The Brussels city gendarmerie had cleared the park half an hour before, so within 800 meters, it was only the seven of them.

Not that they were really alone. Every listening, holo, and cam device in and above the city was making sure what happened was recorded for posterity—or possibly as evidence against the three of them.

"You OK,?" Foue asked as they approached the waiting quad.

"Oh, yeah. I'm just fine. We've got our whole relationship riding on this, so why should I worry?" she said, too quickly and too high-pitched.

"Calm down," Pavoni said. "You're going to do fine."

"You always wanted to be the team lead, so why don't you take over?" she snapped.

"Yes, I thought I should have been the lead. That's not to denigrate your potential. I've got the experience, and you don't. But Gary chose you for a reason. So, just buckle down and do it."

They marched another 50 meters before she said, "Sorry, Norelco. That wasn't fair. I'm just—"

"I know. Don't worry about it. You'll do fine."

It took another minute to cross the wide-open area leading up to the arch. Instead of all four Klethos being abreast, Glinda stood out in front with the other three behind her.

The moment the three humans reached them, Glinda said, "Time is not more. You with your United Assembly of Man are not all of your kind. There exists *d'lessu*, those who have foregone honor. It is now a matter of honor for the Klethos-lee to remediate that honor, as you are abdicating that responsibility.

"Furthermore, by abdicating your responsibility, we now—"

"Ambassador, you are correct," Sky interrupted. "It is not time, and we are ready to take action."

Glinda paused, then took a breath to continue.

Sky didn't let her, cutting her off with, "As the *d'lato* of humanity, we invoke *d'lamma* for our lost brethren."

Glinda's eyes widened in shock, the same way a human's would, and her neck frill fully raised. She actually sputtered before saying, "You cannot! Your *d'lessu* know honor and abandoned it. They are not *d'lamma*."

"I invoke *d'lamma*," Sky repeated, wishing Gary had given her any formal format that should be used. "And I require Klethos assistance in teaching the Brotherhood honor."

All four Klethos had their frills up, including Gary. She hoped that was merely for show, and not that she has screwed up.

"I hear your request. In honor, I must listen, but I do not acquiesce to your contention."

That wasn't expected, so Sky had to play it by ear.

"The Brotherhood have, in fact, acted without honor. But they are like *d'lammo*, children who know no better."

The neck frills on two of the Klethos stood up even straighter, and Sky wondered if she had crossed the line mentioning the Klethos young. She hurriedly went on.

"They believe they are acting within their own honor."

"There is only honor, which is true and unchanging," Glinda said.

"You said you would listen. Now you lecture me. Is this honor?" she blurted out, before thinking of the consequences.

Hell, Skylar. Don't piss her off.

She could almost imagine those huge clawed feet striking out to disembowel her.

Glinda turned her head low, exposing her neck, with all four arms spread out before she straightened and said, "Proceed."

Except Sky had pretty much shot her load. She didn't have anything left in the chamber.

"The Brotherhood does not understand what true honor is, and we will teach them now," she said, simply rephrasing what she had already said.

"And what will you do, Vice-Minister? Will you be teaching them?" Glinda asked.

She was about to say that a team of representatives from the UAM was ready to be dispatched to the Brotherhood home world, but the slightest shift of Gary's expression stopped her. She hesitated a moment and remembered something he'd said, something about "she" who invoked *d'lamma* had to fix the situation.

"I am going to Destiny to teach them honor," she blurted out.

Sky could almost read the disappointment in Glinda's posture—although that was probably wistful thinking. The Klethos were not human, and a scientist could not afford to anthropomorphize them.

"We do not concur," Glinda said, and Sky's heart fell. "Your *d'lessu* knew honor, then abandoned it.

"But honor must be maintained, and you, Vice-Minister, are *d'lato* until declared otherwise. So, we must confer as to the merits of your invocation."

Without another word, the four turned and strode off, leaving the two humans alone.

"Did that work?" Foue asked.

"They didn't declare us *d'lessu*," Pavoni said. "I'd call that a win."

"For now. They are conferring," Sky said. "There's still time for them to do that. Let's get back. Our bosses are probably pissing their pants right now."

"Which they just heard, Sky," Foue said with a laugh.

They'd gone in without any way to communicate, all to give the UAM as a whole plausible deniability, but everything they said was being recorded, and Sky had just said the the ministers—heck, the chairman herself—were soiling themselves. She broke out into a laugh, more from the relief of being finished rather than anything else.

The other two joined in, and they started the long march back to where their handlers were gathering. It took five good minutes of walking, but a host of official hovers were ready to whisk them back to UAM headquarters. Keyshon stood by the first one, holding the door open.

"What now, ma'am?" he said as they took their seats and the autodriver kicked in.

"Get transport for two to Destiny."

"Ma'am?"

"Destiny. Travel for two. You and me. I told the quad I was going."

Sky had thought her part was going to be over after today. She was only a mouthpiece, after all, and she could pass the mantle to the professionals. Now, it looked like she was still in the thick of things.

Why did I say Destiny? Why not Saint Barnabas?

Sky had contact with the Dictymorphs before, and they struck fear into her very bones. Something told her, though, that it had to be Destiny. That was where nexus was, not the Brotherhood homeworld.

Somewhere on the planet was the key to the problem, and it was up to her to find it.

DESTINY

Chapter 33
Hondo

"What's your power reading?" Hondo asked Pickerul. "I can't pull you up."

"I'm at eighty-two percent. Why can't you read me?"

"Don't have a clue. When you're relieved, go find Gunner Moeryanti and ask him to run a check."

The squad's PICS hadn't had their arrival upcheck, what with being diverted to Destiny and then the armory getting all the PICS for the assault force upchecked. The combat suits were pretty robust, but the mere fact that Hondo wasn't picking up Pickerul's readings was proof that something was wrong. It was probably her upload wizard—Hondo could read everyone else's PICS as normal.

Technically, Hondo should send her back now. If he couldn't read her, then she was combat ineffective and admin deadlined. But they were in the rear with the gear, and Hondo doubted very much that the refugees were going to boil out of their camp and assault the Marines. Besides, with everyone else in the squad on post as well, he'd have to ask Cara to send someone to relieve Pickerul, and they'd just gotten off an eight-hour watch.

"Was that the VIPs that just landed?" the PFC asked him.

"Probably. Don't know for sure."

He'd seen the ship's shuttle flare in for a landing twenty minutes before. The lieutenant had told them during the morning brief that some VIPs were expected, but the squad was pretty low on the food chain, and no one had bothered to check in with him to let him know if that shuttle was them.

Hondo was more concerned with what was happening on the other side of the planet. The fighting between the Brotherhood and the Grubs had been fierce. Initial contact between the Marines and the Grubs had been made, but, Hondo didn't know how the Marines were faring. Three Pelicans had made it back to the rear, and Hondo had seen the ambulances streaming from the LZ to the field hospital, but he didn't know how bad or how good things were going.

Once again, he wished he was there. They'd been training to fight the Grubs, and after essentially running away from them on Purgamentium, he had a burning desire to make up for that and to see if the new training and weapons would make a difference.

Instead of the Grubs they'd been gearing up to fight, they'd fought the Brotherhood, and now they guarded Brotherhood refugees. It didn't seem right.

"Sergeant McKeever, did you find what's wrong with PFC Pickerul?" the lieutenant asked over the P2P.

"Roger that, sir. She's at her post, and she's fine. She's at 82 percent. Her PICS isn't uploading."

"Understood. Have her check in with the armory after her watch. Second thing, stay on Alverson. The VIPs are about to go call on the brothers in the monastery, and I want everyone on their toes."

"Is there a threat to the VIPs, sir?"

"Not that I know of. But we're here to provide security, so let's do our job."

"Aye-aye, sir. I'll let everyone know."

Pickerul, Hanaburgh, RP, and Lance Corporal Bill Morales had posts along Alverson, the main road leading from the camp to the town of Berea and passing the monastery. Morales was a stay-behind from 2/14 when his PICS was deadlined, so he was at the main gate in the guard house. Hondo passed the word, then started to walk up the hill to the monastery.

He was curious about the place after the lieutenant had mentioned that some of the weapons the Marines used against the Grubs had been developed based on the research done there. It seemed odd to him that a monastery would be into weapons development, but then again, the Brotherhood was based on religion, and he knew from experience what they could do on the battlefield. His interest piqued, he looked the place up and found out that the Jesuits had a long history of scientific development over the millennia. The brother and sister monks discovered many of the principles that made everyday living possible. If the VIPs were going to pay them a visit, Hondo thought he might be able to get a glimpse of a few of the monks when they came out to meet them.

Hanaburgh had the post outside the gate into the monastery, and he greeted Hondo as he strode up to him.

"Have you beaten off any Grubs?" Hondo asked him.

"Not many. About fifty when I got here, then another hundred or so since then. It's been pretty quiet."

"Well, the monastery is still standing, so I guess you did your job. Keep it up."

"So, who're the VIPs?" Hanaburgh asked.

"Who isn't a VIP now?" Hondo answered with a laugh.

"You've got that right, I guess."

Since the task force had departed, more than a few officials, both UAM and Brotherhood, had come to be briefed by the rear-party commander. These VIPs, though, were probably a little more VIP-ish than the others, given how they had arrived and the interest that was given to them.

"Sergeant McKeever, they've just passed me," Morales passed.

"How many are they?"

"Two beetles," Morales said.

"There're only two beetles," he told Hanaburgh. "So, maybe they aren't all that."

"Only two? Heck, we had ten big black hovers when the provincial staff came."

A beetle was the nickname given to the four-passenger expeditionary hovers that were used to transport personnel back and forth in a secure area. Most VIPs seemed to travel with a retinue whose size corresponded with how important they thought they were. If there were only two beetles, then these VIPs might not be that high on the pecking order, despite the briefing the Marines had received.

Hondo turned back towards the camp, and in time, the beetles appeared from behind the curve. A few minutes later, they arrived, coming to a stop outside the stone-covered walkway that led up the hill to the main gate.

The front door of the first beetle opened, and to Hondo's surprise, First Sergeant Nordstrand stepped out. The first sergeant was recovering well, the plastiflesh peeking out from under his collar the only sign of his injury. He should have been medivaced back to division to undergo regen, but he'd managed to work his bolt to stay with the company, as depleted as it was. There was no way he was combat effective, but the SNCO mafia had ways to bend the rules when they wanted.

The first sergeant nodded at Hondo, then opened the back door. A lanky, older civilian stepped out, stretched, and then took a moment to take in the view of the valley. The second was a younger woman. She looked familiar, and it took Hondo a moment to realize why.

"Doctor," he called out, recognizing her even if he'd forgotten her last name.

Both the man and woman turned to him, as did another woman getting out of the second beetle.

"It's me, Sergeant McKeever, ma'am."

They all looked at him like he was crazy, and then he remembered that he was in a PICS, so how could she remember him?

"During the first battle with the Grubs, I carried you out of the fight. I was a lance corporal then. I was there when you got off Purgamentium, too."

Recognition flooded her face, and she stepped around the beetle and walked up to him, saying, "McKeever, that's right, I remember you. What are you doing here?"

I'm a Marine, so where else would I be? The question is, what are you doing here?

"I'm part of the rear area security, ma'am."

"Wow! It's a small universe." She turned to the man and said, "Jack, this Marine saved my life."

The man automatically held out his hand, saying "Glad to meet you, Sergeant," before hesitating and dropping his hand back a few centimeters.

Hondo stifled a laugh. People tended to forget how big a PICS was, and when a huge gauntleted hand reached out, they suddenly wondered if their hand was going to be crushed. PICS' fine motor-tuning was such that a Marine could hold a butterfly and not crush it. He took the man's hand and gently shook it.

Thirty meters up the path, the gates to the monastery opened, and two monks came out, a brother and a sister. In their black robes, Hondo thought they could have stepped out of the 16th Century, Old Reckoning. Well, not totally. Back then, the Jesuits were only male monks.

"Sergeant, I've got to go meet the mother superior now, but I'm going to be here for a couple of days. I'd like to catch up with you if you've got the time."

"Uh . . . sure, ma'am. At your convenience."

"Foue, Norelco, shall we?" she asked the two who'd gotten out of the second beetle.

The four, along with a woman who had the look of a minder about her, turned and walked up the path to greet the two monks.

"So, you hobnobbing with the bigwigs?" the first sergeant asked, stepping over to stand beside him.

"Ain't like that, First Sergeant. I just remembered her."

"If you say, so," the first sergeant said, rolling his fingertips around to meet the top of his thumb, then taking the "hole" and rotating it around his nose in the universal sign of a brown-noser.

Hondo rolled his eyes. He knew he wasn't going to hear the end of this over the next few days. He knew the doctor had said to meet him, and she had to be pretty high on the food chain, but he swore to make sure he avoided her if at all possible. She'd probably forget it anyway.

"So, Sergeant, I see you've got yourself a girlfriend," Hanaburgh said as he joined them.

"Oh, fuck you, too, Burger," Hondo said, wheeling away to stalk off.

The first sergeant was bad enough, but now a lance corporal was giving him shit?

Two sets of laughter followed him down the road.

Chapter 34
Skylar

Skylar sat on the bench seat in the half-filled dining hall. Some of the monks had on lab coats or overalls, but most of the monks were in their black robes. After the modern labs she'd just toured, the hall seemed a throwback to years gone by. The image of the current pope did not fit with the painting of Christ at the head of the hall, nor with the many images of whom Sky thought must be famous Jesuits from over the last more-than-1200 years.

"Well, Doctor Ybarra, what did you think of our facilities?" the mother superior asked.

"I'm very impressed. They're rather, uh . . . surprising, I guess I would have to say."

"Which is not an unusual reaction, Doctor Ybarra."

"I'm not much of a lab-rat, Mother Superior. I've made my living analyzing the data gathered by others. You would have to ask Dr. Pavoni what he thinks of your facilities. He's climbed the academic ladder in some of the best labs in the Confederation."

Sky had been impressed. The monastery grounds could be used for a 22nd or 23rd Century period piece, and the chapel looked like it was plucked from one of the 16th Century European cathedrals, but the research facilities would rival any she'd seen. She wasn't sure what she'd expected, but it wasn't she'd found.

"I have to say, I was surprised to see so many here who are not of your order," she said.

"We don't discriminate against those who are not guided by a higher power," the mother superior said.

What?

Sky looked at the older woman in surprise before she caught the slight smile and twinkle in her eye.

She's playing with me, she realized.

"Well, thank you for allowing others to bask under your guidance," Sky said.

"It's the least we can do. Actually, at the moment, we have . . . " she started, before turning to a monk sitting across the table from them and saying, "How many visiting staff do we have now, Brother Thanh?"

"As of this morning, we have twenty-one."

"Twenty-one," the mother superior repeated to Sky. "We've had as many as seventy in the past, but with the current situation, some have been recalled by their governments. To be expected, I guess."

Several young men and women, looking somewhat strange to Sky in robes with white aprons attached, pushed carts between the tables. Sky had expected the mother superior to be served first, but each monk was served based on how close they sat to the kitchens.

Sky hadn't eaten since the ship bringing them to Destiny had reached the system. The Dictymorphs had yet to fire on a ship that wasn't attacking them, but there was no use taking chances. Standing well off the planet itself, that had resulted in a four-hour shuttle ride to the planet. Add the two-hour tour at the monastery, and she was starving.

She looked up eagerly at the young monk making his way down the aisle, and when he put a covered bowl in front of her, she took off the lid.

Tempura? Really?

The shrimp and vegetable tempura on a bed of rice would have fit in at any fine Japanese restaurant.

"I didn't expect tempura," Norelco said.

"Did you expect gruel, Doctor Pavoni?" Brother Fa'ad, one of their guides, asked.

"We only have gruel on Monday, Wednesday, and Friday, Doctor Pavoni," the mother superior added.

She's enjoying this, Sky thought. *I think I like her.*

"It is Wednesday," Norelco said.

"So it is, Doctor. So, you are doubly lucky the cooks made a mistake."

Norelco reddened and picked up the chopsticks attached to the lid of his bowl.

Sky fumbled with her chopsticks but managed to lift a piece of shrimp to her mouth without dropping it. It was delicious, without the mealy consistency of the shrimp found so often in lower-quality fabricators.

"Tempura is Jesuit food, you know," the mother superior said as she ate.

"It's Japanese," Sky objected.

"Fifteen-eighty, Old Reckoning, Nagasaki. The Jesuit brothers fried vegetables during Lent when they abstained from meat, using the term 'tempora,' as in 'temporary.' The Japanese acquired a taste for fried foods, and 'tempura' was born. Hence, this is a Jesuit dish. And you're welcome."

Sky didn't know if the mother superior was pulling her leg or not, but she was going to look it up the minute she left.

"So, what's on your agenda next?" the mother superior asked, changing the subject.

She kept eating, but Sky could see the woman was hanging on her answer.

"We are on to Gethsemane to see Archbishop Teluride."

The meeting with the governor would be her first official attempt to bring the Brotherhood into *d'lato* status. The planetary governor knew why she was here, of course, and the back-channels had been heating up, but her meeting was also a bit of show for the Klethos. There had been no communications with the Klethos since the meeting in Brussels, so no one knew what they were thinking, but the secretary-general, with the full concurrence of the heads of the various states, felt that Sky had to proceed with her mission. This had been somehow thrust upon her shoulders, and she had to show the Klethos that the UAM was serious in maintaining honor.

"He's a good man, Doctor Ybarra," the mother superior quietly told her. "This is out of his hands, but he understands the role he has to play."

Sky stared at her tempura, afraid to raise her head. The monastery was an independent enclave on a Brotherhood world. The Jesuits at the monastery were not Brotherhood citizens, but it was not surprising that the mother superior was well connected with the planetary government. What she'd just revealed was the first bit of intel she'd received, something she doubted that her side knew. As soon as she left the monastery, she had to relay that back to Earth.

She was trying to come up with a diplomatic way to acknowledge the advice when another monk entered the hall, searched the sitting monks, and hurried over to the mother superior. He bent over and whispered into her ear, and Sky saw her relaxed expression harden into something almost frightening in its determination.

She stood up, and in a surprisingly piercing voice, yelled out, "Everyone, leave the dining hall and report to your labs to await further instructions."

Sky joined the monks in looking at the mother superior in confusion.

What's going on?

The mother superior's next words struck a primal fear into Sky's heart.

"The Dictymorphs are landing in the valley. We are under attack."

Chapter 35

Hondo

Hondo was still glowering over the razzing from the first sergeant and Hanaburgh when high in the afternoon sky, something caught his eye. He zoomed in, and his stomach lurched. He'd seen the orange-glowing spheres before, on Purgamentium.

The Grubs were landing.

Almost immediately, sirens started blaring, and his display lit up.

"Alpha Company, all hands to Checkpoint Golf," the skipper passed on the command net.

Hondo had already started to run down to the camp, but he turned to go back uphill to rejoin the first sergeant and Hanaburgh. He skidded to a stop, then looked back down. Below him, one of the new plasma cannons—adjusted to become what was essentially a flamethrower on steroids—started to fire, reaching up to splash one of the spheres. The second cannon fired, hitting another, bathing it in a blanket of flame. Both spheres glowed brighter for a moment before they collapsed in on themselves.

"Get some!" the first sergeant said.

No one had known how the new cannons would work, but evidently, they were pretty effective. More and more spheres were appearing over the valley, though. Could two cannons hold them off?

PFC Pickerul pounded up the road to join them.

"What do we do?" she asked.

"Hold on, the skipper's on his way," the first sergeant said.

Hondo watched the cannons shift to more spheres, knocking out four more in a matter of ten or fifteen seconds. As on Purgamentium, the Grubs didn't seem to be able to fire their light weapons while in their spheres.

"They're sitting ducks," Hondo said.

The gods of war are fickle, and as if listening to Hondo, they flipped the script. From the far ridgeline, a finger of light shot across the valley floor to strike one of the cannons. There was an explosion, probably the powerplant going up.

"What the . . ." Hanaburgh said.

The light tendril shifted, tearing up camp buildings as it walked across the camp. The buildings were collateral damage, Hondo knew. The target was the second cannon. He zoomed in his display, and he could see the gun tube start to traverse towards the origin of the Grub beam, but it had barely moved when the light tendril hit it. The tube sagged as if made of wax, then the powerplant erupted in flames.

"The Grubs put a team up there," the first sergeant said. "How the hell no one picked that up . . ."

"We underestimated them again," Hondo said.

"Let's just hope they underestimated us, too," Hanaburgh added, as the first of the spheres landed a couple of klicks outside the camp.

Within moments, the spheres started to dissolve, and the Grubs unrolled themselves. To Hondo's surprise, they didn't immediately launch into the attack, as if they were waiting for the rest of them to land. That didn't bode well. The simple fact that they had somehow inserted a couple of them in the far ridgeline to support the landing told him they were developing coordinated tactics, and that wasn't good news for the home team. Any human success so far had been due to better tactics, not more powerful weapons.

Coming around the bend, a flatbed appeared, flanked by four PICS Marines.

"Here comes the skipper," the first sergeant told them.

Hondo zoomed in, and he saw the company commander and Gunny Gustav on the bed. They'd picked up Morales from the main gate as well. He pulled up his display and saw that the PICS Marines escorting them were Tony B, Joseph, the lieutenant, and RP.

By now, there were a dozen Grubs on the ground, and they started to move off, but not towards the camp. They were heading in the direction of Berea, some 30 klicks down the valley, but sharply visible in the clear air. At the edge of the city was the second refugee camp, and if the Grubs were going to attack, they'd go right through the camp.

"First Sergeant, Camp Bravo," Hondo said.

"What about it?"

He'd forgotten for a moment that the first sergeant wasn't in a PICS, and he couldn't just zoom in.

"The Grubs are heading right for it."

There was a pause, then the first sergeant said, "We've got more Grubs landing here. Just wait for the skipper."

It didn't seem right. Hondo pretty much hated the Brotherhood right now, but those were civilians, and they were going to get slaughtered.

From the city, an aircraft rose. Hondo zoomed in further. It was an Air Guard fighter, but an ancient one, which probably explained why it wasn't on the other side of the planet fighting in the main action.

Except, is that the main action? Hondo wondered. *Or was that a feint to draw all the fighting forces away from here?*

There had been significant discussion about why the Grubs had attacked the more sparsely-populated eastern hemisphere instead of the western. Forty clicks from the assembly area in the other direction was Gethsemane, the planetary capital and largest city, and right behind him was the monastery, which was evidently a center of Grub research.

Hondo thought he might be reading too much into the Grubs, giving them too much credit. The Marines weren't even here when the Grubs landed, so they didn't have to be "drawn off." There had been a strong Brotherhood force, though.

The old Brotherhood fighter rose up a couple of thousand meters, then gracefully turned on itself and started to dive back to the surface. On Purgamentium, a Navy Shrike had blown several spheres out of the sky, but the Brotherhood fighter looked to be three generations older, and instead of the spheres still descending, it went for the Grubs on the ground.

There were flickers of light as the fighter opened up on the Grubs. Hondo shifted his view. He could see the impacts on two of the Grubs, but he couldn't tell if they were having any effect. Light tendrils from three of the Grubs reached out to meet with each other, then a stronger, straighter beam of light shot out from that confluence towards the fighter. Hondo shifted again just in time to see the fighter disintegrate, pieces spreading out as they fell to the ground.

"Shit," Pickerul muttered.

The flatbed slowed down, and Captain Ariç jumped out before it had come to a complete stop.

"Lieutenant Abrams, form your defensive line," she shouted, before starting to run up the path to the gate of the monastery. "I'll be back as soon as I can."

"Sergeant McKeever, I want you on along the road on both sides of the crest here. Push your Marines out 200 meters. Get someone else down the slope to the knob there," he passed, pointing down the hill to the west, perpendicular to the road, where a protruding rock knob gave good fields of fire down the slope.

"Sir, that's a big area. I don't have the troops for that."

"Just do, it, Sergeant," the lieutenant snapped back. "When Sergeant Riordan gets here, you'll shift, giving her from here to the north back towards the camp."

"Aye, aye, sir," Hondo said, surprised at the lieutenant's tone.

"Listen up," the lieutenant continued, this time on the platoon net, which, for all intents and purposes, was now the company net. "We have one mission and one mission only: that's to defend the monastery. Whatever happens below, to the camp, to the refugees, this is our mission. Understand?"

When no one answered, he repeated, "I said understand? I want a positive acknowledgment, now!"

The Marines entered their acknowledgments, both those in Hondo's First Squad as well as Cara's Second who were still donning their PICS back in camp.

"Get to it, Sergeant," the lieutenant passed again on the P2P.

"Uh . . . sir? What about Lance Corporal Morales? He's not in a PICS," he asked hesitantly, not wanting to set his platoon commander off again.

"He's a fucking Marine, Sergeant," the lieutenant said, before cutting the connection.

Lieutenant Abrams had been somewhat moody since the fight with the Brotherhood, but this was the first time Hondo had ever heard him curse. It wasn't like him.

Hondo shook it off and placed his Marines, putting Hanaburgh and his Weapons Pack Four on the knob down the hill, which was the most exposed position, and hence the most dangerous. He could have put RP there, but Hanaburgh had proven himself in combat where the more gung-ho but somewhat flighty RP had not.

Sorry, Burger, but it's got to be you.

"Where do you want me?" the first sergeant asked, which surprised the heck out of him.

First Sergeant Nordstrand was the senior Marine in the company, he was not in a PICS, and he was still wounded. Why was he asking a sergeant where he should be?

"Uh, maybe with the skipper?" he asked, pointing to the gate to the monastery.

"He doesn't need me, son, and you do. You're kind of thin here."

"But you aren't armed, First Sergeant."

That wasn't technically true. The first sergeant had his M99, but that would be ineffective if the Grubs attacked them.

"*Au contraire, mon* sergeant," the first sergeant said, walking over to the flatbed where he reached along the side and pulled out a pike, the same kind that the Marines had used on K-1003.

He handed that to Morales, who was standing looking rather unsure of himself, then grabbed another for his own use. Stepping back to Hondo, he brandished it over his head.

"I'm armed."

Hondo, trying to couch his words, said, "First Sergeant, that's all well and good, but the pikes, they're older technology, and well . . . " he trailed off, pointing at the man's bad right shoulder.

"Lucky I've got two arms, Sergeant. And these might be older tech, but they work. You saw that. Me and Morales, we're ready, right?" he asked, turning to the lance corporal.

Morales did not look like he was ready as he dubiously looked at the pike, but he replied, "Yes, First Sergeant."

Hondo had said his piece, and it had been rejected. The first sergeant outranked him, and if he wanted in on the fight, there wasn't much he could do about it.

"Why don't you two take the gate, First Sergeant?" he asked, although if the Grubs got that far, he was pretty sure the cause would already be lost.

"Yes, sir, *mon* sergeant," the first sergeant said, stomping a foot to come to attention and snapping out an open-palmed salute like a legionnaire.

"He's fucking crazy," Pickerul said, as the first sergeant gathered up Morales and left to take his position. "What was he speaking?"

"Maybe he *is* crazy, but who the hell isn't?" Hondo said. "And I think he was trying to speak French."

"Like I said, crazy," Pickerul said.

He stepped over the edge of the road and looked down to where Hanaburgh was already in position. Over the lance corporal's shoulder, the valley stretched out. A dozen Grubs were making their way south towards Berea. Thirty or forty were out of their spheres, with five heading towards the camp. Another ten or so were still descending. If the dozen still continued on their way, that left about fifty facing the camp and possibly the monastery. Between Hondo and Cara, they had 15 PICS Marines including the lieutenant. The detachment from 2/14 had another 13. That would not be enough, even if the 60 or so cats and dogs were added to the mix. For all the first sergeant's enthusiasm, Hondo didn't think any of the non-suited Marines and corpsmen would stand much of a chance against a Grub.

"Sergeant, the refugees in Camp Alpha are in panic mode," Hanaburgh passed, as he looked down at the camp from his vantage point. "Some are climbing the slope to us."

Hondo stepped off of the road bed and down to him, carefully placing each step. His gyros would keep him upright, but the footing was loose, and he could still start a long fall down to the valley floor. He reached Hanaburgh and looked over the lip of the shoulder. Camp Alpha was located between the Marine camp and the base of the hill. Hundreds, if not thousands, of refugees were streaming out of the camp. With the dozen Grubs visible farther to the west, no one was heading in that direction. Some were running for the Marine camp despite more Grubs being on the other side of it, some were running south along the base of the hill. A crowd, however, was climbing up the steep slope, heading right towards the monastery.

"Sir, we've got refugees heading our way," Hondo passed to the lieutenant.

"Block the road. No one is to approach the monastery."

"Not on the road, sir. They're coming up the slope from Camp Alpha."

"Wait one," the lieutenant said. He came back twenty seconds later and said, "Keep them away. Warn them that they need divert to the south at least five hundred meters where they can get on Alverson."

"What force is authorized if they refuse?" Hondo asked, praying he wouldn't hear what he feared.

No one listened to his prayer, because the lieutenant said, "Lethal force, if necessary."

"Do what you have to do to keep them away from the monastery. They can move down 500 meters, then reach the road," he relayed to Hanaburgh.

"How am I supposed to do that, Sergeant?"

The snap-snap-snap of Chimera missiles reached them. Out in the camp, Marines were engaging the Grubs in the valley.

"I think they're more afraid of them than us," Hanaburgh said, pointing.

"Just do it. Use lethal force if you have to."

"What? They're civilians!"

"Just do it. Lieutenant's orders, and they're probably coming from on high."

Hanaburgh swiveled to look at him, and Hondo could see his expression through the faceplate. He wasn't happy.

"I'm not saying to kill anyone. But if you make them think you will, then they'll steer clear."

"I hope you're right, because I'm telling you now, Sergeant, I ain't going to kill anyone. We're here to protect them. And what the hell's so important about the monastery, anyway?"

"I don't know. Lots of research going on in there. Our grappling hooks came from what they discovered.

"So, evacuate them and be done with it. Bring them to Tarawa and let them work there, for that matter."

"Maybe, but that's not what's happened. Look, the lead ones are halfway up here. Get going."

"I'm not shooting anyone," Hanaburgh said, then he stepped to the edge of the drop-off, cranked up his externals, and started yelling at the people to shift to their right.

The lead people stopped, looked up at him, and shifted ten meters or so.

"That's five hundred meters, Hanaburgh," Hondo said, before he left him and climbed back up to the roadbed.

"Sergeant McKeever, Sergeant Riordan's almost here. She's got Staff Sergeant Rutledge with her. What do you want me to do?" Corporal Johnson asked.

"Shift back to me. We're going to take right here at the gate and back down the road to the south. Ask Sergeant Riordan to take from where you are now and up the road to link with us."

"Roger that. She's coming up to me now."

"Wolf, are there any Grubs to the east of the camp?"

"No, they're out in the valley, but most are closing in on the camp now."

"OK, thanks. I'll see you back up here."

While there at the top of the hill, the view was extensive, the curve of the west-facing slope blocked Hondo's view to the base of it by the edge of the camp. He needed to make sure the approach up the road from the camp was under observation. The Grubs might be big, and they seemed slow, but they had an uncanny ability to show up where they weren't expected.

Wolf showed up ten minutes later, Joseph and RP in tow. Leaving Pickerul right at the crest, he sent the three to fill in along the road as it descended back towards the south. Their frontage was now more in line with the SOP, but this wasn't a defensive line. The Grubs could bypass them entirely and hit the monastery from behind, and there wasn't much the Marines could do about it.

The skipper and two people in white labs coats came out, looked over the valley, then gestured several times at the hillside before returning back inside.

"What was that about?" Pickerul asked.

"Not for us to try and guess."

He did wonder, though. The skipper had looked agitated about something, and if something wasn't right, then it could affect his Marines.

Hanaburgh was doing a masterly job of diverting the civilians. He strode back and forth, his speakers on max as he yelled, cajoled, and threatened them to get them to shift to the right. Several times, like sheep escaping the sheepdog, people would break and try and climb to the road too soon, and his Marines had to try and shoo them back down. Luckily, no one had to fire their weapon.

All the time they were playing traffic cop to the refugees, below them, Grubs continued the unstoppable push toward both Berea and the camp. The Marines from 2/14 were engaging long-range, but the Grubs heading towards the camp were not yet returning fire.

With a scream of tortured air, two Gen 5 Brotherhood Air Guard atmospheric fighters blasted directly over the monastery, inverted, and dove on the Grubs heading for the city. They fired a salvo of missiles before pulling some impossible G's to loop back. From the far ridge, another finger of light reached out, enveloping one of them. A purplish-orange aura coalesced around the plane, but still it flew, scrambling to get clear.

"Come on, make it," Hondo muttered, trying to will the fighter back over the near hills.

It broke up before reaching safety, coming apart into a thousand pieces and splattering the hillside a klick away from them. Hondo shifted to take the Grubs in view, but the same dozen were still moving forward, seemingly unfazed by the attack.

"Nothing's stopping them," Pickerul said. "Look at that."

"They're not within grappling hook range," Hondo said. "Wait until they get closer."

At 500 meters, the front rank of Grubs started sending ropes of light across the nearest camp buildings, as if spraying water from garden hoses. Buildings started collapsing. Inside them, he knew Marines were dying. He couldn't see them, and he refused to zoom in. He still knew it.

The Marines on the front had reported decent results from the modulated sonic cannon. It turned Grubs away and could even kill one of the bastards, but if the 2/14 Marines were using them, they were having no effect. Maybe the distance was still too great, or maybe the Grubs had already adjusted to the weapon.

"Joseph, if they come up here, don't employ your sonics until they get within 150 meters."

Down the road, the PFC waved the bulky, odd-looking weapon in the air and passed, "Roger that, Sergeant."

He was the only Marine in the squad with one of them, and Hondo wasn't convinced as to how robust the thing was. It looked pretty flimsy to him—the bell, in particular, looked like it could be snapped off in a heavy wind. He didn't want Joseph to go crazy with it before the Grubs were within range.

A single stream of fire reached out from the camp's fence line. It fell just short of the nearest Grub, and immediately, two of them shot their light tendrils at the spot. No more flames reached out.

"Steady, guys. Wait," Hondo muttered.

As with the Grubs heading south to the city, the ones moving on the camp were advancing in rough ranks, with eight in the first one. Those first eight sped up as they closed, and several streams of fire arched over the closing distance to splash five of them. Hondo zoomed in when he heard the distant bangs of grappling hooks, spotting at least a dozen reaching out to pin several of the enemy.

How many PICS does Fox have? Not that many, for sure.

Which meant that the cats and dogs, those in the rear party, had to be fighting without combat suits. Hondo had met a Grub in his longjohns and only survived the encounter by a stroke of luck. The un-armored Marines and sailors in the camp had the odds stacked against them.

The Grub farthest from him, upon being hit, swung a pseudopod like a scythe, cutting the line on the hook. The line was a molecularly bonded ceramic—it should not have parted, and the same line had held fast against Grubs before, but it came apart this time as if it was crepe paper.

The grappling hook still gave the thing a jolt, but without the line, no more energy could be passed through. It was one and done.

Where the flamethrowers connected, those Grubs did not seem to be able to cut the lines. One other was hit with three hooks. It managed to cut one before it started going into spastic convulsions.

"Are you watching this?" Hondo passed on the platoon net to both squads. "We've got to double up on them."

Three of the eight Grubs slammed into the camp fence, not even pausing as they flowed into the camp proper. The second rank of Grubs galumphed past the dying in the first rank, just as one of them imploded in a brilliant flash of white light.

The upgrades to the hooks are working, at least.

The previous versions had never killed a Grub so quickly.

Five out of fifty was nothing, however. Within moments, half of the remaining Grubs were in the camp, like Godzilla in Tokyo, using their bulk as much as anything else to flatten buildings.

They're saving their energy, he realized.

In previous battles, the fight had boiled down to making the Grubs expend their energy. Like a PICS when the powerpack ran out, they couldn't fight. Unlike a PICS, though, when a Grub ran out of power, they either imploded and collapsed, or they used the last of their power to go out with a bang. Hondo didn't know the math, but he was pretty sure that simply crushing an expeditionary shelter with their mass used less energy than using their light-based weapons.

The Marines below didn't roll over and surrender. They were putting up a fight, and grappling hooks, flamethrowers, and missiles were fired, but individually, not in a concerted massing of fire. Grubs fell, but more entered the camp.

Hondo had seen a documentary once, of the War in the Pacific during World War II. On one of the islands—Iwo Jima, he thought it was—the Marines had hit the beach. Many of the old films were taken from aboard the ships out as sea, safe and sound, while a couple of klicks away, US Marines and

Japanese soldiers were dying. Hondo felt like that now. He was safe—for the moment, at least—while down there in the camp, his fellow Marines were being slaughtered. True, some Grubs had been killed as well, but not enough.

The camp was going to fall, that was pretty evident. Hondo was pretty sure they'd be next.

"You doing OK?" he asked Hanaburgh, shifting his attention off of the camp.

"It's herding cats, but I'm managing."

The lance corporal had been running back and forth along the fall line, haranguing, begging, and threatening to keep the people moving. Hondo slaved into his display and was shocked. He'd imagined fifty or sixty refugees still climbing, but there had to be a couple of thousand, a mass of panicking humanity. The pack was moving south, some at the bottom, some on the sides of the slope.

"Just keep them going," Hondo said. "The camp is about to fall."

Captain Ariç came out of the monastery with a monk, took the first sergeant under her tow, and came to the road where she could see the camp. She and the first sergeant were having a heated discussion. Hondo was tempted to turn up his pick-ups, but he held back. If the skipper wanted him to know what she was saying, she'd be broadcasting.

After a few moments, the three jogged back up the path: the skipper and the monk to go back in, the first sergeant to resume his position with Morales. Within twenty seconds, the lieutenant was back on the net.

"Change of plans. Staff Sergeant Rutledge, Sergeant Riordan, you're going to get off the road and move to higher ground. We want to canalize the Grubs off of the road and to the ground just above it."

Hondo shifted his gaze. "Just above" the road, the rough terrain was somewhat flat up to a 30-meter wall that ran from 40 meters to the south of the gate and then to the shear rock wall of the bones of the hill 80 meters to the north. He only now noticed a monk—or as he was not in robes, at least a technician—making what looked to be readings along the wall.

They think that's strong enough to hold back a Grub?

He didn't think so.

"We're still going to try and stop them, but if any of them are going to get past us, it has to be right there."

It sounded like a stupid plan to him, but those were the orders. First Squad remained in place, but Cara took her squad and pushed them back along the upper slope. The platoon's line was 400 meters along the road to the south, up to the gate, then breaking west of the road and into the upper slope.

And Hanaburgh, downslope with the refugees.

This isn't good!

Hondo was not wedded to all the Marine Corps pubs on how to fight, but those pubs were out there for a reason. Simple things like mutually supporting fields of fire made sense, and the way they were set up now, that just wasn't there. Tony B, the farthest-most Marine, was left out there hanging, with only RP and Joseph able to support him if it came to that.

"Sir, I'd like to bring Lance Corporal Hanaburgh back up to us," he passed to the lieutenant on the P2P.

There was a pause, and the indicator light let him know the lieutenant was slaved into Hanaburgh's cam. Hondo piggybacked on that, and the mass of refugees on the slope below had not diminished.

"No, leave him there. We can't let the refugees up here." There was another pause, then, "It's safer for them if they don't get caught up in this."

Hondo couldn't tell if the lieutenant was sure of that or trying to convince himself it was true.

"No, belay that. If the Grubs head straight up the hill at him, recall him back, OK? We can't leave him out there alone, civilians or not," he said, to Hondo's relief.

"Roger that. Thank you, sir."

Hondo switched to Hanaburgh's P2P and said, "I just spoke with the lieutenant. If the Grubs come up the hill at you, hightail it back to the road. You aren't going to meet them head-on by yourself."

"What about the people?"

Hondo didn't like that either, and it hurt him to say it, but he had to look at the bigger picture, and if the Grubs came up the hill instead of the road, Hanaburgh wasn't going to be able to keep them alive.

"They're going to have to fend for themselves," he said, then cut off the net before Hanaburgh could respond.

"The Grubs are moving past the camp," Corporal Wojcik, Cara's surviving NCO, passed.

Hondo turned from Hanaburgh and ran down the road until he could see down into the entire camp. Most of the camp was leveled, and sixteen Grubs had passed through the other side and against the base of the hill.

Which way are you going? Hondo wondered as the Grubs milled about, seemingly without a specific target.

He refused to wish that they would head south, to join the ones heading to Berea, but the thought was hovering at the back of his mind.

Five more joined them, and as if that made a quorum, six turned to the south while fifteen headed for the road, jostling each other as they funneled onto it.

"They're on Alverson," Hondo passed, "And coming our way. Fifteen of them at the moment."

Lieutenant Abrams joined him a moment later, then he gave a flurry of orders to Second Squad. Hondo counted five of them on the road before he ran back to Pickerul in front of the path to the gate.

"Get ready," he told her. "They're coming."

"Telltales on," the captain passed. "We've got Shrikes inbound, ETA two minutes, danger close."

"You heard the skipper, telltales on!" Hondo passed, suddenly much more confident.

The Navy Shrikes had proven quite capable against the Grubs on Purgamentium. Hondo knew there was a squadron with the main force, but he hadn't expected the CG to release two to fly halfway across the planet to support them. The Shrikes weren't Marine birds, though, and the friendly identification system did not always synch, so the Marines had telltales, letting the universe know who and where they were. In combat, these would also let the enemy know the same thing, but if the Grubs could even pick up the signals, it was too late to matter now. They already knew.

Hondo couldn't quite see the last two Marines in Second Squad, but he saw a stream of flames reach out to disappear from his view.

Are they already that close?

As a squad leader, Hondo could only slave to his Marines' PICS, not Second Squad's.

Fingers of light reached back up to the Marines. The battle was joined.

Hondo scanned the skies, looking for the Shrikes. They needed the help.

Lance Corporal Hodge's avatar grayed out. He'd been the Marine farthest to the north.

"Cara, how many are on the road?" he asked in the P2P.

There was no response. Hondo wanted to ask again, but he held back. He shouldn't be diverting any of her attention.

Finally, there was a scream of tortured air as the first Shrike popped up from the north. Immediately the Grubs on the far ridgeline shot out their light tendril, which enveloped the aircraft, but still, it bore in, releasing its payload before pulling a barrel roll that took it up and over the monastery and breaking the hold of the Grub's light weapon.

An instant later, all hell broke loose on the hill, shaking the ground under Hondo and making his servos whine to keep him upright. Dust rose up from the hillside where the Shrike's ordnance had hit.

"That took out six for sure," Corporal Wojcik passed. "'Bout took me out, too."

"We've got civilians down," Hanaburgh passed.

"How many?" Captain Ariç asked.

"I don't know. Maybe a hundred? It looks pretty bad."

"Get them moving. We've got the second Shrike inbound."

Below Hondo, Hanaburgh was a madman, running back and forth, screaming at the refugees. Their cries of panic reached all the way to the road. Down past Tony B, the first of them had reached the road and were now rushing to put some distance between them.

The second Shrike started its run, and this time, the enemy on the far side were silent. Hondo hoped that meant that they were low on energy. Smaller tendrils of light reached up, but they had no effect on the plane as it dove down.

It released its payload and pulled up just as a powerful tendril of light reached out across the valley floor, piercing the air just below and behind the Shrike—and the entire sky lit up. The Shrike started tumbling ass-end over the front, smoke pouring from it as the shock wave hit Hondo, rocking him.

"They took out the bombs, not the plane," Hondo said in wonder.

And used its own bombs against it.

The Shrike was in a bad way as her pilot struggled to save her. The plane cartwheeled over the road and disappeared past the crest of the hill.

"Here they come," Corporal Wojcik passed.

"Funnel them to the monastery wall," the skipper passed.

"Pickerul, McKeever, with me!" the lieutenant shouted, as he bolted past Hondo towards Second Squad.

Without thinking, Hondo was on his platoon commander's ass, pounding back up the road. Cara's Marines dotted the upper hillside, and they were letting loose on the Grubs coming up the road, the first just now coming into view as it charged forward.

"Support me!" the lieutenant shouted as he stopped in the middle of the road, legs apart, the very image of an old American west sheriff, waiting for the bandits to ride into town.

Hondo stopped off of the lieutenant's left shoulder, Pickerul to his right. As the lead Grub charged forward, the lieutenant started his flamethrower and marched straight ahead. The flames splashed the Grub, and it contracted slightly as a light tendril reached out to hit the platoon commander.

Hondo had ten grappling hooks in his magazine. He stepped farther to the left so as not to hit the lieutenant and fired, sending the hook into the Grub's side, while Pickerul fired a salvo of shoulder rockets.

Whether it was the flames, hook, or rockets, the Grub swerved left, off the road and right where the skipper wanted them canalized. Hondo started lowering his launcher, but the lieutenant had broken into a run, screaming like a madman, flames sweeping in front of him.

"Keep with him, Tammy!" Hondo yelled at Pickerul.

There were four more Grubs on the road—the rest of the 15 must have been taken out by the first Shrike. As the lieutenant charged, spraying the first with fire, the Grub barely hit him with a light tendril before it left the road as well in trace of the first. One after the other, the next three followed, the lieutenant spraying each as they passed.

"Ooh-rah, Lieutenant!" Pickerul shouted, firing another salvo of three rockets that slammed into the side of the last Grub.

Hondo was slack-jawed in amazement. That was either the bravest or stupidest thing he'd ever seen. Maybe it was both. And the fact that the lieutenant was standing there, upright and alive, was unbelievable. Hell, the fact that all three were alive was unbelievable.

He turned to watch the Grubs close in on the monastery, wondering why they'd been allowed to approach. The lead Grub slowed down, raised its front section slightly, then morphed into a lower, squatter form, reminiscent of a medieval battering ram. It picked up speed and slammed into the smooth wall . . .

. . . and exploded into a fireball or light, heat, and globs of Grub-flesh.

What the hell just happened?

Chapter 36
Skylar

"It worked!" Brother Joplin said, sounding surprised.

Dr. Iolana Ka'aukai leaned over and hugged him, kissing the top of his head and saying, "It sure did."

Sky let out the huge breath she'd been holding. The sight of the charging Dictymorphs, even over the monitor, had dredged up old fears, fears she'd thought she'd repressed.

Now looking at Brother Joplin and Dr. Ka'aukai, she realized that they hadn't been sure the phase-neutralizers would work either, despite what the mother superior had assured Captain Ariç. Sky looked over to the woman, and the cool calm she had been showing was gone—she had taken a seat and had now raised a trembling hand to her brow, her eyes closed. Sky didn't know if she was praying or in shock.

Brother Joplin and Dr. Ka'aukai, a visiting fellow from the Kingdom of Hiapo, had been working on the neutralizer for the last nine months. It hadn't been close to being fielded, but the Dictymorphs had sped up the schedule with their arrival. Even so, this had been amazing.

The theory behind the weapon was sound. They had understood the basic weaponry of the Dictymorphs for some time now; the question was how to combat it.

The Dictymorphs used an organic light, similar to the oxyluciferin created by some Earth funguses. Unlike Earth organisms, however, the Dictymorphs could focus that light much like a laser, and they powered it from energy sources inside their bodies.

Scientists had immediately suggested ways to combat the creatures, one being to attack the wavelengths of the weapons. Some suggested "cancelling" them out in the same way that noise-cancelling headphones worked. Brother Joplin had a different idea: he wanted to resonate with the wavelengths and hit a harmonic frequency. After inviting Dr. Ka'aukai, a renowned expert on bioluminescence, they had progressed in a surprisingly short period of time, and they had created their first beta model for testing. What they didn't have was a projector, a way to weaponize it, but when needs arise, humans can be extremely innovative.

One of the other brothers had suggested using the outer wall as a projector, like a big drumhead. With a flurry of activity, the beta model was moved to the prayer room, which abutted the outer wall.

Sky had joined the monastery's leaders in the main lab while Brother Joplin sat ready to turn the weapon on. Then, almost too quickly to follow, the Dictymorphs were there, big as elephants as they charged. One moment they filled the monitor, the next, the first one exploded.

No, not "exploded." It simply came apart. The "explosion" was just the thing's energy being released.

One after the other, all five of them hit the wall, and all five of them were killed. The monks in the lab cheered and smacked elbows.

"Where are we at, Brother Joplin? Are we ready for more?" the Mother Superior asked, leaning forward, in control of herself again.

"We overloaded the generators, but we can get that back online," Brother Joplin said, looking at his readouts. "And it looks like the propagation isn't what we'd hoped. If they'd hit us another 30 meters to their right, I don't think it would have worked."

"Maybe if we adjusted the D-scrambler, to say . . . zero-point-six?" Dr. Ka'aukai asked.

"That could do it," Brother Joplin replied. "And if—"

"Brother Joplin, before you and Doctor Ka'aukai get lost, when will it be up again?" the mother superior asked.

"I don't know. Maybe an hour?"

Sky shifted to look at the monitors that covered the valley floor. There were still forty or fifty Grubs down there, and already another dozen were moving to the road from the Marine camp. She didn't think they had an hour.

"You've got ten minutes, Brother. Get it done."

Brother Joplin glanced at Dr. Ka'aukai, and she sat down, fingers flying over their control board.

"I'm going to leave you now," Captain Ariç said, coming up behind her and Foue.

"But, what can you do out there? We need you here," Sky said, a touch of panic rising inside her.

Having the Marine captain inside the control lab had been a reassuring comfort. Sky had been rescued by Marines twice, and she trusted them. She didn't want the woman to leave.

"I can't do anything else in here. I know that. And those are my Marines out there. In another five, maybe ten minutes, they're going to be fighting for their lives—your lives, too, I might add. And I need to be there with them."

She gave a curt half bow, then spun around and marched out of the room.

No one seemed to notice her as she left.

Chapter 37
Hondo

"The skipper?" Pickerul said.

"What?" he asked, turning to see Captain Ariç at the flatbed, pulling out a pike.

"I guess the shit's about to get real," Pickerul said.

If what just went down wasn't real, then I'm not sure I want to see it when it is.

The skipper shook the pike a few times, then went to join the first sergeant and Morales at the gate.

Hondo was still trying to process what had just happened. The five Grubs had just blown up, but he hadn't seen how. He asked the lieutenant, but the man just mumbled something unintelligible back at him. The platoon commander seemed dazed, so Hondo had left it at that.

"Alpha Company, the five Grubs that were just killed were because of a new weapon the brothers developed. The thing is, employing it blew the power supply, so it's going to take a bit of time to get it back online. And it only works there on that section of the wall. The gate here, it isn't covered. Until they get the weapon back online, it's up to us to protect the monastery. What they're doing in there—hell, it would blow your mind. The bottom line is that what they're doing could turn the tide. It could give us the upper hand. I think the Grubs know that somehow. I think they want to destroy it. And right now, another wave of them is heading our way."

Hondo spun around to look down the road, but he couldn't see anything.

"Whatever we do, we've got to keep the Grubs out of the monastery until they can get the neutralizer back online."

"Skipper, but you said that weapon is only on that section of the wall. What if they go around?" Cara asked.

"Then we're shit out of luck, Sergeant Riordan, so let's pray they don't."

"Uh, Skipper? I see them. Maybe a dozen or more, and they're coming fast," Corporal Wojcik passed.

"It's time to earn our salaries, boys and girls," the skipper said.

"Sergeant McKeever," Hanaburgh broke in the moment the skipper finished. "I've got six Grubs turning up the hill. They're crushing the civilians in their way."

"Lieutenant! Hanaburgh's got Grubs coming."

The platoon commander didn't respond.

Hondo took matters into his own hand and said, "Pull back. Get to the monastery gate."

"But they're being slaughtered!"

"There's nothing we can do about it now. Get back."

"And if they come all the way up here? They won't be at that magic wall, will they?"

Hondo hesitated. Hanaburgh was right. The gate did not have that weapon there, only three unarmored Marines wielding pikes.

"Sergeant, don't the Marines teach NCOs not to give orders that won't be obeyed? The fuckdicks sure do."

Hondo knew at that moment that Hanaburgh was going to try and stop the Grubs, both to save the refugees and maybe divert them from the gate area. And who knows? Maybe he could delay them enough for some other miracle. He might as well make it so Hanaburgh wasn't breaking orders to do it.

"Go for it, Robert. And hooah!"

"Fuck that, Sergeant. I'm a Marine now. Ooh-rah!" he shouted, before vaulting over the hill's shoulder and disappearing from view.

"He's something," Pickerul said, with what sounded like awe (or was it something else?) in her voice.

Hondo was about to reply, but the first Grubs hit Second Squad's position.

"Wolf, shift back uphill to the gate. Burger's got six Grubs coming up his way.

"Whatever happens, don't let them get past you to the skipper and the first sergeant," he told Pickerul, as he ran back to find the lieutenant, worried about his state of mind.

He could see the platoon commander's avatar, but as a squad leader, he couldn't pull up his vitals.

"Staff Sergeant, do you see the lieutenant?" he asked.

"We're up to our asses in Grubs here. I don't have the El-Tee watch."

Hondo rushed around the bend, afraid of what he might see, but whatever had put the lieutenant in a daze, it was gone. He was charging the Grubs again, a never-ending gout of fire spewing over the creatures. He was being hit in return; his shields had to be failing, but he didn't seem to care.

Hondo stepped forward, readied his hook at the Grub who was locked on the lieutenant, and fired. The hook plunged deep into the thing's side as charge after charge flowed into it.

Swinging around—and breaking the light tendril on the lieutenant—it raised a pseudopod which had flattened almost into a blade and swung down, slicing the line in two. A moment later, it lashed out at Hondo, his suit alarm blared its warning.

Hondo's instincts told him to dive away, but the lieutenant was still alive and fighting by taking it to the Grubs, so Hondo, against all logic and reason, ran forward, firing two more hooks.

The net was full of cat vidclips, some of kittens attacking big dogs that backed down. Hondo felt like one of those kittens, ready to be flattened. To his amazement, the Grub faltered. Hondo could have sworn that it was, well, scared? Did Grubs even feel fear?

The pseudopod from which the light tendril was being emitted flattened into the sword shape and sliced through one, then the other line, but instead of attacking him, it turned on itself and moved uphill, joining the rest of them as they burst through Second Squad's line.

"They're going to hit the monastery from the rear! After them!" Staff Sergeant Rutledge yelled out at max power.

Hondo looked around. Two of Cara's Marines and Doc Kekoa were down, and one Grub, alive but contracting into the ball, was bearing the brunt of the lieutenant's fury when his flame flickered, then petered out. He'd exhausted his supply of fuel.

Hondo turned and bolted back to his Marines. He arrived as Wolf, Tony B, Joseph, Doc Leach, and RP came running from the other direction.

"Nothing gets by us," Hondo said. "RP, Tony B, come with me. We're going to help Burger."

Hondo had been watching Hanaburgh's avatar, which somehow was still a bright, deep blue. But he couldn't hold out. With the Grubs on the road going to the rear of the monastery, the six down the hill facing the Marine were now the biggest threat, so he could justify going to help the former FCDC trooper.

He skidded down the slope, trusting his gyros to keep him upright. As he reached the shoulder, he could see a thousand people, fleeing in all directions. To his right and down the slope, a lone Marine was firing at six Grubs, which were maneuvering to surround him. They were firing back, and Hanaburgh's PICS was glowing under the onslaught.

"Now, move your asses!" he shouted, jumping forward—just as Hanaburgh collapsed, his avatar flickering between light-blue and gray for a moment until it settled on the gray.

Hell, Burger!

"Back up!" he ordered.

He couldn't do anything for the fallen Marine except hope he could be resurrected, and for any chance of that happening, the rest of them had to hold the field of battle.

The three reached the road, and then joined Wolf and the rest, spreading out in a half-circle around the path leading to the gate. Hondo tried to see what was happening to Cara, but they were out of sight. There were sounds of crashing, as if heavy construction crews were at work, and Hondo could imagine the Grubs breaking into the monastery.

Which made their protecting the entrance superfluous, like admiring the lock on the front door while the thieves went in the back window. But the skipper was there, and he knew they had at least six Grubs heading their way.

As if reading his thoughts, the skipper passed, "Another nine are heading up Alverson now."

"Just worry about what's in front of us," Hondo said.

"The six down the hill in front of us, or the nine coming up fucking Alverson in front of us?" Pickerul asked.

"Pick your poison, Tammy."

The sound of sliding scree reached them, and a moment later, the tops of two Grubs appeared.

"Fire!" Hondo shouted, as he sent his fifth hook out, glancing it off the top of a Grub, wasting it.

PFC Joseph, with his sonic projector, stepped up and fired. His target shuddered and contracted, but then with a screech—only the second time Hondo had ever heard a sound from one of them—it launched itself up the last 40 meters of hillside faster than Hondo would have thought possible. He fired another grappling hook, this one biting into the back of the beast, but it didn't seem to notice the current flowing into it.

Joseph took a step backwards just as the Grub slammed into him, almost breaking his sturdy PICS in two. His avatar grayed out immediately.

The Grub swung toward RP, but it was trembling, its movement herky-jerky. Hondo hit it with yet another hook, and this time, it collapsed on itself, deflating like an old balloon.

And then the rest were on them. Hondo fired his last three hooks, frying one of the Grubs and causing it to retreat. After the final hook, he switched to grenades. Wolf was throwing flames, hitting Hondo once, bathing him with fire but doing no harm. What *was* doing harm were the Grubs. Hondo's shields were dropping.

RP backed away, still with nine grappling hooks in his magazine.

"RP! So, help me, if you run, I'll come back to haunt your ass!" Hondo shouted.

In almost slow motion, the rear area warrior turned to Hondo, eyes wide behind his faceplate. He screwed up his face, then with a wordless scream, charged the nearest Grub, launcher out like a pike, and hit it, triggering all nine remaining pikes before his PICS gave out. The Grub stiffened, then blew, the shock wave managing to knock Hondo over before he could scramble back to his feet.

"Sergeant, the skipper!" Doc Leach shouted.

Hondo was moving slowly. His PICS wasn't working correctly, but he didn't have time to run an analysis. He turned to see one of the Grubs advancing on the gate. Morales was down, a wisp of smoke rising from his back, but the skipper and the first sergeant were standing shoulder-to-shoulder, pikes outstretched before them.

Hondo tried to fire his shoulder rockets, but nothing happened.

Snap the hell out of it, McKeever.

He focused on his readouts. He'd fired every piece of ordnance he had.

There were still pikes, though.

Hondo tried to force his balky legs to the flatbed, but the Grub charged before he could reach it. He grabbed one of the four or five pikes that were there just as the Grub reached the end of the path and slammed into the two unflinching Marines, flattening them against the ornate gate itself. The Grub shuddered, but then started pounding on it, using its own body as a battering ram.

With the pike in his hand, Hondo started running forward, his internal alarms blaring. His shields were gone, and power was being shunted to keep the suit moving. The Grub never turned, and one of the massive gates broke open just as Hondo drove the pike deep into its hind end. He let go, triggering the charge.

The result was spectacular, more than he would have expected. The Grub seemed to pull up, as if becoming taller and thinner at the same time. It went stiff, and the right half collapsed, like a Grub stroke victim. The left half still moved, and it dragged the rest of the body to the side where it went still.

All Hondo could figure was that the pikes that the skipper and the first sergeant had impaled it with hadn't activated until Hondo's set them off. All three at once had fried part of the Grub's interior circuitry.

Hondo turned back to get another pike, but for the moment, the fight was over. Joseph and PR were KIA. One

Grub was dead, and the one at the gate was wounded. He had no idea where the other four were.

"What happened? Where are the others?"

"On up the hill. I think they are trying to go around," Wolf said.

Hondo was frankly amazed that only five of them had been killed facing six Grubs. That had to be a record of some sort. But running through the status numbers, they couldn't do much else. Pickerul's PCS was dead, out of power, and she was in the process of molting. Tony B had 11 % of his shielding, while Wolf was at 2%. Doc's shielding was gone, and his power was not much better. No one had much in the way of ordnance.

"Can you raise the skipper?" Staff Sergeant Rutledge asked on the P2P.

"She's dead. First sergeant, too."

"I can't raise the lieutenant or the gunny, either. Well, hell. Looks like I've got the company. Not for long, though. You've got another twenty-one coming your way."

"Any chance of some help, Staff Sergeant? We're kinda running on empty here."

"Sorry, Hondo. We're in the same boat. We've got Grubs tearing up the back of the monastery, and they're almost inside. We've got enough for one last hurrah, but that's it, and there's no way we could make it there in time even if we tried."

"How long?"

"Four minutes. Five maybe?"

"Well, that's it, I guess. Kick some ass, Staff Sergeant."

"You, too, Hondo."

Hondo went over to the flatbed and pulled out the last four pikes, handing one to Wolf, Doc, and Tony B. He kept the fourth.

"What about me?" Pickerul asked.

"That's all we have," he said. "Form on me."

He took a position in the middle of the road while the other four, including Pickerul, came alongside him.

He turned his depleted PICS to her, and she said, "Well, nowhere else for me to be now."

Hondo had faced death twice before, and each time, a sense of calm flowed through him. This time was no different. He didn't want to die, but it came to everyone eventually. If the main body came back and kicked Grub ass, then he might get resurrected if he wasn't messed up too badly, but he wasn't putting any stock in that. If it happened, it happened.

"Shit, here comes more of them," Wolf said as Hondo's PICS' AI registered something behind him—up and behind him.

Hondo spun around, pissed that more Grubs were landing. But the objects descending looked different. It took him a moment to realize what they were: the cavalry.

The Klethos were landing.

Chapter 38
Hondo

"Damn, there's a shit-load of them," Pickerul said.

Hondo picked up a rock and threw it down the slope. He had molted as well, the third time he'd had to do that in combat. That had to be some kind of record as well.

The area was full of Klethos, at least a couple of thousand. Two hundred had landed around the monastery where they attacked the Grubs with their usual ferocity. Within 30 minutes, the hill was clear.

Down in the valley, the fight had taken a little longer, but twenty minutes ago, Grubs started rising in their spheres, a reverse landing. A retreat. The Klethos seemed willing to let them go.

"That's it, then,' Doc Leach said, sitting down beside them.

"How's it look?" Hondo asked, not wanting to hear the answer.

"RP, I don't think so. Morales and the skipper, no. The first sergeant and Joseph maybe. Hanaburgh, I think so."

"Really?" Hondo and Pickerul asked in unison.

"Yeah, really," he said, flipping a thumb back to where the bodies were lined up in the zip-locks. "In fact, I'd go out on a limb and say that there'll be no regen."

"Thank God for that," Pickerul said, leaning back on her elbows.

Hondo would never have thought that Hanaburgh, after facing down six Grubs, would ever have been a candidate for resurrection. But Doc's verdict put him in a better mood, despite the word on the others.

Wolf came to join them. He'd just molted, and he smelled. Pickerul frowned and scooted over a meter.

"What about him?" Wolf asked, pointing at Tony B.

"As long as he's got power, he stays in. It looks like the Klethos have everything under control, but who knows?"

"Oh, thanks, Sergeant," Tony B said over his externals.

Pickerul languidly raised a middle finger, not bothering to look at him.

"Any word on when we get out of here?"

"Nothing. Staff Sergeant Rutledge says to hold tight. We'll probably have to escort the VIPs back down to camp.

"Speaking of which," Wolf said, pointing back to the ruined gate where several people were exiting.

Hondo stood up, stretched, checked his sidearm, and went over to meet them. Three turned to their right and started examining the Grub body, the one that had seemed paralyzed up to the point that the Klethos killed it. But in the other group of seven, Hondo recognized the xenobiologist.

Her eyes widened in recognition as he came up, and she said, "Well, Sergeant McKeever, we keep seeming to meet each other."

"Yes, ma'am, we do."

"Sergeant McKeever has rescued me two times so far, Foue."

"It looks like he might have done it again," the woman she'd called Foue said with a soft French accent, as she pointed to the dead Grub.

"We are supposed to escort your party down to the camp, ma'am," he said. "Transport will arrive, but we aren't sure when."

"Well then, I guess we'll just have to wait." She turned to an older woman and said, "Thank you for your hospitality,

Mother Superior, but I'd just as soon not go through this again."

The older woman—did this grandmotherly-looking woman really run that huge monastery?—laughed, then took the xenobiologist's hand and said, "Things are not usually so exciting. Take care, child. I have a feeling your part in all of this will be significant."

The two women hugged, then the mother superior hugged the other woman and finally one of the men.

The xenobiologist turned to Hondo and said, "We're ready, Sergeant."

"Then let's get you out of here, ma'am."

SAINT BARNABAS

Chapter 39
Skylar

Sky strode along the Cobblestone Way, the 400-year-old stone pathway leading up to the First Cathedral Annex, the seat of government power on Saint Barnabas, the Brotherhood of Servants homeworld. Flanked by Foue and Norelco, the civil patrol kept the gathered crowds out of their way, but the people weren't looking at the three diplomats. Their eyes were locked on the Klethos quad who followed Sky.

Sky tried to exhibit a sense of righteous determination, chin out, eyes forward. Once again, she wondered how she'd landed in this position at a nexus of human—and Klethos—history. She had to produce.

It wasn't entirely on her shoulders. She had both Foue and Norelco, but more than that, on the other side of her earbud were her boss, the Second Minister, the Chairman of the Federation, the Confederation president, the Greater France president, and the UAM secretary-general. They'd been quiet since leaving the shuttle, but it was a nice safety blanket to know they were there.

The crowd was surprisingly quiet as well. There was no shouting, no demonstrations, just a slight recoil as the UAM party came abreast of them. Sky was tempted to yell "boo" just to see them jump.

They reached the 20-meter high double doors, made from the wood of an ancient kauri tree from New Zealand on Earth, which swung open for them as they approached. Sky didn't change her stride but stepped into the dark interior.

"This way, Mesdames Ambassador, Mister Ambassador," a white-robed official said, ignoring the four Klethos behind them.

All three of the humans had been granted temporary ambassador status for the purpose of this mission. It didn't matter to Sky, but it evidently did to the career diplomats.

Sky followed their guide down the Chandelier Passage to the Great Hall. She had no eye for the historical significance of the building. She just wanted to make sure that history was made today, and for the good.

Inside the Great Hall, the first brother sat in the center seat on the dais. She'd always thought that the robes worn by a first brother were rather plain for a head of state, but that was before meeting the Jesuits. Now, as she approached, she could see the detail in the robe that reflected its own kind of extravagance.

Flanking the first brother was the Alliance president, the Freedom Alliance secretary, and the Dentonian CEO.

"Only the first brother and the CEO are real. The other two are holograms," the voice in her earbud told her. "Just focus on the first brother."

Sky scanned the room until she spotted her old adversary, Bishop Van Meter, standing alongside the wall leading up to the dais. She let her gaze slide past him as if she hadn't noticed the man.

"Welcome, Ambassadors," the first brother said, his familiar voice resonating throughout the Great Hall and raising a tiny shiver in her spine.

He was a noted orator, but Sky wondered if he was having a little technical help with his voice. She shook off the shiver, and focused on his face, trying to read into it. His reaction, his decisions, would have grave ramifications.

"Thank you, First Brother. The three of us, and our Klethos allies, appreciate this audience," she answered as Foue stepped to her left and the four Klethos stepped forward into that gap, their sheer size intimidating.

"Wait, and let them absorb our friends," her coach passed.

The first brother's face remained impassive, but she could see the discomfort in some of the other worthies in the hall.

Distaste or shame? she wondered.

"I am here as a representative of the United Assembly of Man, an organization of which you are still a member," she went on, pointedly ignoring the other three representatives.

Everyone knew that it was the Brotherhood calling the shots here, and she'd had her instructions.

The first brother nodded his head, and she continued, "Beyond the UAM, you are humans, part of the broad panoply that is mankind. So, despite your unfortunate and inopportune withdrawal from the task force formed to combat the Dictymorph threat, when your world of Destiny was attacked, the UAM responded with both Federation Marines and our Klethos allies to defend your world and throw back the invaders at a significant loss of life."

"Invaders that were only there because of your interference," the first brother interrupted her.

"We do not know how or why the Dictymorphs select their targets."

"So, you believe it was just chance that they chose to attack Destiny, home to the Saint Peter Canisius Monastery, a center of Dictymorph research?"

"As I said, First Brother, we do not know why . . ."

"Don't argue with him," the voice in her ear said. "The why's don't matter now. We went over this with you."

". . . but what matters now is the fact that twice, now, the Dictymorphs have invaded human space. We believe that this is only the beginning. Just as they have spread through Klethos space, they will push their aggression into our own."

She paused, and when the first brother remained silent, she continued, "It is obvious that your own forces, as vaunted as they are, cannot stand against the threat."

"We are developing better weapons, Ambassador."

"Better does not mean you can defeat them, only that you will take more with you before you all die," she snapped.

She waited for the rebuke from her unseen coach, but he remained silent. So did the Brotherhood, but Bishop Van Meter positively bristled.

"With the full might of the UAM, we believe we can slow the inexorable push into our space, but despite the success on Destiny, we cannot keep this up indefinitely, even moving to a humanity-wide war-footing. We need the Klethos as our allies."

"From your own reports, Ambassador—reports I read with great interest, I might add—the numbers of your Klethos are not great."

She pounced with, "Yet they have been fighting the Dictymorphs for a century, and still they survive. And if I might candidly say so, we needed their assistance on Destiny. Without them honoring their commitment, Destiny would have been lost."

She had been ready with her response, knowing someone would mention the Klethos numbers.

"Even if that was so, Destiny is but one world. Its loss would have been terrible, but not so terrible as to attract even more evil attention from the Dictymorphs."

Sky didn't know why they were fencing like this. The Brotherhood knew what the rest of the UAM wanted. The UAM knew the Brotherhood's objections. The question now was what the Brotherhood would do. All of this posturing was just that. Sky had no illusions that she was going to change anyone's mind standing in the middle of the Great Hall, but appearances had to be kept.

She hoped that what she was going to do when she left the hall, however, might affect their decision.

"Granted that we are in a debt of gratitude to the Federation Marines who sacrificed their lives on Destiny, but beyond our thanks, just why are you here? What are you asking of our four states?"

He pointedly ignored the four hulking Klethos, who were standing impassively beside her while reminding observers that three other governments were there with the Brotherhood.

This is all theater, she thought, but she answered, "Honor your commitment to the UAM task force. Let us combine our strength rather than split us apart."

"Even if that spells our destruction?" he asked.

"Don't answer," her coach said.

Sky stood still.

"Well," the first brother said, after an uncomfortably long silence. "You must be tired after your journey. If you would follow the Right Honorable Williams, he will escort you to more comfortable quarters where you can relax while we consider your request."

Bullshit. You already know what you're going to do, and you're playing to the media.

Sky smiled, gave a half-bow, then turned to leave. Then, as if spotting Bishop Van Meter for the first time, she detoured to him, hand outstretched. Sure enough, instinct took over, and he held out his hand as well.

"Good to see you, Bishop," she said, taking his hand.

"Likewise," he said.

He had to have felt the tiny capsule she'd just pressed into his palm, but he showed no sign of it. He knew the media was watching as well.

This was the tipping point, and Sky knew it could go either way now. The UAM decision-makers had argued long and hard over this. They could have sent the message over normal channels, but no one yet knew the Klethos' capabilities of surveillance, and if the media somehow got ahold of it, panic would ensue. In the end, going against the objections of many, including the Federation chairman, if what Sky heard was correct, they decided that using her as a courier would be the safest bet, and it would also give the first brother a visible reason to make a change of policy. Sky and the others were a cover, for all intents and purposes.

If the first brother agreed. If not . . . ?

That wasn't something she even wanted to contemplate.

✳✳✳✳✳✳✳✳✳✳✳✳✳✳✳

Two hours later, the seven of them were still lounging in a very comfortably furnished room with overstuffed chairs and bookcases full of physical books. Refreshments had been provided, but all for humans. Other than the water, the Klethos hadn't touched any of them, even if some should have been biologically acceptable. They stood quietly in one corner of the large room, their unblinking eyes giving them a statute-like quality.

After a flurry of conjecture between themselves and conferencing with the UAM leaders, the three humans had sunk into the plush chairs and sat, lost in their thoughts.

"Stop it, Foue," Sky finally said. "You're driving me nuts."

She lowered her hand from her mouth where she'd been chewing her fingernails. Two fingers showed signs of blood around the nailbeds.

"Sorry. It's just the waiting."

"Be prepared to wait longer," Norelco said, before leaning back in his chair and closing his eyes.

Sky pulled herself out of the deep chair, then wandered over to the wall-to-wall bookcases. She didn't know if she'd ever seen so many physical books in her life, outside of a library. She reached up to touch one, pulling it out halfway before putting it back and walking along the case, her forefinger trailing along each book in one row. The titles didn't register. Her mind was on the message she'd delivered, and the longer they waited, the more she was sure it had been a big mistake.

Norelco was right, however. Two hours really wasn't that long—it just seemed like it was.

"Interesting that you humans put words onto plastic sheets for storage," Gary said behind her, making her jump.

She was surprised that a being that big could sneak up on her like that.

"We also have them on paper," she said, looking back at the other three in the quad.

None of them were overtly paying them any attention, but being only six or seven meters away, they could hardly miss that Gary, the quiet one, was speaking to her.

"We have never used pressed vegetable matter to store knowledge."

Her interest piqued despite the situation, she asked, "What do you use? I mean, what did you use early in your history?"

"There are many media that provide better storage. Some things are quite small, almost too small to notice, that can be handed to someone else should the need arise."

Sky felt her face blanche as her far-off guide said, "Steady, Skylar. We don't know what that means."

Sky ignored the voice in her earbud and asked, "Why do you say that?"

"I say words that reflect my thoughts and observations."

Oh, shit, they know. I don't know how, but they know.

After long and contentious debate, the UAM leadership had decided to play their trump card, laying on the table that the Klethos were about to extract *lassor*, and there was nothing the UAM could do to dissuade them. The situation was out of the UAM's hands, and the only way out was for the Brotherhood and its allies to come back into the fold, so to speak, and restore honor to mankind.

The UAM had unanimously voted to come to the Brotherhood's aid, should it come to that, but that vote was not relayed in Sky's message.

With better intel on the Klethos, the analysts felt that in an all-out war with them, humanity would eventually prevail, but the cost would be high, and a diminished humanity would be far less capable of standing up to the Dictymorphs.

As sure as she'd ever been, she knew that Gary had just let her know that they knew what was in the message she'd given to the bishop. That left the question of whether they also knew that the UAM would side with the Brotherhood.

Over Gary's shoulders, the other three Klethos hadn't moved nor changed their body language. But they knew he was talking to her, and she was now sure they knew the subject. That left the possibility that when Gary had made that surreptitious meeting with her back in Brussels, it had been all planned by the quad, if not higher in the Klethos hierarchy.

"Sometimes, words are not meant for everyone," she said.

"Words are words, and they cannot be owned."

"Skylar, stop talking until we figure what we're going to do," her coach said.

"No, but their meaning can cause consequences if not all people feel the same, right?" she said, tuning out her earbud.

"Words always have consequences. That is why they are uttered. Even when there is agreement."

Sky felt a surge of hope that pierced the curtain of fear that had taken over her. If she wasn't totally crazy, Gary might have just expressed tacit approval of the message they'd given the Brotherhood.

"Ambassador Ybarra, this is the chairman. Do not say anything else to the Klethos until we process this."

Sky reached up and pulled the earbud out, sticking it in her pocket.

"And if there is agreement? Does that mean previous threats are . . . are rescinded?"

She knew she was treading dangerous ground here. Diplomats were not supposed to be so blunt, but then again, she was not a real diplomat.

To her left, Norelco suddenly sat up straight, and Foue was concentrating on something. She looked over to Sky and started to stand up, but Sky held up a hand, palm facing outward, to stop her. Foue looked confused, but she sat back down, then put out a hand to stop Norelco when he started to get to his feet.

"Words have truth, but action does not. Even when there is an agreement to the words, action does not necessarily follow."

Sky stared at Gary for a moment, trying to pull the meaning out of what he'd just said.

"Honor is paramount," he added, before turning to join the rest of the quad.

For the briefest moment, Glinda's soul-piercing eyes shifted to look at her before turning away.

They want this to work, but if it doesn't, honor requires them to take action. It will be war.

Sky walked back to her seat and sat down.

An anxious Foue asked, "What the hell's going on? I've got the president yelling in my ear that you need to be shut down."

"The Klethos know everything."

"Everything?" Norelco whispered, looking back over his shoulder at the quad.

"Everything."

"Now what? They're going crazy back at home," Foue said, pointing to her ear.

"Now we just sit back and wait."

✶✶✶✶✶✶✶✶✶✶✶✶✶✶✶

"Ambassadors? The First Brother requests your presence," the Right Honorable Williams said, entering the room.

"This is it," Sky muttered, as she stood up.

She had her earbud back in and had spent most of the last hour being both threatened and cajoled by more people in power than she had known even existed. There had been talk of replacing her with Norelco and sending her back to the ship, but like it or not, she was the face of the delegation.

That wasn't to mean that they were ignoring what had transpired. Sky had uploaded the recording, and most of the experts agreed with Sky as to what Gary was conveying. Everyone who was monitoring the situation understood the gravity of what was about to happen.

The Federation chairman had tried to circumvent the proceedings and call the first brother, but her call wasn't accepted. The cards had been dealt, and all that mattered was to see how they played out.

As the quad started to follow the three Earth diplomats, Williams held out a hand and asked them to stay in the room.

Sky exchanged worried glances with the other two, but the Klethos seemed nonplussed and returned to their corner.

"Don't worry about them. We've got two SEAL teams standing by if needed, one for you three and one for the Klethos," her coach said.

She nodded at the other two, and they followed Williams, but instead of heading to the Great Hall, he led them to a non-descript office down a much narrower hall. Sky didn't like the looks of things, but when Williams opened a door, she strode in as if she belonged.

She was greatly relieved to see the first brother, Archcardinal Morraine, Bishop Van Meter, and two other men whom she didn't recognize. If this was an arrest, they were certainly using the top of the Brotherhood heap to make it.

The arch-cardinal was the head of the church. The first brother had previously held the position before becoming the head of state, and the arch-cardinal was generally assumed to have the second-most power of anyone else in the Brotherhood.

"Thank you for meeting us here," the first brother said, as if they'd had a choice in the matter. "We have read the message you passed to Brother Van Meter, and as you can imagine, it caused great consternation. The problem with messages, especially ones passed in secret, is that they can be truth or lies, and in our experience, it is usually the latter. Like flowers, truth blossoms in the light of day, while lies fester in the darkness of secrecy, after all."

Sky kept her face expressionless, but that was not a good opening statement.

"However, what you wrote coincides with what some of us think," he said, nodding towards the bishop, "and we cannot summarily dismiss what could be the truth. Furthermore, we have no credible information that would support that the UAM would lie about this."

Which means your spies cannot find anything.

"We still believe in our stand. Aligning with the Klethos was a huge mistake, one that brought us to the attention of the Dictymorphs. Their attack on Saint Canisius is proof of that.

"We also believe that we cannot trust the Klethos. They have exterminated seventeen races that we know of, simply because they could. They are a barbaric race, one that is an affront to the eyes of God.

"However, there is another threat, and as you so eloquently pointed out in the Great Hall, the simple fact is that, no matter who is to blame, we are in the Dictymorphs' crosshairs."

Sky opened her mouth to agree, but her coach told her, "Can it, Sky. For once, shut up and let him speak."

"We cannot afford to fight the Klethos. Even together, if you would join us, we would be crippled in such a fight, and that would leave us ripe for the pickings when the Dictymorphs come, and come they will. So, needs must be done when the devil drives, as they say, and so we agree to rescind our withdrawal from the UAM task force and will once again contribute our resources to the war effort."

Oh, thank God!

"We do have some conditions, however," he continued, which dampened her relief.

"First is that we are not admitting fault in any form. With the attack on Destiny, we have merely advanced our timeline for what would have happened anyway.

"Second, we are going to demand reparations for the attack on Destiny, as it was the UAM's precipitous actions that resulted in the attack so soon."

What? How about your attack on the Zrínyi? You murdered those sailors and Marines. And what about all those who died on Destiny saving your asses?

"Steady, Skylar. This is politics, and it can all be worked out," her coach said.

"Third," the first brother continued, "our alliance with the Klethos will not be a formal alliance, but merely cooperation in convenience. Brotherhood forces will not be tasked with saving the Klethos from destruction, but merely to fight the Dictymorphs where needed. If that is on a Dictymorph world, so be it."

He stopped, looking at Sky, seemingly pleased with himself.

"I appreciate your candor, First Brother. We will pass your conditions to the secretary general."

"Please, Ambassador Ybarra, you don't need to pass that on. As soon as the words came out of my mouth, he heard. I have my gathered officials in the Great Hall as well as media from a thousand planets. I will be leaving this room and announcing my decision, so what will that decision be?"

"Take the offer, Skylar. We can haggle over the terms later," her coach said.

Sky opened her mouth to pass the acceptance, but a niggling thought broke free. There was someone else in play, too.

"We have a condition, too," she said, while her coach said, "Shit, Skylar, I said accept!"

"Whether it was our message given to the bishop or not that changed your mind, there is something else. I've since learned that the Klethos do not want to go to war with the

Brotherhood. They realize the disaster that would be for the fight against the Dictymorphs."

"For God's sake, Skylar, shut your fucking mouth! You're going to ruin it!" her coach yelled.

The first brother's eyebrows raised as he stole a glance at one of the unnamed men by his side. Sky refused to wonder who the man was or what his eyebrows signified. She knew she had just diminished the importance of cooperating again, but she had to go on.

She heard her coach yell to someone in the background, "She's not shutting up."

"However, and despite that, they will attack to remediate the honor that they feel you threw away. Make no doubt about it, even if it means the end of their race, they will proceed, because to them, without honor, they do not deserve to live as a people.

"You can make all the demands you want, and the UAM will bend over backwards to let you save face to your citizens, despite your complicity in all that has transpired. But it isn't just the UAM that you have to deal with. The Klethos have to agree that you are no longer *d'lessu*, that you are *d'lato* once again. If you don't, then it doesn't matter what the UAM says, because the Klethos are going to fall on your holy asses like the devils you say they are."

One of the men looked confused at her use of Klethos terminology, but she knew the first brother understood. He leaned back, his confidence gone. He started chewing on his lower lip, and Sky could see the gears turning.

"Of course, you can assure the Klethos that we embrace honor."

"No."

"Oh, shit, she's making it worse," her coach said, as she tried to tune him out.

"I can't assure the Klethos of anything of the sort. I can assure them that we are punishing you, that we are administering *lassor* because our honor demands it. I cannot speak for you, nor for the Klethos. You are ignoring them right now as if they don't exist, but they are not our pets to do our bidding. They act on their own as they deem fit."

"Surely you didn't expect us to invite them here," Archcardinal Morraine said, "given the content of your message."

"No, I didn't, even though I found out that they were already very aware of its contents. They chose not to intervene yet, and I'm guessing that's to see if the formalities are met and they can step back with their honor intact.

"No, Arch-Cardinal, I cannot speak for the Klethos, and if I give you the agreement that the secretary-general and everyone else who is yammering through the poor man on the other side of this earbud," she said, pulling it out and brandishing it, "I would be doing a disservice, not to the UAM, not to my Federation, but to humanity. What we say doesn't matter. It is what the Klethos say."

There was a shocked silence, broken only by the tinny-sounding voice emitting out of the earbud she held out at arm's length.

"I must admit," the first brother said after a few moments, "that you have given us—given me—pause. I did not really consider this in those terms. If you will give us until tomorrow, we will discuss your concerns. The Right Honorable Williams will arrange for suitable quarters for you and the Klethos."

"No, First Brother."

"What now, Ambassador? You made your point. Is there more?"

Jonathan P. Brazee

"No, sir. But I have a feeling that tomorrow might be too late. We've been underestimating the Klethos for a century, now."

"No, we haven't—" the bishop started, before Sky continued.

"We admit their fighting prowess, but nothing else. You, First Brother, called them a 'barbarous race,' not three hours ago. Yes, they like to fight with swords, yes, they like to fight in the ring, but don't forget, they were plowing through our forces with ease before General Lysander broke the code of gladiatorial combat.

"What we forget is that their technology is superior to ours. They can render our weapons useless. They can travel through space without ships. They can read a tiny encoded capsule that I gave the bishop.

"Why do I bring that up? Because maybe I fear they are listening to us now, no matter what suppression fields you have in this room. My superiors can sure hear me," she said, holding up her earbud again. "Maybe it's nothing more than a gut feeling, but I believe tomorrow will be too late. I believe that the Klethos quad will report to their superiors today whether you have re-embraced honor or not. My fear, which makes me tremble in the very core of my being, is that without the quad's acceptance, we will be at war within hours."

It wasn't just her inner core, but her whole body was trembling. She tried to bring her hands behind her to hide it. She'd given her plea, all the time not knowing if she was even right. She had broken specific orders, and by doing so, might have drawn humanity into a war.

"So, what do you suggest we do?" the first brother quietly asked.

"Ask the Klethos. Tell them you understand honor."

The first brother looked to the archcardinal, who gave him the slightest of nods.

"Foue, can you go get the Klethos and bring them here?" Sky asked.

"No," the first brother said. "I will go to them."

He stood up and walked across the room, flanked by the other five men. Stopping to take off his shoes at the door, he then motioned Williams to open it.

"You are playing big games, girl," Foue whispered, as they fell into place behind the Brotherhood leadership.

"Do you think I'm wrong?"

"*They* do," she said, pointing at her ear. "I'm hearing words like 'treason.'"

"Words are words," she whispered to herself, quoting Glinda, then asked Foue, "But do you think I'm wrong?"

"No, I think you nailed it, and that might have saved us."

Sky wanted to throw up as they marched down the hall, and she felt faint. The die was cast, and things were out of her hands, and that made it worse.

When Williams opened the door, the four Klethos were standing in the middle of the room in their diamond formation, upper arms folded as they faced the door. Sky knew at that moment that she had been right. They knew what had transpired in the room. What she didn't know was how it had been received.

The first brother walked straight up to Glinda and immediately went prone, face-down. The other five followed suit. Sky, taken by surprise, started to go down as well until a soft touch from Norelco on her arm kept her upright.

His face on the ground, the first brother said, "Ambassadors, I humbly offer my sincere regret for our misguided actions. We misunderstood what was honorable and what wasn't. In good faith, we withdrew from the rest of mankind, foolishly thinking that to interfere with others was not honorable. When our own world of Destiny was invaded, however, we learned what true honor is. Despite our abandoning you, and despite abandoning the rest of humanity, both of you came to defend us. Both Klethos and humans lost their lives for those of us who spurned you.

"I am ashamed of this, and I humbly ask of you the chance to regain our honor. Let us show you what we have learned. Let us prove ourselves."

With his arms outspread and his face on the ground, Sky was struck at how much he looked like the Klethos gladiator Sally Mae when she offered herself to the Purple Sledgehammer, the act that initiated the Klethos-Human alliance. Sky wondered if the first brother had done that on purpose.

He was a wily politician, so she would bet on yes.

His apology and request to regain honor seemed specious and simple theater to her. It wasn't up to her, however. It was how the Klethos received it that mattered.

And for a long moment, they said nothing, all four standing motionless. Sky wondered if they were just thinking, if they were conducting their own set of theater, or if they were in communications with their bosses.

Finally, Glinda spread all four arms and said, "Honor lost is not easily regained. Make sure you achieve your goals, *d'lamma.*"

As one, the four stepped forward, parting around the prone men to leave the room.

Gary, the back position in the diamond, reached out and pulled Sky in as he passed, saying, "You understand, Skylar Ybarra. You have honor enough for all, and I thank you," before he straightened and followed the other three out of the room.

"Where are they going?" Bishop Van Meter asked, raising his head.

"I imagine back to Earth, or their homeworld. Who knows?" Sky said, an unbelievable wave of calm sweeping over her. "They don't need to wait for our ship, after all."

"But, what's happening?" the first brother asked. "Did they accept?"

"She called you *d'lamma*," Foue said.

"I'm afraid I don't know that term."

"It is like a child, one who doesn't understand things such as honor, someone who needs to be taught."

"So, if we need to be taught, I take it they are not about to launch an assault on our worlds?" he asked, standing and brushing off his robe, all hint of remorse gone.

"I think that would be a safe assumption," Norelco said.

"Then, before I return to the Great Hall, do we have a deal?" he asked, hand out to Sky.

He hadn't been entirely sincere, she knew, only debasing himself to save his people. She resented the Brotherhood's attacks and the loss of life on Destiny. And she was positive that he was going to make no mention of honor in the Great Hall. But stakes were too big for her personal feelings.

And as he'd said, needs must be done when the devil drives.

She was probably already fired, so she didn't bother to get back on her earbud. Let them arrest her when she got back. She looked him dead in the eyes and took his hand.

"Deal."

AEGIS 2

Chapter 40
Hondo

"Man, oh, man, this sure tastes good," Pickerul said as she drained the entire cider, then slammed the stein back down, smacking her lips.

"Slow down, Lance Corporal," Hondo said. "We've got all night."

"Then no reason to wait now, huh? I mean, Sergeant, sir!" she said, snapping off a sloppy salute. "Me and Tony B are buying, so you just drink there."

"To lance corporals!" Tony B shouted, raising his beer.

That brought a round of cheers, and more than a few steins were drained. Both Marines had been promoted on the ship on the way back to Camp Walters, but this was the first opportunity since then for a wetting down.

"To fallen comrades!" Wolf shouted, standing up.

"To fallen comrades," the rest shouted, a little more subdued.

Alpha Company had taken horrendous losses, many lost to the black after the *Zrínyi* was hit, more in the fighting because they were too far gone for resurrection. First Squad had made it through with five Marines and Doc Leach, which was the most of any squad in the company. Doc had been right about Hanaburgh, though. He was one of the six survivors, having been brought back on the ship and only given a week of rehabilitation.

Second Squad's four Marines made it the second-largest squad left. The scuttlebutt was that the company had suffered more combat losses of any Marine Company since the War of the Far Reaches. The scuttlebutt was also that the company was being put in for the Chairman's Unit Citation, something that had only been given out to a company-sized Marine unit three other times.

Hondo didn't know much about that. He'd just as soon have his Marines back and skip the award. But there seemed to be an inordinate amount of interest in the company. Each of them had gone through extensive debriefings, starting on the way to J-Point, and that hadn't stopped until they'd arrived back on Aegis 2 that morning.

The company was being held up as a "hero" company, not only highlighting the fight against the Grubs, but also as a shameful reminder to the Brotherhood.

Screw it, he thought, taking another swallow of beer. *I don't want to think about all of that tonight.*

Other Marines in the club were giving their group a wide berth, but Hondo could catch their surreptitious glances. It was probably to be expected, but he was grateful that at least for now, they were given the chance to celebrate alone, celebrate not only the two new lance corporals, but just being alive.

"Hey, Jones, where's your squad leader?" he asked one of the Second Squad Marines. "She's falling behind."

"She's meeting her sister. She said she's still coming, though."

"She'd better make it," Hondo said.

Hondo grabbed a handful of popcorn out of the basket. As a kid, he'd never really liked popcorn, which rather set him apart, but as every two-bit fabricator in every bar could make the stuff without pause, he'd gotten used to the salty taste to complement his beer. It wasn't going to fill his stomach, but they had pizza coming as soon as the staff sergeant and lieutenant made it there.

Hondo wasn't sure he'd ever seen an officer in the E-club. It just wasn't done. But until the powers that be decided what was going to happen to Alpha Company, Lieutenant Abrams was the only officer, just as Staff Sergeant Rutledge was the only Staff NCO. This might officially be a lance corporal wetting down, but every one of them wanted all of them to raise a glass together, the lone officer included.

He thought the lieutenant needed it. It was pretty obvious that the man blamed himself for all the losses. He'd been almost unapproachable since leaving Destiny, locked up in his stateroom unless some specific duty pulled him out. After he finished, he was right back inside—brooding, for all anyone knew. The staff sergeant was concerned about the man, but he thought that getting together with the survivors like this would do him a world of good.

Hondo understood the lieutenant's feelings. He felt the same thing. His job has been to get all of his Marines back safe and sound, and in that, he'd failed. But that was part of being a Marine. You toasted fallen comrades, you kept their memory alive, but you marched on, ready to march to the sound of guns again.

"Sergeant Riordan, you're a pitcher behind!" Wolf shouted.

Hondo swiveled in his seat to see Cara and a woman who looked exactly like her in tow, all heading to their table. He stood up, not quite sure why. That was Cara, after all, just one of the guys.

"Sorry to be late. Lauren here kept me gabbing. I haven't seen her in two years."

Lauren was a petty officer in the Navy, Hondo knew, but not much more than that. She did look exactly like Cara, but somehow, it registered to him differently. He stood, saying nothing, as Cara went around the table, naming everyone.

"And this big lug is Hondo McKeever," she said, after coming around the table to him.

"I've heard a lot about you," Lauren said, her eyes sparkling with a force of personality.

"Don't believe a word. I swear I didn't do it," Hondo said, his standard retort while the rest of the table laughed.

"Yes, he did!" Wolf said. "We know the truth."

"Well, are you going to offer two thirsty souls a drink?" Cara asked.

Tony B, as one of the two hosts, jumped up, holding pitchers of beer and cider. Cara took the cider, Lauren the beer. Cara wormed her way between Wolf and Hondo, shoving the corporal away with a butt-swipe, and she and Lauren sat down.

More drink flowed, and the popcorn was replaced a couple of times. Hondo's stomach was growling, and the beer was getting him a little tipsy on his empty stomach, but he was happy, sitting with his fellow Marines. Doc Leach got up, shoved his way between Lauren and Wolf, and started talking Navy talk, all about promotions and such, and Hondo felt a pang of, well—not jealousy, for sure. He just wanted a chance to get to know the sister of his good friend.

"Hey, when's the pizza coming?" Hanaburgh asked.

"Not until the lieutenant and staff sergeant get here," Cara said. "We agreed to that."

"Well, they'd better get here soon."

Hondo checked his PA. The two of them were late. He quickly typed a *Where are you?* to Staff Sergeant Rutledge, who replied a minute later with, *On my way to the Q. The lieutenant's not answering.*

OK, hurry up. We're waiting on you for the pizza.

Cara got up to use the head, and suddenly, Lauren was sitting next to him. He didn't know what to say, so he listened to the rest of the Marines while Lauren and Doc Leach were lamenting the time it took to make E5. When Cara came back, she came around to the other side and sat on Hondo's left, which scooched him closer to her sister. As he and Cara chatted, he was *extremely* aware of his thigh touching Lauren's.

"So, what do you think of my sister, Hondo?" Cara asked suddenly.

He felt his face burn, feeling guilty for some reason he couldn't explain.

"Uh . . . she seems nice," he said lamely.

"Nice? Ha! You don't know her yet. Hey, Lauren, Hondo thinks you're nice. Are you?"

Lauren tilted her head back in laughed—not a dainty, feminine trill, but a full-throated guffaw.

"Nice? I'm afraid no one's ever called me nice. Lots of other things, but never nice."

"I'm sorry, I didn't mean anything," Hondo said, trying to rush out the words.

"Oh, don't worry," she said, putting her hand on his forearm. "It's just a family joke. It's fine."

Hondo wasn't sure it was fine, but he wanted to talk to her.

She pulled her hand away and just started to turn back to Doc when he blurted out, "So, how long are you going to be here?"

"Here? On Aegis? I'm on a week's leave, but I report in to Holcomb Station after that."

"No shit? Holcomb?"

"Yeah, so I can keep an eye on my sister, there."

"Or I can keep my eye on you, you mean," Cara said.

"Whatever."

Holcomb Station was the naval base that supported the system. It was only a short shuttle ride to the planet's surface.

Hondo was about to say that they were going to be neighbors or some other inane comment when he was saved by a chant of "Pizza, pizza, pizza" that grew in volume.

"What do you think?" Cara asked. "Do we wait?"

Hondo shot off another message to the staff sergeant, and when there was no reply, he told her, "We might as well order. I don't know what's going on."

"You two lance corporals, it's your call. I'm not sure when the lieutenant's going to make it."

Pickerul and Tony B looked around the table, then Tammy said, "Let's get it. We can get another when they get here."

She punched in the order to the cheers of the rest.

"So, what is your designator in the Navy?" Hondo asked Lauren to keep the conversation going.

"I'm a cryptologist," she answered.

Hondo had heard the word before, but he didn't exactly know what it meant, so he kept his mouth shut and nodded knowingly. This was pretty much what he kept doing as she went on about her last duty station, aboard the giant *FS Canada*, one of the newest battleships in the Navy.

The pizzas arrived, not via the server tunnel, but carried by the E-Club manager himself.

"They're on the house," he said. "We're all so proud of you."

Hondo should have felt happy, but that hit him with a touch of melancholy. From the looks of it, a few of the others felt the same way. They thanked him, though, and he left with a satisfied-looking smile.

"You got off cheap," Wolf said. "I think you owe us another."

"This is the wetting down, corporal, and you get what you get," Tony B said.

There were good-natured hoots at that, and things got rolling again.

Hondo filled Lauren's stein when Cara said, "Finally, here's the staff sergeant."

Hondo looked up, ready to call out when the look on the staff sergeant's face as he approached them stopped him cold.

Pickerul, though, grabbed a used stein, tipped it over so the last drops of someone else's beer ran out, and filled it before holding it up and saying, "Here you go, Staff Sergeant. Better late than never."

Staff Sergeant Rutledge ignored the drink and said, "All of you, listen up." A few of them kept talking, so he shouted, "I said listen up!"

"I just came from the lieutenant's quarters."

"When's he coming?" Pickerul asked, still holding the full stein of beer.

The staff sergeant's fingers were trembling, something Hondo focused on. He was drifting, almost an out-of-body experience. Somehow, someway, he knew what his platoon sergeant was going to say.

Staff Sergeant Rutledge took a deep breath of air, and as Hondo expected, he said, "He's not. He just killed himself."

Epilogue
Hondo

Newly promoted Gunnery Sergeant Roy Rutledge lowered the company's colors, and the commanding general attached the Chairman's Unit Commendation to the headpiece. Conscious of the press recording the ceremony, Hondo stared straight ahead, but he watched with his peripheral vision.

Company colors did not normally display battle streamers, so the commendation ribbon looked lonely hanging there as the general saluted and the gunny raised them. It should look odd. Only two other Marine companies had been so honored in the past; Alpha Company, First Battalion, Fourteenth Marines, made it three.

Hondo felt a deep sense of pride, but that was mixed with the melancholy that had permeated his thoughts, more so since Lieutenant Abrams had committed suicide. The Navy Cross that now hung on his chest, pinned on just 20 minutes ago by the new Second Vice-Minster, Skylar Ybarra herself, didn't do much to alleviate the depression.

Alpha Company had boarded the *Zrínyi* with 163 Marines and sailors. Standing with Hondo were twenty-two others: the survivors. Except for entire Marine units lost when ships were destroyed, Alpha and Charlie Company had suffered the highest casualty rate for a company since the War of the Far Reaches.

Alpha was now one of the most decorated companies in Marine Corps history as well. The awards ceremony had been going on for 45 minutes now, as every surviving member was awarded at least a Bronze Star. Doc Leach, Tammy Pickerul Tony B. Good, Robert Hanaburgh, Lorenzo Marasco, Cara Riordan, and Hope Running Fox from Second Squad received Silver Stars—Running Fox's and Lorenzo's posthumously. Hondo, Staff Sergeant Rutledge, and Curtis "Wolf" Johnson were awarded Navy Crosses, as were First Sergeant Nordstrand and Captain Ariç, the latter two posthumously.

Then there were the two Federation Novas. One went to Hanaburgh to go along with the Silver Star he'd been awarded for the fight on Lore ten minutes before.

Not bad for a hooah FCDC trooper, Hondo had thought, as he listened to the Nova citation.

Like most Marines, Hondo referred to the FCDC troopers as "fuckdicks," but if they could produce Marines like Burger, then he vowed to stop doing that.

Then there was the second Federation Nova, awarded to Second Lieutenant Armando Abrams, United Federation Marine Corps. That had been bittersweet. Hondo understood now that during the battle, the lieutenant was already in a deep depression, and he'd been trying to get killed by the Grubs, only his fighting spirit wouldn't let him when he had his Marines to defend.

PTSD had been around since man first began to fight each other. "Battle fatigue," "the thousand-yard stare," "shell shock," and "soldier's heart" were all terms used before medical science began to codify the disorder. Modern medicine could do wonders to combat it, but a sufferer had to seek treatment—and those around them had the duty to get the sufferer help. Even today, after centuries of fighting the disorder, fighting men and women often couldn't face the fact that they needed help.

It was a sign of weakness, it was a sign of not being up to the task—that was the thinking. Marines (sailors, soldiers,

Legionnaires, Guardsmen, host, etc.) were strong, and they never needed help, right?

But the same serviceman or woman would think nothing about going through regen to replace a missing leg, to grow new eyes. Somehow, the shame was still there, that someone suffering from PTSD was at fault for their thoughts.

Hondo and Staff Sergeant Rutledge had gotten stinking drunk the day after the lieutenant had killed himself. They had both seen it in their platoon commander, and neither had reported it to the battalion commander, the battalion surgeon, or even the chaplain. Neither wanted to ding on their commander, a man they'd admired tremendously. If they had, however, then the lieutenant might possibly be still alive and being treated. He'd be standing next to Hanaburgh right now, the Federation Nova around his neck.

Raising their fifth or tenth beer, both men had vowed to each other that they would never ignore the signs of PTSD again. Even in death, their lieutenant would possibly be saving future lives, and they owed him that.

In the center of the parade deck, Gunnery Sergeant Rutledge handed the company colors to Private Batbayar, the junior Marine in the company, who took her position behind him and to his left. He performed an about-face, waiting for the general's orders. This would be his last moment as acting company commander. In formation behind them, Captain White and more than 150 Marines waited, ready to be formally assigned to the company.

Hondo had been surprised that the twenty-three of them had been left alone so long. He knew it was politics. The situation with the Brotherhood was still shaky, and the public affairs bureaucrats evidently thought that keeping the survivors together made for better propaganda, to remind them what the UAM—and the Klethos—had done to protect the same Brotherhood that had abandoned the fight.

Politics or not, Hondo had appreciated the chance to stay isolated, spending as much time as they could in the field training. He just hadn't been ready for a new Alpha Company.

Ten more minutes, and that new company will be here.

He still wasn't sure how he would feel when Rutledge handed the colors to Captain White. Not that what he felt would change the course of the company.

Behind the general, the adjutant called out the order to commence with the change of command.

"Ladies and gentlemen, we now begin the second part of today's ceremony where Gunnery Sergeant Roy Rutledge will relinquish command of Alpha Company, First Battalion, Fourteenth Marines, to Captain Harris L. White," the narrator said.

Meanwhile, Cara stepped five paces forward, did a left-face, and marched forward to stand beside the gunny, while Captain White and his first sergeant marched forward alongside the massed Marines, then performed a left-turn and marched across the front of the formation to come to a halt next the gunny and Cara in the box formation.

The narrator started giving the standard spiel about the history and meaning of command, but Hondo's mind started to wander. His thoughts were on those who had fallen. He knew Greg Ling's family was in the stands observing, as were Antman Acevedo's, and he wanted to see them when this was over. The first sergeant's wife wasn't. Hondo, along with the rest of the company, had helped Guang Nordstrand pack up her base housing the month before, and she'd left Aegis 2 to return home.

A flurry of motion registered in his peripheral vision, but he didn't budge. The gunny was passing the company colors to the captain.

The old Alpha was gone, long live the new.

The gunny and Cara marched back to the rear of the formation, while Captain White took his place as the new company commander. And that was that. After the general gave the command, Captain White dismissed the company—*his* company now.

Immediately, the civilian handlers rushed forward to gather the "old" Alpha Marines for a photo-op and questions from the press, and for the next ten minutes, Hondo joined the rest in posing with the first minister and the general while answering questions about how proud—and humbled—they were. The handlers had spent several hours prepping them over the last two days, so they were ready and knew what was to be expected. Even Pickerul kept to the script without any snide comments.

Hondo kept scanning the crowd, so he was surprised when he heard a "Hey, Solider, looking good!" from behind him.

"BK, glad you could make it," he said, edging back so he could see his good friend.

"Wouldn't miss it for the world," she said, lifting the Cross from his chest with a finger, before letting it back down and giving him a crushing hug. "I miss you, big guy," the petite Marine whispered in his ear.

"How did you get permission to come? I thought you guys were on work-ups?"

"We are. But I just happened to give an interview to the local station, which was picked up by the UP. I told them about how we came up together, how close we are, how everyone looks up to you. You know, all the bullshit."

"Don't tell me, your command thought they'd get some good press if you came."

"Got it in one. And one of those newsdrones hovering over us like fucking gnats is on us now . . . oh, don't worry, you guys listening now can edit out my nasty language," she added, looking up at the mass of tiny drones that were recording the ceremony.

She turned him around to better display his Navy Cross, then spoiled it by raising her middle finger.

"BK!"

"Ah, don't worry about it. I'm serious about them editing it. But let's give them something they can use," she said before jumping into the story about how the two of them had to molt from their PICS on K1003 and then attack one of the Grubs in their longjohns.

To listen to her, Hondo just about saved the entire universe from utter destruction. Hondo just listened and nodded, letting her go on.

"Hondo!" another voice called out, and he turned to see Lauren coming over, one arm dragging Cara, who was still talking to a reporter who kept following her and asking questions. She was in her Navy whites, the first time he'd seen her in a dress uniform.

Hondo wasn't sure if the bright light in her eyes faded a few lumens when she saw BK's arm around his waist.

"Uh, Lauren, hi."

"Congratulations on your Navy Cross," she said.

Hondo just nodded, then said, "Lauren, this is BK. BK, this is—"

"I know who this is," BK said, an almost evil grin coming over her face. "This is your—"

"BK!"

"Well, it's true, big guy. You've already told me about her."

She turned to Lauren and said, "Pleased to meet you. I'm BK. Hondo and I go way back. And take it the sergeant you're dragging over here is Cara?"

"Can you give me a moment?" Cara asked the persistent reporter and said, "Good to meet you, Sergeant. I saw that interview you gave on the net. I'd like to hear more about Hondo fighting the grubs in his longjohns. That's an image that's burning in my mind."

"Hey, BK. How long are you going to be here? I'd like to speak to Lauren for a few moments, if I can."

"Until zero-dark-thirty tomorrow. So sure, maybe I'll tell Cara here about K1003. But you're taking me out to dinner—that is, unless your girlfriend objects."

Shit, BK, give it a rest!

He was beginning to doubt the intelligence of spilling his life secrets to his best friend.

He looked at her shit-eating grin, then rolled his eyes.

"I'll catch up to you in half an hour. Try not to get into any trouble."

"Me? Trouble? You wound me!" she said, linking her arm through Cara's and leading her away from the anxious-looking reporter.

"Girlfriend?" Lauren asked when they were alone, or as alone as two people could be while standing on the parade deck with people milling about.

"That's just BK. She loves to yank people's chains."

Lauren shrugged, but she didn't look convinced, if the tiny smile that tilted the end of her mouth was any indication.

"I just wanted to let you know that I'm leaving the company."

"I know, Cara told me."

Cara was keeping Second Squad. There would be seven new Marines in the squad, and she said she wanted to make sure the new Second was as good, if not better, than the old.

"So, you're going up to battalion headquarters? That's what she said."

"Yes, for three weeks."

Lauren raised an eyebrow and asked, "And what's after that?"

"I've been talking to people, you know. And I need a change. I know Cara's staying, but for me, it isn't Alpha anymore. Wolf and Tammy are leaving, too."

"So, you've been talking to people? And what do these people say?" she asked, her voice sounding just the tiniest bit apprehensive to him.

"Well, I just decided this morning, and I told the sergeant major. I'm going to recon."

"Recon? she asked, sounding surprised.

"Well, RTC, that's the Reconnaissance Training Course. I have to make it through the eight weeks to get the MOS."

"Wow. I didn't expect that."

"RTC's on Tarawa. All it does is see if we've got what it takes, weeding out those who can't. And then there's MSOC, where we actually learn the skills for the job. That's another twenty-four weeks."

"That's a long time," Lauren said, her voice subdued. "After that, then what? You coming back to Fifth Division?"

Which he knew she meant Camp Walters on Aegis-2.

"I don't know. I can't select that."

"Well, I . . . I don't know what to say."

Hondo had been dreading this moment. He'd enjoyed Lauren's company for the last few months. She'd come down to the planet, and he'd spent two weekends up on Holcomb Station—the first time along with Cara, the second time alone, just Lauren and him. She was fun, and a good friend. He wondered sometimes if she might become something *more* than a good friend. But now he was telling her that he wasn't going to be around.

He could have easily gotten a job at battalion or one of the higher headquarters, but Hondo had to get away. There were too many memories, both good and bad, that were filling his thoughts to the bursting point. He didn't think he had PTSD, but the lieutenant and his problems were heavy on his mind. He'd finally spoken with one of the Navy psychiatrists, who had ruled out classical PTSD, which was a relief, but suggested that maybe he needed a change of scene. The more he'd thought about it, the more he thought that was a good idea. Then a chance meeting with a recon gunny had piqued his interest. The idea of pooping and snooping out on his own, with only a small team instead of a full squad, had a strong allure. He asked for a screening, which he passed (barely), and with his record, he'd been accepted.

He still hadn't signed off on the orders, but his meeting with the sergeant major had convinced him to pull the trigger. Immediately he felt as if a load was taken off his shoulders, and he was excited to begin.

That didn't answer what his relationship with Lauren was, or if there even was a relationship. Military romances were difficult at any time, but with her in the Navy and him joining recon, that would be a pretty difficult obstacle to overcome.

He wanted to try, though.

"And you really want recon? You aren't simply running away from the past six months?"

"I thought I was at first, but no. I really want to do this. I want to prove myself."

She nodded, her eyebrows scrunched up.

"Three weeks, huh?" Lauren finally asked him.

"Yeah. I leave on the 18th."

"Do you have any leave saved up?"

"Well, yeah. It's been hard to take any of it with the tempo around here."

"I think I can manage ten days. What about you and I taking leave together?"

What? Hondo wondered, looking over at her.

She was staring straight ahead, her body as still as a statute.

"I . . . I think that would be great," he managed to get out.

A smile crept across her face as her posture relaxed.

"Yes, it would be," she said, as she reached out and took his hand in hers.

Thank you for reading *The Price of Honor*. I hope you enjoyed this book, and I welcome a review on Amazon, Goodreads, or any other outlet.

If you would like updates on new books releases, news, or special offers, please consider signing up for my mailing list. Your email will not be sold, rented, or in any other way disseminated. If you are interested, please sign up at the link below:

http://eepurl.com/bnFSHH

Other Books by Jonathan Brazee

The United Federation Marine Corps' Lysander Twins
Legacy Marines
Esther's Story: Recon Marine
Noah's Story: Marine Tanker
Esther's Story: Special Duty
Blood United

Coda

The United Federation Marine Corps
Recruit
Sergeant
Lieutenant
Captain
Major
Lieutenant Colonel
Colonel
Commandant

Rebel
(Set in the UFMC universe.)

Behind Enemy Lines
(A UFMC Prequel)

Women of the United Federation Marine Corps
Gladiator
Sniper
Corpsman

High Value Target (A Gracie Medicine Crow Short Story)
BOLO Mission (A Gracie Medicine Crow Short Story)
Weaponized Math

The United Federation Marine Corps' Grub Wars
Alliance
The Price of Honor
United (Working title—coming soon)

The Return of the Marines Trilogy
The Few
The Proud
The Marines

The Al Anbar Chronicles: First Marine Expeditionary Force--Iraq
Prisoner of Fallujah
Combat Corpsman
Sniper

Werewolf of Marines
Werewolf of Marines: Semper Lycanus
Werewolf of Marines: Patria Lycanus

Werewolf of Marines: Pax Lycanus

To The Shores of Tripoli

Wererat

Darwin's Quest: The Search for the Ultimate Survivor

Venus: A Paleolithic Short Story

Secession

Duty

Non-Fiction

Exercise for a Longer Life

Author Website
http://www.jonathanbrazee.com

Made in the USA
Columbia, SC
11 January 2018